By Len Deighton

FICTION
The Ipcress File
Horse Under Water
Funeral in Berlin
Billion-Dollar Brain
An Expensive Place to Die
Only When I Larf
Bomber
Declarations of War
Close-Up
Spy Story
Yesterday's Spy
Twinkle, Twinkle, Little Spy
SS-GB
XPD
Goodbye Mickey Mouse
MAMista
City of Gold
Violent Ward

THE SAMSON SERIES
Berlin Game
Mexico Set
London Match
Winter: A Berlin Family 1899–1945
Spy Hook
Spy Line
Spy Sinker
Faith
Hope
Charity

NON-FICTION
Action Cook Book
Fighter: The True Story of the Battle of Britain
Airshipwreck
French Cooking for Men
Blitzkrieg: From the Rise of Hitler to the Fall of Dunkirk
ABC of French Food
Blood, Tears and Folly

LEN DEIGHTON

Horse Under Water

HARPER

Harper
An imprint of HarperCollins*Publishers*
1 London Bridge Street,
London SE1 9GF
www.harpercollins.co.uk

This paperback edition 2015
1

First published in Great Britain by Jonathan Cape 1963

Copyright © Pluriform Publishing Company BV 1963
Introduction copyright © Pluriform Publishing Company BV 2009
Cover designer's note © Arnold Schwartzman 2009

Len Deighton asserts the moral right to
be identified as the author of this work

A catalogue record for this book is
available from the British Library

ISBN: 978 0 00 812479 3

Set in Ehrhardt

Cover designer's note

In creating cover designs for the new publication of Len Deighton's quartet of spy novels, I came up with the metaphor of the chess game as it relates to the spy game. Three enamel U-boat sub-mariners' cap badges became pawns on the chessboard.

A constant feature of Deighton's nameless protagonist's Charlotte Street WOOC(P) office was the ubiquitous pack of Gauloises cigarettes and the ever-present tin of Nescafé. (This very same street was used as the location for the HQ of the nest of spies in Alfred Hitchcock's *Foreign Correspondent*.) The Swiss had invented instant coffee prior to World War II, but it only became available in the UK in the 1950s, so when freeze-dried soluble grains were introduced a while later they became the beverage of choice for the Swinging London set. My search for a UK Nescafé tin of that period ended when I located one in far-off Australia!

Finding a contemporary, key-opened Portuguese sardine tin became virtually impossible. Discovering the illustration of a sardine on a cigarette card and a crested souvenir spoon from Lisbon became much easier, thanks to eBay!

My wife, Isolde, who produces all of my art work, and is a dab-hand at Photoshop, reproduced the period British

European Airways ticket, incorporating the exact flight number described in the book.

One obsession of Deighton's nameless protagonist is solving crossword puzzles. Since I have kept copies of the illustrations I produced for the London *Sunday Times* during the 1960s, I was able to find among the pages of the newspaper a crossword puzzle of the period.

The 1943 German postage stamp on the spine of the book depicts a German U-boat. The group of cigarette cards on the back of the cover spells out in semaphore K.U.Z.I.G. and Y. The nautical interpretation of these letters is referred to in the book as 'Permission granted to lay alongside'.

Some years ago, given the possibility of producing a feature film on the subject of the Nazi plan to flood the Allied economy with counterfeit money, I purchased a fake £20 note.

On meeting a survivor of the Sachsenhausen concentration camp where, as an engraver, he was forced to produce the counterfeit bank notes, I showed him my note, which he held to the light and proudly proclaimed, 'Yes, it's one of ours!' I photographed the jacket set-up using natural daylight, with my Canon OS 5D digital camera.

Arnold Schwartzman OBE RDI

Introduction

The Ipcress File, my first book, was written in two separate sessions. It was started when I was on vacation in the South of France. Porquerolles is an island off Toulon. In those days there was very little to do there other than sit and look at the Mediterranean, and eat and drink at regular intervals. So I whiled away the sunny days writing a story.

I have always enjoyed being in France. As a moderately successful illustrator, I decided to live there. I had an energetic and encouraging artist's agent in London and she sent work to me. My overheads were small, for the isolated cottage I lived in was Spartan accommodation for hunters. It was high on a windy hillside in the Dordogne and the forest that provided game for the hunters started within inches of the door. It had no heating other than a wood stove and drinking water was drawn from an ancient well about three hundred yards away. Day began with getting the stove started and going for water. Until the wood was burning bright, there could be no hot tea.

Rural life was enchanting but it was too good to last. Art directors of advertising agencies and magazines all preferred to deal with artists they could shout at in person. As the flow of illustration jobs diminished, I had more time for writing. But money diminished too and I reluctantly gave up my idyll and returned to London. (Not so long ago I went back to find the little cottage. It was still exactly as I remembered it but no smoke rose from the chimney. It was unoccupied and the windows were unwashed. I shed a tear and stole away.) But in those weeks of waiting for work to arrive I had continued writing the uncompleted story I had begun in Porquerolles. By the time I left for London, the story had become a book and it was more or less complete. But being almost broke I had no time for anything other than work. The manuscript of *The Ipcress File* was put on a shelf and forgotten until I met a literary agent at a party in London's Swiss Cottage.

It was when *The Ipcress File* was accepted by a publisher that I took seriously the idea of writing books for a living. They were even talking about making a film of it. By that time I had done enough drawings to be solvent again, and with enough money to be on vacation in a dramatically situated, but somewhat shabby, cliff top apartment in Portugal. It was there on a balcony overlooking the Atlantic that I started scribbling in longhand the story that became my second book, *Horse Under Water*. In those days Southern Portugal was a remote region. There was no airport nearer than Lisbon and the journey from there to the south coast was gruelling. But it was worth it. The Algarve, on the very edge of Europe, is a pictorial region and I always delight in being there.

Many of the ideas in the book dated from earlier times. In the nineteen thirties, when I was a small child, my father had taken me to many museums but I particularly enjoyed the War Museum. To me the tanks, artillery pieces and aircraft were like gigantic toys and I have never lost my fascination with large examples of machinery.

So when I moved into the Elephant and Castle neighbourhood of London – where I lived for many years – the War Museum in Lambeth was within easy walking distance and it became a haunt of mine. It was a time when the Army, Navy and RAF, and many civilian agencies, began passing over to the War Museum books, films and documents that had become history rather than operational reference. A proportion of these items were technical ones seized from various German archives at the end of the war. I found it fascinating but the Museum found them an almost overwhelming burden.

In the final year of the war, there had been tremendous scientific advances in undersea warfare and I pursued these reports – British, American and German – with particular zeal. The War Museum's librarian asked me to help by categorizing the material I examined, so that I became an unofficial member of the Museum staff. At the time, I had no idea that the notes I made would be used for anything other than my interest in history. It was during my stay in Portugal, when I was asking local people about German activity there during the war, that I recalled all that underwater warfare material. The book's plot fell into place and I started writing.

Like *The Ipcress File*, this second book was started with a fountain pen and locally purchased school exercise book. I had not named the hero of *The Ipcress File*. A Canadian book-reviewer said it was symbolic and pretentious but in fact it was indecision. Now, writing a second book, I found it an advantage to have an anonymous hero. He might be the same man; or maybe not. I was able to make minor changes to him and his background. The changes had to be minor ones for the WOOC(P) office was still in Charlotte Street and Dawlish was still the hero's 'chief'. There were very few modifications but I realized that (although Deighton is a Yorkshire name, and I had lived briefly in the city of York) identifying him as a northerner would make demands on my knowledge that I could not sustain. It would be more sensible to give him a background closer to my own.

The indomitable Harry Saltzman, who had coproduced

the James Bond films and was making *The Ipcress File*, solved everything with the sort of unhesitating practical move for which he was renowned. Michael Caine was cast to play the hero of that film and Michael was a Londoner, as I was.

He was named Harry Palmer. It was the right decision. Michael and the man of whom I'd written fused perfectly. I am indebted to Michael for the dimensions his skill and talent provided to my character. Having no underwater skills, knowledge or experience, I went to the Royal Navy and asked for help. Everyone at the Admiralty was one hundred per cent helpful. They sent me to the Royal Navy's diving school and this experience is described here more or less as it happened. It was only when I was half-way through the course, and up to my neck in water on the ladder of the diving tank, that I confessed that I could not swim. They were shocked and apprehensive on my behalf but as I said: 'What is the point of wearing all this scuba gear if you can manage without it?' The chief instructor gave a grim smile and nodded me down into the water. Those were the days when you didn't have to wonder why health and safety allowed the war to be won!

Len Deighton, 2009

Solution

1	Parley		30	Entreaty
2	Nostrum		31	Aid
3	Air		32	Old
4	Me		33	Nods
5	Pistol		34	Rude
6	Gib		35	Guard
7	Brief		36	Black
8	Road		37	Reread
9	Gun		38	Gas
10	U		39	D.D.
11	Aid		40	A.I.T.C.
12	Frog		41	Film
13	Read		42	Reason
14	Sim		43	Sex
15	Um		4	UNO
16	Bills		45	Deep
17	Lore		46	Life
18	Fado		47	Forgo
19	Die		48	Sings
20	Foe		49	Echo
21	Sin		50	File
22	Sex		51	Shoes
23	Boat		52	Set
24	Yarn		53	Baix
25	Yes		54	Yo
26	Ball		55	Jam
27	All		56	Beep
28	Tip		57	Ail
29	Pray		58	Tack

I cannot tell how the truth may be;
I say the tale as 'twas told to me.

SCOTT

Perhaps the worst plight of a vessel is to be caught in a gale on a lee shore. In this connection the following... rules should be observed:

1. Never allow your vessel to be found in such a predicament...

CALLINGHAM, *Seamanship: Jottings for the Young Sailor*

Sunday 26th January,
1941.

Dear Walter,

     I shall ask you to burn this the moment you have read it. Tell K.E.F. that he will <u>have</u> to supply <u>anything</u> from the factory in Lyon that you ask. Remind him that it wasn't the French Resistance that have paid his wages for the last ten months. I want the chimneys smoking again at the earliest possible moment <u>or I will sell the whole plant.</u>

     Would your Wehrmacht people be interested in buying the place? Should you be interested I will appoint you as the agent at the usual rate. Surely a factory in the Vichy Free Zone could be useful in the light of this 'Trading with the Enemy Statutory List'?

     I think these people here are beginning to realize which way the wind has blown and already a little of the bravado has disappeared. You can mark my words that should your fellows actually come into conflict with the Soviets we British will not be long in understanding what must be done.

     Our plant in Latvia has gone down the drain now that they have been subverted by the Bolshies and I can only say how glad I am that the plans for the Bukovina place didn't materialize.

     I am forming a 'Brains Trust' (as they say these days) of people who see eye to eye with me on these points so that when the country finally comes to its senses we will be in a position to do something about it.

     You are right about Roosevelt's crowd: now that he's safely in for the third time they will foment the spiteful retaliatory attitude of the socialist mob here. However, Roosevelt isn't America you know, and as long as your people don't do anything foolish (like dropping a bomb on New York) only a small number will be willing to pick up a gun if it means putting down a cash register.

     Burn this now,

     Yours,

     Henry

Horse Under Water

Secret File No. 2

1 Sweet talk

Marrakech is just what the guide-books say it is. Marrakech is an ancient walled city surrounded with olive groves and palm trees. Behind it rise the mountains of the high Atlas and in the city the market place at Djemaa-el-Fna is alive with jugglers, dancers, magicians, story-tellers, snake-charmers and music. Marrakech is a fairy-tale city, but on this trip I didn't get to see much more of it than a fly-blown hotel room and the immobile faces of three Portuguese politicians.

My hotel was in the old city; the Medina. The rooms were finished in brown and cream paint and the wall decorations were notices telling me not to do various things in French. From the next room came the sound of water dripping into the stained bath tub and the call of an indefatigable cricket, while through the broken fly-screens in the window came the musical sound of an Arab city selling its wares.

I removed my tie and put it over the back of my chair. My shirt hung suddenly cold against the small of my back and I felt a dribble of sweat run gently down the side of my nose, hesitate and drop on to 'Sheet 128: Transfer of sterling assets of Government of Portugal held in United Kingdom, Mandates or Dependencies to successor Government'.

We sipped oversweet mint tea, munched almond, honey-sticky cakes, and I took comfort in the idea of being back in London inside twenty-four hours. This may be a millionaire's playground, but no self-respecting millionaire would be seen dead here in the summer. It was ten past four in the afternoon. The whole town was buzzing with flies and conversation; cafés, restaurants and brothels had standing room only; the pickpockets were working to rota.

'Very well,' I said, 'availability of thirty per cent of your sterling assets as soon as the British Ambassador in Lisbon is satisfied that you have a working control within the capital.' They agreed to that. They weren't delirious with joy but they agreed to that. They were hard bargainers, these revolutionaries.

2 Old solution

The W.O.O.C.(P) owned a small piece of grimy real estate on the unwashed side of Charlotte Street. My office had an outlook like a Cruikshank illustration to *David Copperfield*, and subsidence provided an isosceles triangle under the door that made internal telephones unnecessary.

Dawlish was my chief. When I gave him the report on my negotiations in Marrakech he laid it on his desk like the foundation stone of the National Theatre and said, 'Foreign Office are going to introduce a couple of new ideas for tackling the talks with the Portuguese revolutionary party.'

'For *us* to tackle them,' I corrected.

'Top marks, my boy,' said Dawlish, 'you cottoned on to that aspect of their little scheme.'

'I'm covered in the scar tissue of O'Brien's good ideas.'

'Well, this one is better than most,' said Dawlish.

Dawlish was a tall, grey-haired civil servant with eyes like the far end of a long tunnel. Dawlish always tended to placate other departments when they asked us to do something difficult or stupid. I saw each job in terms of the people who would have to do the dirty work. That's the way I saw this job, but Dawlish was my master.

On the small, antique writing-desk that Dawlish had brought with him when he took over the department – W.O.O.C.(P) – was a bundle of papers tied with the pink ribbon of officialdom. He riffled quickly through them. 'This Portuguese revolutionary movement …' Dawlish began; he paused.

'*Vós não vedes*,' I supplied.

'Yes, V.N.V. – that's "they do not see", isn't it?'

'"Vós" is the same as "vous" in French,' I said; 'it's "*you* do not see".'

'Quite so,' said Dawlish, 'well this V.N.V. want the F.O. to put up quite a lump sum of money in advance.'

'Yes,' I said, 'that's the trouble with easy payment plans.'

Dawlish said, 'Suppose we could do it for nothing.' I didn't answer. He went on, 'Off the coast of Portugal there is a boat full of money. It's money that the Nazis counterfeited during the war. English and American paper money.'

I said, 'Then the idea is that the V.N.V. boys get the money from the sunken boat and use it to finance their revolution?'

'Not quite,' said Dawlish. He probed the hot pipe-embers with a match. 'The idea is that *we* get the money from the sunken boat for them.'

'Oh no!' I said. 'You surely haven't agreed to that. What do F.O. Intelligence Unit* get paid for?'

'I sometimes wonder,' agreed Dawlish, 'but I suppose the F.O. have their troubles too.'

'Don't tell me about them,' I said, 'it might break me up emotionally.'

Dawlish nodded, removed his spectacles and dabbed at his dark eye-sockets with a crisp handkerchief. Behind him on the window ledge the sun was rolling dusty documents into brandy snaps.

* Foreign Office Intelligence Unit, part of M.I.6.

In the street below a man with a twin horn was dissatisfied with the existing disposition of traffic.

'V.N.V. say that off the Portuguese coast there is a wrecked ship.'

Dawlish could never tell you anything without drawing a diagram. He drew a small formalized ship on the notepad with a gold pencil. 'It was a German naval vessel en route to South America in March 1945. Inside it there is a considerable amount of excellent counterfeit currency, sterling five-pound notes, fifty-dollar bills and some genuine Swedish stuff. It was for high-ranking Nazis seeking exile, of course.' I said nothing. Dawlish dabbed his eyes and I heard the traffic outside begin to move again.

'The V.N.V. want us to help them retrieve these items. For "help them retrieve" you can read "present them with". F.O. see this as a way of supporting what they think is an inevitable change of power, without implicating us too deeply, or costing any money. Comment?'

I said, 'You mean the Portuguese revolutionaries are to use the counterfeit U.S. money and the genuine Swedish stuff to buy guns and generally finance a political Paul Jones, but the English money they can't use because the design of the fiver has been changed.'

'Quite so,' said Dawlish.

I said, 'I'm cynical. Do you have the name of the ship, charted position of the wreck and German bills of lading from Admiralty Historical Department?'

'Not yet,' said Dawlish, 'but I have confirmed that there have been a fair number of counterfeit fivers in that region. They may have come from a wreck. Also V.N.V. have a local fisherman who is confident about locating it.'

'Item 2,' I continued, 'the idea is that we mount a subversive operation in Portugal, which is a dictatorship whichever side of the dispatch box you rest your feet. This in itself is a tricky enterprise, but we are going to do it, in cooperation with, or on behalf of, this group of citizens whose openly avowed aim it is to overthrow the government. This you tell me is going to cause H.M.G. less embarrassment than planting a few hundred thousand into a bank account for them.'

Dawlish pulled a face.

'O.K.,' I said, 'so don't let's have any false ideas about motivation. It's a way of saving money at a considerable risk – our risk. I can see the working of the P.S.T.'s* eager little mind. He is going to organize a revolution while the Americans have to finance it because there are so many counterfeit dollars turning up all over the world. But Treasury are wrong.'

Dawlish looked up sharply and began tapping his pencil on the desk diary. The twin horn had nearly reached Oxford Street. 'You think so?' he said.

'I know so,' I told him. 'These Portuguese characters are tough guys. They have been around. They will get rid of the British stuff all right, then the Treasury will be all long faces and little pink memos.'

We sat in silence for a few minutes while Dawlish drew a choppy sea above his drawing of a boat. He swivelled his chair round so that he could see through the dingy windows, jutted his lower lip forward and beat it with his pencil. In between this he said 'Ummm' four times.

He turned his back to me and began to speak. 'Six months ago O'Brien told me that he knew of one hundred and fifty experts on world currency. He said there were seven who knew all the answers about moving it, but when it came to moving and changing it illegally, O'Brien said that you would be his choice every time.'

* Permanent Secretary of the Treasury: Head of the Treasury and therefore holds the title 'Head of H.M. Civil Service'.

'I'm flattered,' I said.

'Perhaps,' said Dawlish, who considered illegal talent a dubious virtue; 'but Treasury may have second thoughts, if they know how strongly you are against it.'

'Don't sell tickets on the strength of it,' I told him. 'What F.S.T.* will pass up a chance of saving perhaps a million pounds sterling? He probably has the College of Heralds designing a coat of arms already.'

I was right. Within ten days I had a letter telling me to report to the R.N. Instructional Diving School (Shallow Dive Course No. 549) at H.M.S. *Vernon*. The F.S.T. was going to get an earldom and I would get an Admiralty diving certificate. As Dawlish said when I complained, 'But you are the obvious choice, old boy.' He inscribed the numeral 'one' on his notepad and said, 'One, Lisbon 1940, many contacts, you speak a bit of the lingo. Two,' he wrote 'two', 'currency expert. Three,' he wrote 'three', 'you were in on the first contacts with the V.N.V. in Morocco last month.'

'But do I have to go on this frogman course?' I asked. 'It will be wet and cold and it'll all take place in the early hours of the morning.'

'Physical comfort is just a state of mind, my boy, it will make you fighting fit; and besides,' Dawlish leaned forward confidentially, 'you'll be in charge, you know, and you don't want these blighters nipping below for a crafty smoke.' Dawlish then uttered a curious polyphonic sound, rather high-pitched at first, ending in a vibrating palate and terminated by the distribution of tobacco ash throughout the room. I stared incredulously; Dawlish had laughed.

* Financial Secretary to the Treasury, who deals directly with the Prime Minister and directs the Treasury to implement decisions of the Government.

3 Undersea need

There is a point on the A3 near Cosham at which the whole of Portsmouth Harbour comes suddenly into view. This expanse of inland water is a vast grey triangle pointing to the Solent. The edges are sharp serrated patterns of docks, jetties and hards enclosing the colourless water.

A penetrating drizzle had been leaking through the low cloud since I had joined the A3 at Kingston Vale about 6.45 a.m. Window display men were junking polystyrene Xmas trees and ordering gambolling lambs. On their way to work people were sneaking a look at shop windows to see how much their relatives had paid for the presents they had received.

The snow had been around a long time. Layer upon layer had crystallized and hardened into abstract shapes. Now it sat like a delinquent child glaring at passers-by and daring them to try moving it. The ground had absorbed so much cold that rain made a slippery layer on the ice. I slowed as crowds of factory and dockyard workers swarmed across the streets. I turned into the red-brick gate of H.M.S. *Vernon*. A rating stood there in oilskins that gleamed like patent leather. He waved me to a halt. I walked to the porch where half a dozen sailors in damp saggy raincoats sat huddled together, hands in pockets. From the brittle Tannoy came a message for the duty watch. I knocked at the counter.

A young rating looked up from the assorted parts of a bicycle bell that lay before him on the table.

'Can I help you sir?'

'Instructional Diving Section,' I said.

He asked the operator for a number and sat, eye-glazed, waiting to be connected. On the notice board I read about the Q.M. of the watch being responsible for boilers when there were men in cells. Under it hung a copper bugle with highly polished dents. I signed into the visitors' ledger 'Time of arrival 08.05', a drip of rain spattered on to the page. Inside the office were the highly polished lino and blancoed belts that go with military police systems everywhere in the world. A two-badge seaman took over the phone and clobbered the receiver rest a few times. A P.O. emerged, holding a brown enamel teapot. He looked at my Admiralty authority.

'That's all right – take him over to Diving.' He disappeared still holding the teapot in both hands.

The rain hammered the concrete roadways and paths and large freshly painted ships' figureheads dribbled pensively. The Instructional Diving Section was a barn-like building that echoed to the noise of metal drums being moved. Behind a wire screen was a hardboard counter and a muscular rating.

'Course 549?' he asked.

'Yes,' I said. He eyed my civilian raincoat doubtfully. Over the Tannoy came the clang of one bell in the forenoon watch. A tall one-stripe hooky exchanged a Gauloise cigarette for half a cup of dark brown tea and I warmed my hands on the enamel sides of the mug. I knew it would all take place in the early hours of the morning.

The grey winter light and wet fog crept through the tiny windows and illuminated the rigid lines of school desks, engraved with hearts, patterns, and initials. I looked around the classroom. At the other desks were quiet, smooth-faced

N.O.s with carefully dirtied gold stripes wrapped around brushed blue worsted. They talked quietly together in a well-bred clubby sort of way. I found my cigarettes and lit up. Behind me someone was saying ' … and the bedrooms will be all G-Plan too …'

'Here we go,' someone else said. The door clicked open. With a smooth legerdemain perfected amid the tyranny of gunrooms the class came to attention on half-smoked cigarettes.

The golden arm of a senior officer waved us back to relaxation and gave us some 'team spirits', some 'work hard and play hards' one 'welcome aboard' and then gave us Chief Petty Officer Edwards.

C.P.O. Edwards was a pink man. His face was the same shade all over, neither more pink at the lips nor less pink around the eye sockets. He clasped a pink right hand inside a pink left hand and thrust them floorwards as though trying to cope with an almost unmanageable weight. His hair was short and the colour of 'tickler' and he was anxious to find out how high he could lift his chin without losing sight of his class.

'Seeing how this is an officers' course some young gentlemen may feel that the due care and attention in respect of hours of commencement need not be observed. I would like to correct this impression right away. Late arrivals will not, repeat not, enter the classroom after the door is closed but will report to the Lieutenant-Commander's office. Third door on the right down the corridor. Any questions. Right.' There could be no questions.

On the lapel of C.P.O. Edwards's serge jacket was a star, a diver's helmet, a crown of red thread, and a small C. C.P.O. Edwards was a professional diver, an expert, a 'Clearance Diver'. He walked to the rear of the class and put large cardboard boxes on each desk. 'Don't you dare touch till you are told to,' he shouted to the young paymaster lieutenant in the front row, adding, some moments after, 'sir.' A couple of the officers grinned at each other but I didn't see anyone start opening a box.

'Right, have–your–notebooks–ready–and–I–don't–want–anybody–asking–for–a–pencil,' he said, probably for the thousandth time. 'This is your kit, check it; sign for it. I don't want anybody asking me for a spare hood. Look after your gear and it will look after you. Lose something and come and tell me about it and you know what I shall do? Do *you*, sir? Do *you* know what I will do?' The Chief was talking to the officer with the G-Plan bedroom.

'I'll larf, sir, that's what I will do; larf.' The Chief gave no sign of laughing either now or at any future time: I thought for a moment that LARF was some strange nautical verb.

There are lots of different degrees of diving skill. The first dives are done with the divers on the end of a leash like a well-bred poodle taking a dip. At the end of three weeks we would be shallow-water divers – the lowest form of submarine life. We were training to be amateurs.

Any member of ship's crew could volunteer for this course and become the one to do inverted pressups on the barnacles to discover a foreign limpet of destruction. Others might stay here at *Vernon* to shake off the leash of authority and swim alone in the dark sea as a Free Diver; but it was the Clearance Divers who spent long professional years to learn the whole box of tricks from copper helmet to rubber flippers. C.P.O. Edwards was such a man.

Finally we were allowed to open the big brown boxes while the C.P.O. sang the contents to us.

'Combinations, blue woollen, one. That's it, son. A blue woollen man knitted by an old maid. Frocks, white woollen, one. That's it – I know it's a roll-neck pullover but you sign for a Frock. I'm not responsible for Naval Nomenclature. Helmet, blue woollen, one. Keep your head warm – one of the first rules of diving. Right. Mittens, free flooding, one pair. Right. Neck ring, one. No, that's your neck *seal*. A neck ring is metal.' He made a clucking noise in the throat and walked across the room, in tacit protest at an appalling state of ignorance. 'Right. Neck clamp, one. Metal, son, the thing that fits on your neck ring. Right. Neck seal, one. Well where did you put it? Look, he's got it on *his* desk,' then in a louder voice, 'look after your gear, already you are mixing it all up. I'm telling you, the rating divers on the other course will pounce on you lot like a jaunty onto a Crown and Anchor game.'

By now everyone was examining the gear like kids on Christmas morning. There were the one-piece black rubber suits, with two-way stretch and tight-fitting wrists, and the belt and the undersea knife. By now the classroom looked like a war-surplus store.

'Do we have the rest of the day off, chiefie?' someone asked.

'There's a couple of things on the agenda,' said C.P.O. Edwards. 'Muster at the sick bay for a medical, half an hour with the recompression chamber and a quick dip into the tank for all of you.'

'Today?' said G-Plan. He looked out of the window; across the roads of the depot the rain was bouncing back up and making a thick pile carpet of wetness.

'Yes, you'll be snug and dry in the tank,' said Edwards. 'It's no depth, son, do you the world of good. Next. Instruction period Two: (a) dealing with wet gear, (b) stowing wet gear and (c) underwater signals.'

'We aren't going to have much time for lunch,' said G-Plan. The chief relished this moment. He smiled a calm old-fashioned smile.

'Lunch will be served at the diving position, sir. 'Hot coffee and sandwiches.' There was a bustle of comment. 'It's better in the long run you'll find,' the Chief said to no one in particular. 'You won't be running up a lot of mess bills and if you are going to be divers it's not a lot of good to you all that drinking at the wardroom bar.'

If one pressed flat against the wall, which I was learning to call a bulkhead, only a small portion of the heavy rain hit you. Behind us the Artificer Divers were welding and hammering at the benches. After we had been in the tank they would resume the same tasks under water. The diving tank was a grey-painted gasometer, reinforced with crisscross girders. Above us in a boiler suit 'dhobied' almost white was the tall one-stripe hooky. He called down to us, 'Ready for number four.'

The sub-lieutenant with the G-Plan bedroom shuffled forward, awkward in the flippers. The wind cut a thin rasher of water from the top of the tank and slopped it over the side. It hit the concrete with a crack and splashed around our black rubber legs. Number four was at the top. The tall leading seaman mouthed instructions that were kicked aside by the wind and swept across the harbour. Number four nodded and began to descend the ladder into the tank.

I looked through one of the glass panels. It was the size of a large TV screen. The sea water inside was cloudy green and small flecks of animal and vegetable matter swayed in neutral buoyancy. I watched number four stumbling across the floor of the tank. The suit suddenly ejected a stream of bubbles from the relief valve on his left shoulder. He had allowed the counter-lung to build up too much pressure. In war time such a mistake could cause instant death. They were tricky to use, these oxygen sets, but skilfully operated no tell-tale bubbles ever reached the surface. The diver breathes in and out of the rubber bag using the same air over and over, topping it up with oxygen while absorbing the CO_2 by means of the absorbent canister. Number four was learning how to move under water now, leaning forward as though in a powerful headwind, but his over-inflated rubber lung had lifted him clear of the floor. He was almost horizontal before he had gripped the metal ladder. Now the sailor on the ladder tapped a signal and G-Plan began to haul himself upward.

Soon he was back under the leaky lean-to, dripping wet, smiling and wiping the back of his hand across his face before putting a cigarette in it. He drew on the fag and breathed out of an open mouth, revelling in the dirty warmth of the smoke. We awaited his verdict.

'Nothing to it,' he said. 'My kid could do it.'

'That officer there,' the voice of C.P.O. Edwards came effortlessly along the whole length of the jetty, 'neglecting his diving gear.' The whole place sprang to life, the sibilant sound of fags being doused, equipment tidied and welding torches lit echoed around the hut.

'Leading seaman Barker. Get these trainees on the ladder.' Edwards's sentences ended on an authoritative high note, and the leading hand almost toppled into the tank in his haste, as Edwards's metal-tipped heels moved ever closer.

'Number eight, please,' said the leading seaman rather plaintively. Our numbers were painted across each and every metal part of the equipment. 'Eight,' I heard the hooky say again. I looked at my own absorbent canister. I was number eight. 'The civilian officer, sir, who is always late.' I was No. 8.

'Nice and cosy', the L.S. made sure the square wraparound mask was watertight, and the mouthpiece between my teeth, then gave me a gentle slap on the arm. Through the eyepiece everything was enlarged and I found difficulty in even locating the ladder's top step. The water was dense and very cold.

Only when one's eyes descend below the waterline is one suddenly under water. A few large white bubbles sped upward past my eyes, escaping from the folds of the rubber suit. The water closed upon me like a green trapdoor and light shimmered and danced as the wind's rough file tore notches in the smooth surface.

'Wanch Wanch.' The noise of the air rattling around the breathing bag was deafening. I touched the soft black rubber of the counter-lung across my chest, and, deciding it was too soft, turned the brass tap of the bypass. The compressed oxygen roared through the reducing valve and an explosion of white bubbles rushed past my left ear. Too much. It was tricky. Still listening to my breath I noticed that I was breathing faster just as the instructor said everyone did. I deliberately held my breath for a moment. Shallow breathing didn't give the CO_2 absorbent enough time to do its job and could result in CO_2 poisoning, which in turn causes one to breathe shorter until intoxication, giddiness and blackout occur. I must stop even thinking about such things. By holding one's breath the slight sound of the wind upon the water, the creak of the metal, and the noises of the people outside became audible. I went close to the vision panels. I felt the pressure of the water constricting my arms and legs. The rain still swept across the jetty. I breathed out, the air clattered like a bundle of firewood. Across the floor of the tank the light made patterns of green and white.

My right sock had wrinkled underfoot. I raised my leg and found I could lean forward on the water. I walked two steps but the density prevented me making progress. I bobbed. I leaned forward again and made a paddling motion. I noticed how clear my hands were. They and everything else around me had taken on a new interest and wonder. I studied the small scar on the palm of my right hand. It was like seeing a colour transparency of it. I looked up at the surface of the water and tried to guess how deep I was. It was difficult to judge shape, size or distance down here.

I wondered what the time was and walked back to the glass panel to try to see the dockyard clock. Two 'art divers' were standing in the way. I decided to 'guff up' again and gave the bypass valve a little twist. It was a better attempt and although I bounced a couple of feet off the bottom little or no air came out of the relief valve. The other trainees were making a lot of noise. The clatter of them around the tank competed with the noise of my breathing. It was the hooky tapping a spanner upon the top rung of the ladder. A signal for me to ascend. I remembered what Edwards had said; men become forgetful and complacent under water.

As my head broke the surface the light was dazzling and the reflections from the water almost painful to my eyes, which had adjusted to the gentle green underwater conditions. A hooter sounded somewhere across the harbour and I was suddenly aware of all the noisemakers. I dragged my heavy body and its three oxygen bottles out of the water. Down below G-Plan had a large medicine bottle. It contained rum. Watching until Edwards had gone across the jetty he passed it to me.

'Gulpers,' he said and I thanked him sincerely. The gentle warmth raced around my veins like a hot-rod Ford.

In the hut there were warm towels and dry clothing and C.P.O. Edwards. I could hear his voice while I dressed. ' … practical working. Theory five: the physiology of diving and Artificial Respiration. Wednesday, Theory six: recognizing an under-charged set – it's dangerous to risk an almost empty bottle – and then the practical at Horsea Island in the afternoon. Thursday: Symptoms of CO_2 poisoning, of Oxygen poisoning (or anoxia) – what the Navy call "Oxygen Pete", of

Air Embolism or what divers call "chokes", of Decompression Sickness – what we call "staggers" but what you've probably heard them in films calling "bends". And lastly Shallow Water Blackout – what the quack calls "syncope" just fainting really but it's more frequent when you are on Oxygen.'

It made me feel like I'd just had all of them.

'That leaves Friday,' Edwards's voice continued, 'for a morning of diving and a simple revision and written test in the afternoon.'

G-Plan said, 'We will have learnt it all by then, chief? What are you going to find us to do on Monday morning?'

'Monday morning you start all over again,' said Edwards. He stepped outside the door and raised his powerful voice. 'They're spending too much time on the ladder, Barker. They aren't on the steps of the Prince Regent's bathing machine.' Then turning back into the hut again his voice lowered. 'Yes, you'll be starting all over again on Monday. Theory seven: Preparation and service of Swimmers' Air Breathing Apparatus. That's the aqua-lung works with a demand valve and compressed air – quite different to these oxygen sets. And by the way, Stewart,' that was G-Plan's name, 'if the officer of the watch comes round, you'll keep that medicine bottle of yours out of sight. I wouldn't like him to think any of my divers were not well.'

'Yes Chief,' said Stewart. He had eyeballs in his buttons that Edwards.

4 Man with a tail

Some heavy lorries making smoke at Horndean, a sharp rain-storm rolling across Hindhead, grass as green as crème de menthe, and then bright sunshine as I came on to the Guildford by-pass. I watched my mirror, then tuned the radio to France III.

Putney Bridge and into King's Road; shiny, shoddy and deep-frozen. Bald men with roll-neck pullovers. Girls with bee-swarm hair-dos and trousers that left nothing to the imagination. Left, up Beaufort Street, past the Forum cinema and on to Gloucester Road. Men with dirty driving gloves and clean copies of *Autosport*, and landladies weighed down with shillings from insatiable gas-meters. Left again, on to Cromwell Road Clearway. Now I was quite sure. The black Anglia was following me.

I turned again and pulled up by the phone box on the corner. The Anglia came past me slowly as I searched for a threepenny piece. I watched out of the corner of my eye until it stopped perhaps seventy yards up the one-way street, then I got quickly back into my car and backed around the corner on to Cromwell Road again. This left the black Anglia seventy yards up a one-way street. Now to see how efficient they were.

I drove on past Victorian terraces behind which unpainted bed-sitters crouched, pretending to be one grand imperial household instead of a molecular structure of colonial loneliness.

I stopped. From under the front passenger seat I reached for the 10 × 40 binoculars that I always store there. I wrapped a *Statesman* around them, locked the car and walked over to Jean's flat. Number 23 had peach curtains and was a maze of corridors down which the draught got a running start at the ill-fitting doors. I let myself in.

A fan heater provided a background hum while Jean tinkled around the kitchen fixing a big jug of coffee. I watched her from the kitchen doorway. She was wearing a dark-brown woollen suit; her tan had not faded and the hair that hung across her deep forehead was still golden from the summer sun. She looked up; calm, clear and as still as a three-quarter-grain Nembutal.

She said, 'Did you straighten out the Navy?'

'You make me sound pragmatic,' I said.

'And it's not true, is it?' She poured the coffee into the big art-pottery cups. 'You were followed here, you know.'

'I don't think so,' I said quietly.

'Don't do that,' said Jean.

'What?'

'You know very well. It's your Oreste Pinto voice. You say things to provoke a fuller reply.'

'All right. All right. Relax.'

'You don't have to tell …'

'I was followed by a black Anglia, BGT 803, maybe all the way from Portsmouth, certainly from Hindhead. I've no idea who it is, but it could be the Electrolux company.'

'Pay them,' said Jean. She stood well back from the window still looking down towards the street. 'They *could* be from the refrigerator company; one of them has an icepick in his hand.'

'Very funny.'

'You have a wide circle of friends. The gentlemen across the road feature an azure Bristol 407. It's rather dreamy.'

'You're joking, of course.'

'Come and see, child of Neptune.'

I walked to the window. There was a Bristol 407 of brilliant blue, sufficiently muddied to have done a fast journey down the A3. It was awkwardly parked amid the dense mortuary of vehicles in the street below. On the pavement a tall man in a flat peaked cap and short bold-patterned overcoat looked like a wealthy bookmaker. I focused the Zeiss and studied the two men and their car carefully.

I said, 'They aren't working for any department we know, judging from the tax bracket they're in. Bristol 407 indeed.'

'Do I detect a faint note of envy?' asked Jean, taking the binoculars and looking down upon my would-be companions.

'Yes,' I said.

'You wouldn't join the enemies of democracy and threaten the existence of freedom-loving western capitalism for a Bristol 407, would you?'

'What colour?'

Jean was looking out of the tall narrow window. 'He's getting back into it again. They are going to park outside 26.' She turned back to me. 'Do you think they are Special Branch?'

'No: only West End Central cops have big cars.'

'Do you think they're friends?'*

'No, they wouldn't let an overcoat like that through the front door of the H.O.'

Jean put down the field-glasses and poured out the coffee in silence.

'Go on,' I said, 'there are plenty more security departments.' Jean handed me the big cup of black coffee. I sniffed it. 'It's Continental roast.'

---

* 'Friends': jargon for employees of M.I.5, which is not run by the military (in spite of the title) but by an offshoot of the Home Office.

'You like Continental roast, don't you?'

'Sometimes,' I said.

'What are you going to do?'

'I'll drink it.'

'About the men.'

'I'll find out who they are.'

'How?' asked Jean.

'Well, I shall go upstairs, climb out along the roofs, find another skylight, go down through the house. You, meanwhile, put on my overcoat and move about near the window so that they catch sight of what they think is me. At a prearranged time-lapse, say twenty minutes, you will go across and start up the engine of my VW. They will have to pull out the Bristol in order to have any chance of catching my car before it disappears. Got it?'

Jean said, 'Yes,' very slowly and doubtfully.

'By that time I shall be in the porch of, say, Number 29. When they get their car started I will take a potato, which I shall have taken from your vegetable basket and, running forward, crouching very low, I shall jam the raw unpeeled potato on to their exhaust pipe and hold it there. It's only a matter of moments before the pressure builds up enough to blow the cylinder head off with a tremendous crash.' Jean giggled. 'There they will be with an expensive disabled car. They will never get a taxi at this time of day at Gloucester Road cab rank, so they will have to ask for a lift in the VW, which by this time will have had the heater going long enough to make it warm and comfortable. On the way to wherever they wish to go I shall say – quite casually, mark you – "what are you two young fellows doing in this neck of the woods on a Saturday midday?" and from one thing and another I shall soon find out who they work for.'

Jean said, 'It's not had a good effect on you, that Naval Depot.'

I dialled the Ghost exchange number and switchboard

answered. I put a hand over the mouthpiece while asking Jean, 'What is the code word for the week-end?'

'Fine pickle you'd be in without me,' she said from the kitchen.

'Don't carp, girl. I haven't been in to the office for a week.'

'It's "cherish".'

'Cherish,' I said to the switchboard operator, and he connected me to the W.O.O.C.(P) duty officer, 'Tinkle' Bell.

'Tinkle,' I said, 'cherish.'

'Yes,' said Tinkle. I heard the click of the recording machine being switched into the circuit. 'Go ahead.'

'I have a tail. Anything on W.M.?' Tinkle went to look at the Weekly Memoranda sheets that came from the Joint Intelligence Agency at the Ministry of Defence. I heard Tinkle's outsize brogue shoes pad lightly back to the desk. 'Not a sausage, old boy.'

'Do me a favour, Tinkle.'

'Anything you say, old boy.'

'You have someone you could leave in charge if you nipped down to Storey's Gate for me?'

'Certainly, old chap, pleasure.'

'Thanks, Tinkle. I wouldn't bother you on Saturday if it wasn't important.'

'Precisely, old boy. I know that.'

'Go up to the third floor and see Mrs Welch – that's W-e-l-c-h – and tell her you want one of the C-SICH* files. Any one. I tell you what, make it a file we're already holding. You with me?'

---

* C-SICH: Combined Services Information Clearing House. Part of the Ministry of Defence's Joint Intelligence Agency. It is a funnel through which all British and Commonwealth intelligence matter is sorted, filed, and distributed. The commercial organizations (which have men to steal secrets from their competitors and safeguard their own) furnish a great volume of matter to C-SICH.

'Sinking fast, old boy.'

'Ask her for some file we already have and she'll tell you we already have it, but you say we haven't. She will show you the receipt book. If she doesn't offer to, raise hell and insist that she does. Get a good eyeful of all the receipt signatures down the right-hand column. What I want to know is who receipted file 20 W.O.O.C.(P) 287.'

'That's one of our personal dossiers,' said Tinkle.

'Mine, to be precise,' I said. 'If I know who's handled my file lately I have a lead on who might be tailing me.'

'Very crafty,' said Tinkle.

'And, Tinkle,' I added, 'I want a quick check on two car registrations, a black Anglia and a Bristol 407.' I waited while Tinkle read back the numbers.

'Thanks, Tinkle, and ring me back at Jean's.'

Jean poured me a third cup of coffee and produced some pancakes with sugar and cream. 'You are a bit careless on an open line, aren't you?' she said. 'C–SICH and file numbers and all that.'

I said, 'If anyone listening isn't in the business it will be gibberish, and if they are, they were taught that stuff in Dzerzhinski Street.'

'While you were on the phone your Anglia arrived.'

I walked to the window. Four men were talking, well down the road. Soon two of them got into the Bristol and drove away, but the Anglia remained outside.

Jean and I spent a lazy Saturday afternoon. She washed her hair and I made lots of coffee and read a back issue of the *Observer*. The TV was just saying ' … a Blackfoot war party wouldn't be using a medicine arrow, Betsy …' when the phone rang.

'It was the Director of Naval Intelligence,' I said into the phone before he could speak.

'Blimey,' said Tinkle, 'how did you know?'

'I thought D.N.I. would screen a visiting civilian pretty thoroughly before letting him into their diving school.'

Tinkle said, 'Well, good thinking, old boy. Central Register* and C-SICH both booked your files out to D.N.I. on September 1st.'

'What about the car registrations, Tinkle?'

'The Anglia belongs to a man named Butcher, initials I. H., and the Bristol to a Cabinet Minister named Smith. Know them?'

'I've heard the names before. Perhaps you would do an S6 report on both of them and leave it in the locked "in" tray.'

'O.K.,' said Tinkle and rang off.

'What did he say?' Jean asked.

'I'm riding shotgun on the noon stage,' I said. Jean made a noise and continued to paint a finger-nail flame orange.

Finally I said, 'The cars belong to a Cabinet Minister named Henry Smith and to a little thug named Butcher who does a cut-price service in commercial espionage on the "seduced secretary" system.'

'What a lovely system,' Jean said.

'You haven't seen Butcher,' I said. 'My file, incidentally, went to D.N.I. on September 1st.'

'Butcher,' Jean said. 'Butcher. I know that name.' She painted another nail. Suddenly she shouted, 'The ice-melting report.'

What a memory she had. Butcher had sold us an old German laboratory report about a machine to melt ice at an amazing speed. 'What can you remember of that report?' I asked her.

---

* Central Register: a collection of dossiers on two million people including foreigners. Central Register is run by M.I.5.

'I couldn't understand it properly,' she said, 'but the rough idea was that by rearranging the molecular structure of ice it would instantaneously become water. Or vice versa. That's something the Navy might be keen on now that there are missile submarines that have to find a hole in the polar ice-pack before they can fire them.' She held her hand at arm's distance and studied the orange nails for a minute.

'Yes,' I said, 'Butcher had the report. Navy want the report … That's the connexion. I'm a genius.'

'Why are *you* a genius?' Jean asked.

'For getting myself a secretary like you,' I said. Jean blew me a kiss.

'What about Mr Smith the Cabinet Minister?' Jean asked.

'He's just having his car borrowed,' I said. But I wasn't sure about that. I looked at Jean and stubbed out my cigarette.

'My nails are still wet,' Jean said, 'you mustn't.'

5 No toy

My two weeks at Portsmouth passed quickly and I came home with a small Admiralty shallow-water certificate suitable for framing, and incipient pneumonia, although Jean said it was a sore throat. Monday I stayed in bed all day. Tuesday was a cold bright morning in September that warned you that winter was all set to pounce.

A letter from the Admiralty arrived authorizing me to take possession of the R.N. underwater gear from the school and charged it to me! The same post brought me another bill for the repair of the refrigerator and a final demand for the rates. I nicked my chin while shaving and bled like I'd sprung a leak. I changed into another shirt and arrived at Charlotte Street to find Dawlish in a quiet rage because I had made him late for the Senior Intelligence Conference that takes place in that strange square room of the C.I.G.S. the first Tuesday in each month.

It was a terrible day and it hadn't even begun yet. Dawlish went through all the rigmarole of my new assignment: radio code words and priorities for communicating with him.

'I've persuaded them to give you the equivalent authority to Permanent Under-Secretary, so don't let them down.

It might be useful if you deal with Denning[*] or the Lisbon Embassy. You'll remember that after last year they said they would never give us a rank above Assistant Secretary again.'

'Big deal,' I said, eyeing the papers on his desk. 'P.U.S. and they send me on a Night Tourist aeroplane.'

'All we could get,' said Dawlish. 'Don't be so class-conscious, my boy, you don't want us to demand that they off-load some unfortunate taxpayer; why, you'd have the whole of Gibraltar polishing its blanco – or whatever soldiers do.'

'All right,' I said. 'All right, but you don't have to be so bloody gay about it all.'

Dawlish turned over the next paper on his desk. 'Equipment.' Before he could read on I interrupted.

'That's another thing, they've put about two thousand quids' worth of Admiralty equipment on my personal charge.'

'Security, old chap, don't want those career-mad Admiralty people to know all our little secrets.'

I nodded. 'Look,' I said, 'I'll need your signature if I am to draw a pistol from War Office armoury.' There was a long silence, broken only by the sound of Dawlish blinking.

'Pistol?' said Dawlish. 'Are you going out of your mind?'

'Just into my second childhood,' I said.

'That's right,' said Dawlish, 'they are nasty, noisy, dangerous toys. How would I feel if you jammed your finger in the mechanism or something?'

I picked up the air ticket and underwater-gear inventory and walked to the door.

'West London 9.40,' he said; 'try to have the Strutton report ready before you leave, and …' He removed his glasses and began to polish them carefully. 'You have a pistol of your

[*] Director of Naval Intelligence.

own that I am not supposed to know about. Don't take it with you, there's a good chap.'

'Not a chance,' I said, 'I can't afford the ammunition.'

That day I completed my report for the Cabinet on the Strutton Plan. The plan was to have a new espionage network of people feeding information back to London. All of them would be telephone, cable, telex operators or repair engineers working in embassies or foreign government departments. It meant setting up employment agencies abroad which would specialize in this type of employee. As well as describing the new idea my report had to outline the operations side, i.e. planning, communications, cut-outs,[*] post boxes[†] and a super-imposed system[‡] and, most important as far as the Cabinet report was concerned, costing.

Jean finished typing the report by 8.30 p.m. I locked it into the steel 'out' box, switched on the infra-red burglar-alarm system and set the special phone system to 'record'. Next door was our telephone exchange: Ghost, used in the same way that the Government used Federal exchange. Anyone dialling one of our numbers by mistake heard about a minute and a half of the 'number obtainable' signal before it began ringing. After that the night operators next door challenged the caller, then our phone rang. There were advantages; I could for instance call a number on Ghost from any phone and have the operator connect me to anywhere in the world without attracting attention.

Jean put the typewriter ribbons into the safe. We said good

[*] Construction of the network to ensure that one detected person doesn't lead to another.
[†] Places where messages are deposited so that collector and depositor do not come face to face.
[‡] Method of checking network.

night to George the night man and I put my tickets for B.E.A. 062 into my overcoat.

Jean told me about the carpet she'd bought for her flat and promised to fix me dinner when I returned. I told her not to leave the Strutton Plan report with O'Brien, suggested at least three different excuses she could give him, and promised to look out for a green suede jacket in Spain, size 36.

6 Ugly rock

The airport bus dredged through the sludge of traffic as sodium-arc lamps jaundiced our way towards Slough. Cold passengers clasped their five-shilling tickets and one or two tried to read newspapers in the glimmer. Cars flicked lights, shook their woolly dollies at us and flashed by, followed by ghost cars of white spray.

At the airport everything was closed and half the lighting switched off to save the cost of the electricity we had paid seven and six airport tax for. A long thin line of passengers shuffled down the centre of the draughty customs hall while Immigration men snapped passports in their faces with impartial xenophobia. In the lounge a blonde with smudged mascara played us a gay tune on her teeth with a ballpoint pen before we were sealed into the big, shiny, aluminium pod.

Sitting near the front of the aircraft was a plump man in a plastic raincoat. His red face was familiar to me and I tried to remember in what connexion. He was bellowing loudly about the air conditioning.

The surrounding airport was twittering with Klee-like coloured lights and signs. Inside the cabin the strongest had fought for and won their window seats, sick bags were ready and cabin temperature control set at 'Roast'. Starters whined, dipped the cabin lights to half strength and heaved at the propeller blades. The big motors pounded the wet air, settled into a roar and dragged us up the black ramp of night.

The automatic pilot took control; white plastic cups danced and shuddered across the little stage clipped before me, shedding plastic spoons and large wrapped sugar segments.

I could see the back of the plump man's head. He was shouting. I tried to remember everyone who had been involved in the ice-melting file transaction, and wondered if Dawlish had checked this passenger list.

Eight thousand feet. Beneath us green veins of street-lighting X-rayed Weymouth on to the night. Then only the dark sea.

Thin damp triangles of bread clung helpless across the pliable plate. I ate one. The steward poured hot coffee from the battered metal pots in appreciation. Constellations of city lights merged with icicles of stars suspended in the cavern of the sky.

I dozed until – *Plonk Plonk* – the undercarriage came down and cabin lighting was turned fully bright to open sleep-moted eyes. As the plane rumbled to a halt anxious holiday-makers clasped last year's straw hats and groped towards the exit door.

'Goodnightsirandthankyou … goodnightsirandthankyou … goodnightsirandthankyou …' The stewardess bestowed a low communion upon departing passengers.

The plump man edged his way along the plane towards me. 'Number 24,' he said.

'What?' I said nervously.

'You are number 24,' he said loudly. 'I never forget a face.'

'Who are you?' I asked.

His face bent into a rueful smile. 'You know who I am,' he shouted. 'You are the man in flat number twenty-four and I am Charlie the milkman.'

'Oh yes,' I said weakly. It was the milkman with the deaf horse. 'Have a good holiday, Charlie. I'll settle up when you get back.'

'Coaches for Costa del Sol,' the loudspeakers were saying. The Customs and Immigration gave a perfunctory sleepy nod and stamped '30 days' on the passport.

I could see a square, solid, British figure fighting through the Costa del Sols. 'Welcome to Gibraltar,' said Joe MacIntosh, our man in Iberia.

7 Short talk

Joe MacIntosh drove me out to one of the married-officer accommodations along Europa Road past the military hospital. It was 3.45 a.m. The streets were almost empty. Two sailors in white were vomiting their agonizing way to the Wharf and another was sitting on the pavement near Queen's Hotel.

'Blood, vomit and alcohol,' I said to Joe, 'it should be on the coat of arms.'

'It's on just about everything else,' he said sourly.

After we'd had a drink Joe promised to brief me in the morning before he went on ahead. I slept.

We had breakfast in the mess and the water supply wasn't quite as salty as I remembered it. Joe filled in some of the details.

'We have been hearing about this counterfeit paper money for some years; it's being washed up out of the sea.'

I nodded.

'I've made a little sketch map.'

Joe opened his wallet and pulled out a page of a school exercise book. On it was drawn a shaky tracing of the south-western quarter of the Iberian peninsula. The Straits of Gibraltar were in the bottom right-hand corner. Lisbon was near the top left. Small mapping-pen crosses had been inked in along the coastline. The 100-kilometre stretch between

Sagres (on the extreme south-western tip) and Faro curved, in a 100-kilometre-long bay. Trapped into the curve like bubbles were most of Joe's little marks.

Joe began to tell me the arrangements he had made. 'The nearest town to the wreck is Albufeira, here ...' Joe hadn't changed much from the tall, muscular, Intelligence Corps lieutenant who came to Lisbon as my assistant in 1942. ' ... This is a list of all the wrecks that have happened between Sagres and Huelva and ...' Scores of young Intelligence Officers came to Lisbon in '41 and '42, all anxious to spend one strenuous week bringing the Axis to its knees. Mostly they fell prey to the simplest little security traps we set or they got into arguments with Germans in cafés. We hooked their new boys and they hooked ours, and old timers (anyone who had spent more than three months there) exchanged sardonic smiles with their enemy opposite number over thimbles of black coffee. ' ... using an Italian civilian frogman with whom I have worked before. He is perhaps the best frogman in Europe today. If you stop overnight in the town I have marked I'll phone him to meet you there. Code word: conversation. I'll be going by another route.'

'Joe,' I said. Through the window I could just see Mount Hacho on the North African mainland across the clear air and sunny water of the Straits. 'What have you been told about this operation?'

Joe slowly brought a packet of cigarettes from his pocket, took one and offered them.

'No thanks,' I said. He lit his own and then put away his matches. His hands moved very slowly but I knew his mind was working like lightning.

He said, 'You know the Wren with the rather large ...'

'I know the one,' I said.

'She's the cipher clerk,' Joe said. 'I was chatting her up

the other day when I noticed a clip-board with carbons of all the messages I've sent from here to London over the last two months. They all had BXJ in the corner. I'd never heard of that priority before, so I asked her what it was.' He dragged on the cigarette. 'They are sending all our signals traffic to somebody in London for analysis.' Joe looked at me quizzically.

'Who?' I said.

'She's only the clerk,' Joe said, 'it's the signals officer that redirects them, but she …' He tailed off.

'Go on.'

'She's not sure.'

'So she's not sure.'

'But she thinks it goes to somebody c/o the House of Commons.'

I signalled for some more coffee and the Spanish waitress brought us a big jug. 'Have some coffee,' I said, 'and relax; it'll all work out.'

He gave me a shy Li'l Abner smile. 'I wanted to tell you,' he said, 'but it sounds so unlikely.' We went down to Andalusian Cars in City Mill Lane to pick up a grey Vauxhall Victor for me and a Simca for Joe. He started out for Albufeira and would be there before evening. I had some things to attend to in Gibraltar and my journey would be in two hops.

It was still the same squalid town that I remembered from wartime. Huge barrack-like bars with everything breakable long since removed or broken. Accordion music and drunken singing, red-necked military policemen bullying fat soldiers, thin-lipped army wives weaving among the avaricious Indian shopkeepers on the sun-bright pavement. The secret of enjoying Gibraltar, a ship's doctor had once told me, is not to get off the boat.

8 I hit it

The end of Gibraltar's High Street is Spain. Grey-suited frontier guards nodded, looked for transistor radios and watches, then nodded again. I drove through a couple of hundred yards of dead ground, then through the second control post. The road winds back through Algeciras, and looking across Algeciras Bay one sees the whole of Gib. lying there like a wedge of stale cheese; from the heights where the apes stare down to the airport, to the south where the Ponta de Europa drops away to the sea.

After Algeciras the road began to climb. At first it was dry as burnt toast, but soon white steamy cloud twined through the wheels or sat in heaps on the quiet road. To the left a cliff top was as jagged as a picnic tin. The road descended and followed the beaches northward. It was 3 p.m. The sky was as blue as the Wilton diptych and the warm air drew the smog from my lungs.

Sucking nourishment from the Seville highway, Los Palacios is a huge, gangling village that would be a town if it could afford the paving stones. Great loops of underpowered electric bulbs stared fish-eyed into the twilight as I drove in. One café had a new Seat* 1400 outside it. The name EL DESEMBARCO was painted in gaunt letters, deep set into the dark doorway. I put my foot softly on to the brake. A big diesel lorry hooted behind me as I pulled off the roadway. The lorry parked too and the driver and his mate went inside. I locked up and followed.

There were about thirty customers in one huge barn-like room. Smoked hams and bottles were strung across the walls, and large mirrors with gold advertisements hung from the wall and gave curious sloping dimensions to the reflected drinkers. A glittering Espresso machine roared and pounded. On the black matt counter-top bills were chalked and computed by boys with damp white faces who darted between the gigantic barrels, stopping only to wring out their aprons in gestures of despair, and shout plaintive entreaties to the kitchen in high waiters' Spanish that cut through the clouds of smoke and talk.

I girded up my conversation.

'Deme un vaso de cerveza,' and the waiter brought me a bottle of beer, a glass and a small oval plate of freshly boiled shrimps, moist and delicious. I asked him about rooms. He slipped his white apron over his head and hung it on a hook under the Jayne Mansfield calendar. I hate to think what it might have been advertising. The boy led me out through the rear door. To my right I saw the flare of the kitchen and caught the piquant smell of Spanish olive oil. It was almost dark.

There was a sandy courtyard at the back, partly covered with bamboo from which hung rusting neon lights. Down one side of the courtyard a glassed-in stone corridor gave access to small, cell-like rooms. I negotiated a pram and a Lambretta motor scooter and entered my room. It contained an iron

---

* Seat: A Fiat produced in Spain under licence.

bedstead with crisp clean sheets, a table and a cupboard for a chamber-pot.

'*Veinte y cinco – precios fijos si v gusta,*' said the waiter. A fixed price of twenty-five pesetas seemed O.K. to me. I dumped my overnight bag, gave a Gauloise to the waiter, lit both our cigarettes and went back to the noisy restaurant.

The waiters were serving wine, coffee, sherry, and beer as fast as they could go – putting a squirt of soda into a glass from a distance of two feet, slamming down little plates of smoked ham, salt biscuits or shrimps, arguing with the drunks while adroitly serving the sober. The big tent of sound throbbed against the rafters and hammered down again.

All through the fish soup and omelette I waited for my contact. I asked who owned the new car outside. The boss owned it. I had more Tio Pepes and watched the lorry driver who had hooted me doing a card trick. At 10.30 I wandered out front. Three men in overalls sat on the unpaved ground drinking from a flagon of red wine, two children without shoes were throwing stones at the big diesel truck and some men were arguing quietly about the market value of a used motor-cycle tyre.

I unlocked the door of the car and reached under the dashboard for the .38 Smith & Wesson hammerless 6-shot. The grips were powerful magnets. I pulled it away from the car body, folded it into the car documents, locked up and walked back to my room.

My overnight bag still had my used match lying on it, but before going to sleep I opened the little cupboard and put my gun under the chamber-pot.

9 I sit on it

The sun was scorching the courtyard in which I took Thursday's breakfast. Potted geraniums surrounded the well, and pink convolvulus climbed along the bamboo roofing. Half concealed by the limp washing, a large pockmarked Coca-Cola advert was bleached faint pink by the sun, and the church tower from which nine dull clanks came was toylike in the distance.

'A friend of Mr MacIntosh, is it not, yes?'

Standing beyond my tin pot of coffee was a squat muscular man, about five feet six. His head was wide, his hair dark and waved. His face was tanned enough to emphasize the whiteness of his smile. He carried his arms in front of his body and continually plucked at his shirt cuffs. He flicked his fingers across a large area of green silk pocket-handkerchief and tapped three fingers of his right hand against his forehead with an audible tap.

'I have the message for you which your friend request I should deliver in person.'

His manner of speaking had a strange, jerky rhythm and his voice seldom became lower at the end of each sentence, which led one to expect a few more words to appear any moment. 'Conversion,' he said. I knew that the real code word was 'conversation'.

He reached inside his short pin-stripe jacket and produced a hide wallet as lumpy as a razor blade, and from it slid a business card. He replaced the wallet, smoothed his dark shirt, ran fingers slowly down his silver tie. His hands were short-fingered, powerful, and curiously pale. He offered me the card from his carefully manicured hand. I read it.

S. Giorgio Olivettini
Underwater Surveyor
MILAN   VENICE

I shook the card a couple of times and he sat down.

'You had breakfast?'

'Thank you, I have already consumed breakfast, you permit?'

Señor Olivettini had produced a small packet of cigars. I nodded and shook my head at appropriate intervals and he lit one up and put the rest back into his pocket. 'Conversation,' he said suddenly, and gave a vast smile. He seemed to be my passenger to Albufeira.

I went into my room, put the gun into my trouser pocket, picked up my bag and fixed the bill. Señor Olivettini was waiting by the Victor polishing his two-tone shoes with a bright yellow duster.

For about thirty kilometres I drove in silence and Señor Olivettini smoked and contentedly filed and buffed his nails.

My pistol had worked its way under my thigh. It was an uncomfortable thing to sit on. I let the car lose speed.

'You have planned to stop?' said Señor Olivettini.

'Yes, I am sitting on my gun,' I said. Señor Olivettini smiled politely. 'I know,' he said.

10 Sort of boat

This was Giorgio Olivettini, the man who had thrown Gibraltar into a panic during the war when as an Italian naval frogman he had operated across Algeciras Bay from a secret base in an old ship.[*]

'We are to take cargo from a U-boat, huh?' Giorgio asked.

'Not a U-boat,' I corrected gently.

'Oh yes,' said Giorgio confidently. 'Your Mr Joe MacIntosh send me Kelvin Hughes echo-charts of the wreck. She is a U-boat.'

'You're sure?' I asked.

'The MS 29 is a fine echo-recorder system. I work with her before. I tell you, is a big big U-boat. You will see.'

I certainly hoped it would all become clearer to me.

'Yes,' I said, 'I will see.' Ahead I could see the roofs of Ayamonte, in the Sector de Sevilla entrusted to Brigada MCVIL.

The River Guadiana forms the frontier between Spain and Portugal. Splashed along its Spanish bank is the little white cubist town of Ayamonte.

I let the car roll down a cobbled side street until the slow-moving river lay in front. I turned and drove along the

[*] See Appendix 4.

quayside, negotiating the litter of nets, broken packing-cases and rusty oil-drums. Señor Olivettini produced a U.N. passport and we both went into the tired old building that houses the officials. They looked at our passports and stamped them. On the wall was a vignetted photo of a dark-shirted officer. It was signed in a big looping signature and dated a year before the outbreak of the civil war. One man looked inside the car and I was worried about the pistol. That was just the sort of thing that would cause Dawlish to do his nut. The guard said something to Giorgio and hitched his automatic rifle higher on his shoulder. Giorgio spoke rapidly in Spanish and the brittle face of the guard splintered into loud laughter. By the time I reached the car the guard was inhaling on one of Giorgio's cheroots.

I drove down the sloping jetty on to a splintered boat. The weight of the car strained the ropes on the hand-made bollard and the water sagged under the burden. The boat grumbled across the oily grey water as the little white buildings floated slowly away. Getting the car on to the land of Portugal is a job for at least twelve helpers, all shouting 'Back, left-hand down, a bit more,' etc., in fluent Portuguese. I told Giorgio to get out and make sure they had the narrow planks correctly placed under the wheels. I wasn't keen to learn the Portuguese for 'too far'. The car wasn't square on the boat, and as the rear wheels rolled on to them, one of the planks shot away like a bullet. I let the clutch right in and punched the acceleration. The car leapt forward and hurtled up the steep corrugated ramp like ten thimbles across a washboard. I waited for Giorgio. He walked up the ramp smacking imaginary dust from his impeccable trousers. He looked into the window of the car, his hands nervously engaged in twisting his gold rings. He smiled briefly, took his small, new briefcase from under his arm and put it into the car. I hadn't noticed him remove it.

'Valuable,' he said.

Portugal is a semi-tropical land; cared-for, cultivated, and geometrical. This is not Spain, with leather-hatted civil guards brandishing their nicely oiled automatic rifles every few scorched yards. It's a subtle land, without sign of Salazar on poster or postage stamp.

'What about equipment?' I said. 'If you are going to look at this submarine do you think you can operate in forty metres?'

'The first, Mr MacIntosh is bringing for me; the second, yes, I can operate in forty metres. I will use compressed air, it is simple. I am a great expert in the underwater working. Sixty metres I could do.'

The westbound Estrada Principal Numero 125 out of Loule continues the descent the road has been making since S. Braz. A small police-truck hooted twice and sped past us. The road south from this junction leads only to the fishing town of Albufeira; we turned left and headed past the canning factory.

Albufeira is a town built on a ramp. The streets slope steeply uphill and the sound of low gears engaging is constantly heard. The houses that lie along the top of the ramp have their white backs inset into the top of eighty-foot cliffs.

Number 12 Praca Miguel Bombarda is one of the few houses that have private steps leading down to the beach. From the large patio at the rear of the house one can see a couple of hundred yards to the west, and the other way perhaps two miles to Cape Santa Maria, where at night the lighthouse flashes. From the front of the house the little low window – set as deep as a cupboard into the thick stone wall – looks across a triangle of cobbled space at a bent tree and an upright lamp-post. As I parked the car under the tree Joe MacIntosh looked out of the door. The church bell was striking 9 p.m. Thursday.

The night air pressed its damp nose to the window pane. Ocean sand and water were thrashing together in endless permutations, and somewhere in the depths beyond was the sunken wreck that had brought us here.

11 Help

On Friday morning an old black Citroën came down from the embassy in Lisbon. Driving it was a clean-cut fair-haired lad, wearing knee-length shorts and a cream Aertex shirt. He knocked at the door. I answered.

'Lieutenant Clive Singleton. Assistant Naval Attaché, British Embassy, Lisbon.'

'O.K.,' I said, 'no need to use a loud hailer, I'm only eighteen inches away. What's biting them?'

'My information is for the ears of your Commandant.'

'I've got news for you, Errol Flynn, I'm my own Commandant. Now weigh anchor and cast off.' I began to close the door.

'Look here, sir, here,' he said through the crack, his big blue eyes wet with anxiety. 'It's about the ...' He paused and hissed the word 'sub'. By now the door was so nearly closed that he was playing it like a woodwind. 'You must retrieve the log book.'

'Come in.'

I let him into the tiled hallway. Enough light filtered through the two thicknesses of lace curtain for me to take stock of him. About twenty-six, lank fair hair, wiry figure, five foot eleven, leather sandals, blue Austin Reed socks, a black document case with a crest on it. This boy was blue-blazer-with-a-badge-on-it material.

'O.K.,' I said, 'you're in – what's your message?'

He spoke very rapidly. 'I'm seconded to work with you, sir, on account of my skin-diving experience. I've brought my equipment in the car … .'

'I can see you have,' I said. Sitting in the car was a young blonde.

'Yes sir.' He ran his hand through his hair and smiled nervously. 'Charlotte Lucas-Mountford – Admiral Lucas-Mountford's daughter.' I said nothing. 'London told us that we should send someone with underwater experience and someone to look after the household. Charlotte speaks fluent Portuguese and I have the …'

I closed the door and slowed him to a standstill with my eyes. I took a long time lighting a cigarette and I didn't offer them.

'Sit down, sonny,' I said, 'sit down and dust off your mind. You think you're on a ripping little fun-jaunt, don't you?'

'I'm a Clearance Diver, sir, R.N. certificate. You'll need an underwater expert for this job.'

'I will, will I?' I said. 'Well, I don't know what you call "expert", but the man we already recruited spent nearly four years as an Italian frogman. He once spent a night standing in pitch darkness on the floor of Gibraltar Harbour mending a timing device while the Navy threw every grenade they could find into the harbour. They only stopped in the morning because they calculated no one could be alive down there. Then he swam up under the North Mole, fixed a charge weighing 550 lb. to a tanker and swam back to Algeciras. He did that twenty years ago when you were wearing a Mickey Mouse gas-mask and saving your coupons for a Mars bar. If you are going to work here there's not going to be any half-way for ladies and it'll mean being a lot smarter than you've been so far. Why do you think London sent that message in code to the embassy? Why do you think Lisbon couldn't send me a wire? They trusted you with it because they wanted to make sure it didn't get intercepted, and yet as soon as I bend a little muscle at you you broadcast it.' I waved down his explanations. 'Go and get your equipment,' I said.

Giorgio made some quiet remarks about Clive's bright-green undersea gear, but it was much more professional than I feared it might be. As for Charlotte, I'd never seen her before, but there were two things about her one could never forget. However, she set to work in the kitchen in a way that surprised me. They were both dying to prove how efficient and tough they were.

After breakfast we had a conference. Joe spread the linen Admiralty charts across the table and showed us the way the U-boat was lying. The echo-sounder charts were strips of electrolytic paper about seven inches wide. Down each was a thick black uneven band (the ocean floor) and a thin black uneven band, separated by a quarter-inch of white. The thinner of the two bands was fish or objects lying along the ocean floor. On one chart a shape could be interpreted. I was prepared to take an expert's word that it resembled a U-boat.

According to Singleton, Naval Intelligence were very keen to get the log of the U-boat as it was of a new type about which they had very little information. I asked Giorgio and Joe what the chances were.

Joe said, 'If the log wasn't dumped overboard before the sub. sank, it's easy.'

'You know where to find the log book? I can ask London about stowage procedures.'

Giorgio said, 'It will not, I think, prove necessary. I have encountered some experience of the life aboard the German craft.' We exchanged thin grins.

'And if they did jettison it?'

'In that case it depends upon: one,' Giorgio tapped his index finger, 'how far the boat traversed between the jettison and sinking, and two, if the Kelvin Hughes apparatus will encounter such a small flat objective which will likely submerge into the mud, and three,' the gold ring on his finger flashed in the bright sunlight, 'if the boat has been moved much distance by means of the underwater currents which I suspect are strong.'

After that Giorgio asked Joe about tidal movement at surface, absolute slack-water times and slack-water duration, and they discussed ways of setting out a diving timetable in order to use those facts to advantage.

Charlotte brought in a large tin pot of coffee and a plate of black figs. She said, 'After I've drunk my coffee I'll go and do the bedroom.' There was a moment or two in which we were all alone with our thoughts.

There was no point in getting the boat into position so late in the day. I told everyone to relax that afternoon, we'd have another briefing that night and go out on the morning tide for a reconnaissance.

Dawlish had cleverly realized that the way to prevent someone deserting from a situation was to put him in charge of it.

The sea was kicking idly at the beach that Friday afternoon. Charlotte was nearly inside a white bathing suit, Giorgio was doing handstands that had her oo-ing and clapping her brittle little hands together, and Singleton was jumping in and out of the water like a yo-yo. I told Giorgio to swim out to sea with Singleton and let me know what sort of endurance he had.

'Go out about two hundred and fifty yards and come in again. Don't hurry him, but let him know you're watching him.'

'Yes, it is understood,' said Giorgio, and went to tell Singleton.

I watched them run across the soft damp sand lengthening the curved imprints that marry space and time in huge dotted arabesques. Then Joe talked about the echo-sounder.

'I put the sounder in when we first got a whisper of this job three – no, nearly four – weeks ago; we've used it for fishing ever since. It's deadly efficient and some of the fishermen have been talking about buying them for themselves.'

'Isn't there a possibility that they'll follow us out to locate the fish?'

'No, I disconnected it yesterday and I told the old man to say it had gone wrong.' He paused, carefully designing a sentence that wouldn't sound impertinent. 'Why doesn't London do this operation through official channels – and get local cooperation?'

'The whole thing stinks, Joe. To tell you the truth, I have an awful feeling that we are sitting out here bleating like a goat in a tiger trap. That message Singleton brought about the log book. It doesn't ring true. The only department still interested in Nazi U-boats is the Historical Department. How could it be of importance to a modern intelligence department?' I told Joe about my being followed by the two cars, and how one of them belonged to Henry Smith, the Cabinet Minister. I told him about Butcher, Smith's dirty-work man who had sold us the ice-melting documents. I told him that I thought it all connected up. 'And what about this Giorgio character?' I finished. 'Why does he have to meet me at a weird little place like Los Palacios?'

'He's been doing a job underwater inside a gasometer in Seville.'

'Where is his equipment?' I said immediately.

'He leaves a set there,' Joe said. 'It's a contract job. He really is O.K.; he's been checked and re-checked, but there is an American living here in the village that I'm not at all sure about …'

As he said it Giorgio and Singleton came out of the water. Giorgio was tanned dark-brown and moving like he'd just come out of the shower. He brushed his chest as though still wearing his silver tie. Singleton had his mouth open and was gulping down deep draughts of air, throwing his head back and running an open hand through his long fair hair. They walked slowly up to where Joe and I were sitting and waited for words of praise.

'How do you feel, Singleton?' I asked.

His white chest heaved. 'O.K., sir … absolutely … first rate, sir.'

'Then I want you to go out half as far – but swim underwater there and back. Break surface only when you have to, that means I don't want a train of foam and bubbles. If you have any difficulties tell Giorgio immediately. I'm not recruiting dead heroes, I prefer live cowards. And Giorgio, stay close.'

They both nodded. 'Joe and I are going upstairs to watch you and count the number of times you come up for air. And one more thing, Singleton, you're not on parade, so try to look like an English tourist …' They turned back towards the sea … 'that is to say miserable,' I shouted after them.

'Do you think you're being a little hard on Singleton, sir?' Joe asked. We walked up the whitewashed steps to the patio.

'Probably,' I said. 'He reminds me of people who sing "There's a hole in my bucket" to a guitar at Chelsea parties.'

We went on in silence and then Joe said, 'You may be worrying for nothing, sir. It might be as easy and straightforward as it seems.'

I didn't think so.

12 Sort of man

The next great green Atlantic wave sucked the wooden boat out of the surf. The old fisherman used the oars to keep it at right angles to the beach. Joe tugged the lanyard on the outboard motor. Another wave held us high in its open palm and hesitated before dashing us back on the sand. I was high in the prow and Joe was below me in the steeply angled boat. He flung his arm out and I heard the splutter of the motor like a sewing machine. The water foamed at the stern and we headed out into the Atlantic as the screw bit the sea.

The fisherman was a walnut-faced man of eighty. He flashed his brown teeth at me as I helped him ship the oars, and scuttled over to the echo-sounder to reconnect it. From the big picnic hampers Giorgio and Singleton produced clear polythene bags, removed the folded rubber suits, and began to pull them on. We chugged westward.

The green skirt of the sea dashed its frilly petticoats at the yellow rocks. Each rock has its dangers and its name – 'the Castle', 'the Pig', and the long stretches of vertical strata called the 'Bibliotek'. As we passed them the old man yelled the name at me and pointed at them. His finger was like a bent cigar. I repeated the name and he smiled a big yellow smile at me. The most dangerous rocks are the ones that are completely covered at high water, the huge flat stone called 'the Tartar' or the two finger-like monoliths called 'the Wolves'.

I watched the echo-sounder. It clicked away, scratching arcs across the strip of paper, building a picture of the ocean bed. Giorgio was smoking one of the cheroots he favoured. The old man was smoking one too, smiling and tugging on the lobe of his ear – in a gesture of pleasure. He guided the boat by sighting the uneven top of Penha de Alte mountain to the north and the distant Cape Santa Maria to the east.

Joe was watching the scratching sounder needle and the compass. He shouted something to Giorgio, who shrugged, and Joe walked along the boat towards me as we turned through a hundred and eighty degrees.

'We've missed it, I'm afraid,' he said, 'we are going across again. I could have put a marker buoy down yesterday, but …'

'No, you did right,' I told him, 'let's keep it discreet.'

Joe heard the sounder change note and the rusty multi-prong anchor (a great luxury in a district where most boats use a slab of concrete) splashed overboard. The old man was on his feet holding the anchor rope as it snagged the wreck and pulled us into position over it. Giorgio adjusted his compressed-air bottles. I tapped his arm. Under the rubber suit his muscles were as hard as stone. Irregular white patches of the chalk in which the suit had been carefully packed emphasized the strange non-human garb.

'Check that anchor line first thing when you descend.'

Giorgio listened carefully and nodded. I went on:

'Singleton is under your personal orders: he goes down only when and if you want.'

'The boy is good. I tell you that in truthfulness, very good,' Giorgio said. He handed his half-smoked cheroot to the old man, who puffed delightedly at it.

He pulled his circular face-mask down, eased his feet into

the gigantic rubber flippers and carefully put one leg over the side. In spite of the sunshine the Atlantic is cold in October. Giorgio pulled a face behind the mask and dusted a patch of talc from his arm before dropping gently overboard. The water surged over his shoulders and he pushed away from the faded blue side of the boat, kicking out his black legs.

His chunky silhouette shattered into a dozen black moving patches as he sank, and a gush of white bubbles ripped the surface. In parts of the Pacific one can see well over two hundred feet, and in the Med. a hundred is nothing remarkable. But Giorgio had quickly gone.

The old man switched off the motor. It spluttered like a candle, and there was a brief silence before the sea began its background music. Left to the disposition of the ocean the little boat was handed from wave to wave like a rich patient between specialists. At its higher movement I could see a big tanker making a lot of smoke on the horizon. Singleton tried to light a cigarette, but the wind and movement foiled him each time until he flicked the long white shape away, somersaulting it in a curve over the water. The old man saw him waste the cigarette in tacit incredulity. The bubbles continued to rise, break and disappear by the million. He gazed back towards the oyster beds that he had three times asked Giorgio to raid for him. I watched him size up Singleton with a view to tackling him on the subject.

I called Joe over. 'If Giorgio gets a reasonable idea of what sort of shape it's in we'll give London the "contact made" signal tonight. There's nothing wrong, is there?'

Joe wasn't so lively today. He said, 'I'm not so satisfied with our communications.'

'The set's O.K.?'

'Oh, the set is all right. I raise Gib. easily enough, but it's the delay between Gib. and London. Last night, for instance,

I asked for a check on Singleton and the girl as you requested, but this morning they were still deciphering the reply. I had to wait while it came through. It didn't matter being across water, but it's things like that …'

'You are right, Joe. Next time cease transmission.'

'Well, tonight I'm going to go on the air an hour early. I did think it might be better to transmit via the Lisbon embassy because Gib. are probably leaving us at the bottom of the pile.'

'Don't. There are too many ears open between here and Lisbon – the Republican Guard stations, police radio, armed forces. It's too risky. It would be crazy to be picked up for the sake of this foolish little job. Keep contact through Gib. and we'll raise hell with London if we have any trouble. Give tonight's message a TA8 priority and send the message "one cup of coffee 9.40 Yellow".'

Joe raised an eyebrow. 'I'll call them at seven and fill up the car …'

Then the old man called 'pronto pronto' and I saw the anchor rope juggling up and down, and dark patterns in the waves glued themselves into one shape as Giorgio's black-rubber head broke the surface. He unstrapped a big lantern from his wrist and passed it into the boat. He removed his dark-green flippers under water and threw those into the boat too. They landed with a wet thud. Then he grasped the gunwales with his white, bloated hands. With one great heave he came unstuck from the wave-tops and toppled into the boat. Joe had the Thermos flask of hot red *vinho verde* ready, and Giorgio emptied it in one gulp and held it out for more. Having finished that, he produced antiseptic from the hamper and poured it over his swollen hands. Blood was still coming from a bad cut on his left hand, and he stamped the floor of the boat with pain as the antiseptic hit the bloodstream and the brown mixture dropped from his fingers.

After that he stripped off the rubber suit and rubbed himself with camphorated oil and a rough towel. He carefully parted his hair with the aid of a small pocket mirror, slipped into a pair of carefully pressed blue cotton trousers, white shirt and black cashmere pullover before he turned to me and said, 'It is not extremely difficult.' He said there was no need for Singleton to dive, and distributed black cheroots. The old man spun the motor and wound in the anchor and we began to wonder what Charlotte had fixed for lunch.

After lunch Giorgio used a magic marker pen to show the position and condition of the U-boat.

'This is a rock-sided trench. There is what I judge to be a five-knot current pressing the hull against it ... thus.' Giorgio's command of English was on firmer ground when dealing with reports like this. He made arrow marks across the white paper.

'This is a type XXI U-boat,' Giorgio continued. 'Luckily this is something which I know from drawings, although this is the first I have seen. It is about eighty metres long with about seven metres' beam. That makes it a big boat. But all this ...' On his side view of the submarine Giorgio now drew a line along the middle and indicated the area under his line. ' ... is filled with batteries. The space beneath the conning-tower has to be the control room. Beneath that are the magazine and compression tanks. Aft of it accommodation and galley. Aft of that: motors and engines. Forward of the control room there is crew accommodation. That's there. Nearly sixty sailors on this sort of boat. At that bulkhead the battery-storage ends. The next compartment uses the full depth of the hull and is very big. This is the torpedo stowage compartment. Don't get hurt going through that bulkhead – it's a long drop to the floor. This is all full of armed torpedoes, and there is a large break in the hull there,' he indicated the rear of the T.S. compartment, 'at the torpedo tank. Six tubes – three each side of the bow. All bow caps closed.'

I noticed that the cuts on the back of Giorgio's hand were bleeding again.

'The boat is lying at a slight angle; this section is completely collapsed. The main engines have fallen through the pressure hull and jammed together with broken hydroplane into this rock fissure. Lucky the engine compartment is no concern. The rear-most section is torn completely open and many bodies of men in advanced decomposition are visible inside here. The hull here is very sharp and is dangerous bacteriological risk due to the corpses. Anyone diving here must treat even a small cut immediately.

'The control section can be searched in twenty diving hours unless the floor has collapsed. There are ways in which the floor can fall that would make searching under it impossible without lifting apparatus. Another risk is that the hull has been rolled along the ocean floor by water movement subsequent to the control-room floor collapsing. But this is to look on the blackest side of the coin. Tomorrow I shall go inside the hull, if the weather stays as good.'

13 More to do

In the West London air terminal they have electric coin-in-the-slot razors. There was time to shave before Jean came to meet me in Dawlish's old Riley. It was 9.39 a.m.

'Whatever could you have done for Dawlish that he loans you England's answer to the space race?'

Jean said, 'He ripped the bumper off my Mini-Minor yesterday morning. Don't mention it – he's still very touchy.'

'It's a wonder he didn't make you use the car pool.'

'We've been having a little argument with the car pool since you headed into the sunshine.'

'Don't say it,' I said. 'What was it that Bernard's file on the C.I.A. estimated they spent per year? And *we* are having difficulty with the car pool.'

'Never mind,' she said, overtaking a post van, squeezing past an oncoming bus, tuning the radio and lighting a cigarette. 'How are things in Portugal?' She glanced at me. 'You don't seem any more relaxed.'

'I was all right until I entered this car; anyway I've been up since three a.m.,' I said. The rain beat heavily against the windows. Outside Woolworth's a woman in a plastic raincoat was smacking a child in a Yogi Bear bib. Soon we stopped at Admiralty Arch.

'Admiralty Library,' said Jean. 'You must leave here by three forty-five at the very latest if you are going to get that BE 072 back to Lisbon this afternoon.'

Inside the library it was jumping with books. A girl read a *Daily Express* headed 'A Commonwealth Tour for Tony?'

'You remember all that stuff I sorted through for the Weapons Co-ordination Committee last year?' I asked.

'Yes sir,' she said. She folded up *Woman's Realm* and the *Daily Express* and tucked them under a pink cardigan and a bottle of hand-lotion in a little secret shelf under the desk.

'I'll want some of it again,' I said. The whole place smelt of damp melton overcoats. 'I'm trying to trace details of a scientific discovery made by a high-ranking officer, or perhaps a scientist who sailed from Germany during March or April 1945. Also I'll want to see the Assessment Board Reports[*] during that period.' There was a lot to be done before I caught the plane back to Lisbon.

---

[*] Assessment Boards judged the claims of Allied ships and aircraft in the matter of U-boat sinkings. They were remarkably accurate.

14 Portuguese O.K.

Giorgio worked exactly on schedule. He began the search of the control room. The hull was badly silted up and Giorgio decided that looking around haphazardly wouldn't do, so he began at the control bulkhead, port side. I'd told him to look for currency of any sort, or any documents, the log book or the metal cases that German naval ships' papers were kept in.

Within a few days we had a comfortable routine. We would rise about 7.30 to watch the sun come up and have coffee. Then we would go out in the boat and Giorgio would do forty minutes. Singleton would go down for another forty, then Giorgio would do about twenty or so before they came back. By that time mud had been raised so badly that the beam of light wouldn't penetrate the water. We'd get back for lunch about noon and Charlotte would have been to market, tidied the house and fixed lunch.

Singleton had been pressing for a second dive in the afternoons; but I thought it would look too odd, and Giorgio said that it would bring the air consumption over a twenty-four-hour period up to a point where slow surfacing would be necessary in order to be safe from 'decompression sickness'. So afternoons everyone sunned themselves on the beach by order. But the following Saturday clouds were flitting around the sun like moths around a candle, and there was a bite in the air whenever the sun vanished. Charlotte said she'd go up to the house and make tea, when I noticed someone walking towards us up the beach. He was a muscular figure, perhaps a little overweight. His black hair was cropped close to his skull and his chest featured more hair than his head. A small gold crucifix dangled from a hair-fine chain around his neck. He wore a small pair of yellow swimming trunks and carried a white towel which he rubbed against his head as he walked. It was only the towel and shorts that marked him as a visitor, for he was tanned to the same ancient-furniture colour as were the local fishermen.

He shouted, 'Is that a little piece of old England I see there?'

'Little piece?' said Charlotte, and she wrinkled her nose and pouted her mouth.

'Kondit,' he said, and extended a large, hairy-backed hand to Giorgio, who said, 'Kondit?'

'Yes, Harry Kondit.' He laughed. 'I'm from the United States – I was hearing that Albufeira had gotten itself some winter visitors. Look, that's the end of sunshine for today, why don't you nice people join me for a drink? I'll go back to the house and scramble into some clothes and I'll knock you up in thirty minutes. Knock you up in thirty minutes – isn't that what you say in England? Ha, ha, ha.'

Charlotte was all for it, of course, and Giorgio seemed keen to break the monotony of handstands. Joe said, 'He's a bull-dozer, that man; he's the American I mentioned.'

I said, 'He's very nice: check on him.'

The Jul-Bar is the most modern bar in Albufeira. It has plastic, chromium, and mosaic, a G.E.C. refrigerator as big as a phone booth, and an Espresso machine. It is situated half-way down a wide stairway that leads to 'the Gardens', which is the main market place and square. As we walked Harry Kondit ('just call me Harry') explained to us.

In the market place was a huge 'transport collectivo' diesel bus. It had brought farmers and their produce into town. They sat by little heaps of mauve sweet potatoes, green lemons, cabbages, eggs, brown speckled beans and tomatoes.

The black peasant garb is being relinquished from the feet upwards. Few people wear all black, but almost all have a black trilby hat. The old women wear one on top of their head-scarves. A horse with an embroidered harness set with broken mirror and tinkling bells tapped and tinkled past us like a Salvation Army tambourine. Under the trees local lads kicked their Perfectas and Dianas into angry roars and they cavorted in angry bravado across the steep cobbles.

One passed us with a noise like a Cup Final rattle, and Harry Kondit, who seemed to know everyone in this town, shouted to him, 'George Porgy – how's about a drink, kid?'

The little motor bike popped to a halt. On it there sat a white-faced man with a wide moustache and very light blue eyes. He wore the inevitable black trilby with bow at the back, and a grey Spanish-style waistcoat with long sleeves and pointed front.

Almost before the bike stopped he had whirled his hat off and held it across his chest like a shield.

'Let me do the introductions,' said H.K. 'This here is Senhor Jorge Fernandes Tomas. Do I have that right, Fernie?'

'Sim,' said Fernie.

Fernie was a thin, neurotic man of perhaps forty years. Although it was late afternoon Fernie was newly shaved, as is the custom in southern Europe. He wore his hair long, and one sideburn half concealed a small scar noticeable around his ear.

61

'We're going to the Jul-Bar, Fernie,' and H.K. walked on, taking it for granted that he would follow. Fernie propped his two-stroke against the baker's shop. Through the doorway I saw rosy men, lop-sided loaves and flaming tinder.

We walked up the stone stairway to the café. Brightly painted metal chairs shrieked their protest as H.K. arranged them on the pavement.

H.K. had Charlotte under his wing by now. It took him no time at all to discover that Charlotte had been called 'Charly' at school. From that moment on, no one called her by any other name.

H.K. was in no way bashful about describing himself. 'I said Harry you'll soon be nudging fifty and what are you? A small-time publishing exec. making twenty-five grand and not much chance of pushing it past thirty. And what are you getting in return? Three weeks in Florida once a year and a hunting trip to Canada if, repeat, if you're lucky. So what did I do?'

I could see Charly was still converting twenty-five thousand dollars per annum into pounds per week.

'Were you here in Europe in the Army, Mr Kondit?' she said, cutting across his narrative with feminine disregard.

'No, I was not. You remember how General MacArthur told the people of the Philippines "I'll be back"? Well I was back about eight hours before he was. They weren't waiting on the beach with dry pants when I hit the surf. No sir. You're not drinking – I'll order some more wine! – *Chefe dos moços! Estas Senhoras desejam vinho seco.*'

I saw the young waiter catch Fernie's eye, for, quite apart from the extraordinary pronunciation, he had used pompous phrase-book Portuguese. We got the wine.

We went back to H.K.'s for pre-dinner drinks. He lived a long way down the Praca Miguel Bombarda. It was a simple house with a red-and-white tiled entrance hall. The dark furniture did a heavy dance as we walked across the uneven plank flooring. From the entrance hall one could see right through the house to where the light-grey sea, dark clouds and white-washed stone balcony hung like a tricolour outside the back door. From the kitchen emerged a smell of olive oil, pimento, cuttlefish, and a wizened woman of sixty who did for H.K. I could detect her feminine hand in the hydrangeas that stood around in terracotta bowls.

'Hi there, Maria – this way folks,' said Harry, 'I'm the only American in the world that doesn't have an icebox.' He had fixed the patio with green plants and a parasol. From his balcony one could see the new hotel that was being built. H.K. swirled his drink and looked across at it regretfully. 'This place is going to be way outside my tax bracket when they get that baby finito.'

Fernie, who hadn't spoken much until now, asked Giorgio for a cigarette and Giorgio pressed a black cheroot upon him. Fernie's few words were in clear, fluent Italian, and H.K. noticed me listening. 'And he speaks German and Spanish just as well as you and I speak our mother tongue, don't you, Fernie?' He patted him affectionately on the shoulder. 'Used to own three boats, Fernie did, but the Government took them away from him. One morning he goes down to the wharf, there's a padlock on his office door and two men in grey standing by his boats. No law court – nothing – just seized.'

Singleton said, 'What reason did they give?'

'None,' said H.K.

'They must have said something.'

H.K. laughed. 'You've not been long in Portugal, sonny. The day the Government hands out explanations is the day after husbands start telling their wives where they've been. No sir, there's nothing like that in this country.'

'Do you think there was a reason?' Singleton asked.

'Me? Now that's a different thing entirely. Sure it was because Fernie here fought against that son-of-a-bitch Franco in the Spanish business. He was at the siege of Malaga.'

'Really?' I said. 'There weren't many Portuguese fighting in Spain.'

'They've fought everywhere, these Portuguese,' said H.K. 'They say, "God gave the Portuguese a small country as their cradle and all the world as their grave."' Fernie Tomas gave no sign of understanding the conversation.

Singleton said, 'If he fought in Spain I suppose that explains it.'

'Explains it,' said H.K., 'you mean makes it understandable.'

'In a way it makes it understandable,' said Singleton.

'It does, eh?' said H.K. softly. 'Let me tell you something, kid. A lot of my buddies were in the Abraham Lincoln brigade and they weren't Commies either. They were just guys getting themselves dead so that you wouldn't have to wear a black shirt and kick in the window of a Jewish candy-store on the way to school. *Nuestra guerra* they call it over there in Spain, but it wasn't their war, it was his war, my war and, whether you know it or not, your war. It was their war too; the ones that came back Stateside and found a lot of people who'd like to do to them what Fernie's people did to him – and more. But they didn't – which was lucky all round – because in 1942 people who would prepare Fascists for wooden overcoats were back in fashion again. So don't be so tolerant and understanding, you just never know when you might be out of fashion.' H.K. was still speaking quietly but all other conversation had stopped. The evening Nortrada began to shuffle the leaves of the little palm tree. H.K. touched Singleton on the shoulder in avuncular fashion and said in a different voice, 'We're getting a little serious, aren't we – how's about another drink? Come and help me fix it, Charly.'

They disappeared into the kitchen. Fernie began talking Italian to Giorgio across the far side of the balcony.

'What do you know about that?' said Joe quietly.

'Ask London for an S.8 on him, and check Singleton again. You can't be too careful, and that Singleton's just not for real.'

I watched the waves moving down on to the shore. Each shadow darkened until one, losing its balance, toppled forward. It tore a white hole in the green ocean and in falling brought its fellow down, and that the next, until the white stuffing of the sea burst out of the lengthening gash.

Charly and H.K. emerged from the kitchen with a big tray of glasses and a jug with can-can girls and *vive la différence* painted on them in gold.

As they came through the door H.K. was saying, ' … it's the only thing I really miss of the New York scene.'

'But I'll do them for you,' Charly said.

'Willya really honey? I sure would be grateful. Just one a week would be great. My girl can do the cotton ones O.K., it's the synthetic fibres that they burn. They have the iron too hot, y'see.'

Then Charly said in a loud clear voice, 'Mr Kondit – Harry I mean – has made us all a special Martini, and he has got a refrigerator after all.'

'Now you promised that that would be a little secret between the two of us,' H.K. said in a mock stern voice, and he pinched Charly's bottom.

'That's an un-American activity,' said Charly.

'Oh no,' said H.K., 'we still got a couple of things that have to be done by hand.'

Outside, the waves were tripping over, crashing on to and falling through the foamy, hissing scar-tissue of their predecessors. I wondered how long before we would begin doing the same.

15 Reaction in the market

It was another hot sunny day on Monday. I stayed behind in the house, which Charly described as 'just cosy'. I said I thought that she had her hands full of H.K. and Giorgio and she said how did I know it wasn't the other way about. I didn't. Charly borrowed my comb, fixed her hair and returned the comb within one minute and a half. We walked down to the market place. She had established terms of easy familiarity with the men while not alienating the women. She spoke Portuguese with a natural fluency, even knowing the local names for some of the vegetables and fish. The women saw in her the emancipation they all sought, while the men watched her and wondered if she was something they could deal with over either table or pillow.

She wore a pale-pink sleeveless dress that made her arms look very tanned. Her hair was an unbleached white, the colour of Portland stone. She paused to pat a dog that sat in the middle of the hot road. She whistled after the gas man, and the vegetable boy let her work the shredding machine, piling cabbage into heaps of wire wool and sending razor-blades of carrots and pumpkin to join the hairpins of beans.

She cleaved the yellow hands of bananas with a jab of the knife, criticized the garlic, prodded the tomatoes and put nail marks into the beans. They liked her.

We walked through the fish market. The flat concrete benches were ashine with bream and gilthead, pilchards, sardines and mackerel. Outside, the sun reflected off the sea with a million flashing pinpoints of light, as though every bird was sitting there on the ocean top flashing angry white wings.

The painted fishing boats were drawn up high from the water's edge and packed as densely as the finish line at Ford's. Most of them were a vivid ultramarine-blue inside. Outside were bands of light green, faded pink, black, and white. On the prows signs were painted: an eye, a horse or a name. Some carried a big mop of animal hair for luck. The boats that had been out in the rain on Sunday night now, their headsails slackly raised, made an encampment of pointed canvas shapes. Here and there were men checking the nets for holes or rearranging them under the hot sun.

As we left the fish market the little bell clanged for the tax assessor. In the sunlight moray eel was drying, and on the cobblestones a man in a shirt either dark-blue with light-blue patches or vice versa was scrubbing the big wooden fish-weighing machine. Charly asked him if he had sold out. He said 'yes', and when she called him a moderately rude Portuguese name he ran off to fetch the spider crabs that he was pretending he hadn't saved for her.

Even the policeman hitched up his patent-leather belt and smiled, and Charly's stock went even higher. No one had seen him smile before.

Each year the building with the bell is painted a mustard colour and the bar next door a deep tomato red, but the sun bleaches them lighter every day until the colour all but disappears. Inside the bar the star-patterned tiled floor joins the star-patterned tiled walls. The sunlight that lies inside the doors like two white mats reflects coolly among the marble-topped tables and crippled blue chairs, and framed colour pictures of Glamis, the Tower of London and the Queen with Salazar. In happy co-existence is a big sleepy ginger cat and a noisy white cockerel named Francois. The sailors were calling, 'Sing, Francis' to make it crow for Charly when Joe MacIntosh came in. He said, 'We've raised one canister – are you coming?'

Fernie came into the bar just as we were leaving. He watched us with unblinking gaze.

16 One too many

The window shutters were closed. In the dark front room Giorgio was sitting waiting for us. Singleton was tidying the boat and gear. He'd be back any moment.

Joe said, 'We decided to wait for you, sir.'

'Thank you,' I said, like I was taking the helm of the *Queen Elizabeth*.

Over the newspaper-covered table the 60-watt bulb shone on to the green steel canister. The edges and corners were rounded and sealing compound joined two equal-shaped sides.

I told Joe to get the Polaroid Land camera. He brought it complete with flash and a green filter to give us a maximum detail in the green paintwork. He took six shots. The prints were satisfactory.

Joe took a small pair of pliers and applied himself to the canister until it creaked open on its ancient hinges. None of us, I think, was expecting much, but we did expect something a little more rewarding. There were a couple of handfuls of chalky cotton wool, not very good quality, a tattered piece of canvas about as large as a man's handkerchief, some torn pieces of white paper, and a twenty-dollar bill, crumpled and dirty. Charly reached across for the twenty-dollar bill, but as she picked it up the racket of a two-stroke motor cycle became louder, until it cut immediately under the shuttered window.

Charly mouthed the word 'Fernie', and sewed a frown in hasty tacks across her forehead.

It didn't matter, of course, we merely hid the canister before letting Fernie in, then took him to the kitchen for coffee. He accepted a cup in his polite laconic manner, smiled pleasantly and said he was bearing 'a message of a confidential nature from the first citizen of the region'.

I asked him who the first citizen of the region was. Fernie answered, 'Senhor Manuel Gambeta do Rosario da Cunha, a very great gentleman if you will allow me to tell you, sir.'

I heard Singleton's voice from the balcony calling, 'So what was in it?'

'I have a principle, Senhor Fernandes Tomas, of allowing anyone to tell me anything at any time.'

'Me too, sir,' he said. He gave no sign of having heard Singleton, then he gave me an address to which I was invited at 5 p.m. to 'learn something to advantage'.

'I shall meet you there.' He picked up his black trilby from the marble hallstand and kicked up his bike. He sped past the narrow whitewashed walls of the cobbled street. He didn't look back.

Inside the house I found everyone sitting around looking at *two* twenty-dollar bills. The serial numbers were twenty-three digits apart.

'Two,' I said. 'I thought there was only one in the container.'

'There was,' Joe said. 'Charly brought in its twin brother out of the dirty-linen cupboard.'

I looked at Charly.

'It was in the pocket of one of Harry Kondit's dirty shirts,' she said lamely. 'I'd offered to wash them for him.'

I said nothing.

'Not all his shirts, just the synthetic fibres,' she said.

'O.K.,' I told her, 'but don't get so friendly that you'll miss him if he suddenly disappears.'

17 Da Cunha lays it down

West of Albufeira there is a view across gently sloping fields of ash-grey fig and vines to the blue sea three kilometres away.

A patio rings with the voices of fishermen and shopkeepers of Albufeira. On the sun-bleached wooden tables are plates of black cuttlefish and moray dried in the sun and fried crisp. The new crop of wine is drunk and discussed and drunk and discussed until the next crop appears. Pressed in the old Moorish fashion (while still in the jute sacks) the cloudy rosé catches the throat like a *fado*. On the next hill white tower-like windmills, their canvas sails furled, am asterisks upon the horizon. Beyond them the station marks a spot where the railway from Lisbon grasps towards Albufeira and fails to make it by six kilometres.

Fernie shook hands amid tearing of bread and lifting of glasses. He pulled the stiff door beyond the terrace and it sang a choir-like note, echoing and vibrating. Inside the door it was dark. Barrels dribbled into bottles for the drinkers outside. Past tubs of black olives and bowls of green ones were boxes overflowing with figs. Fernie ran his hands through the sack and gave me a handful. We walked out through the far door. To the left and right low white walls provided picture frames around the red soil. Ahead, olive trees marked a brightly tiled path to a pale-blue building with complex white decorations. It sat across the landscape like a Wedgwood teapot. It was one of the old baronial houses or *montes* that dominate estates of cork, olive and fig. Black pigs snuffled under the olive trees and from behind the building a dog barked as if expecting no reply.

Fernie pushed open the wrought-iron gate and, holding it open for me, said in slow, careful English, 'You *are* in contact with Mr Smith?'

'Of course I am,' I lied quickly.

He nodded silently and left me alone at the house of Senhor Manuel Gambeta do Rosario da Cunha, first citizen of the region.

By 5 p.m. in October the sun is well down. To the north the mountains were intensely mauve and the sun, hitting the higher of the white houses, made them as pink as the potted geraniums along the walls.

The last rays of the sun did a spray job on one side of da Cunha's bony head, and behind him the gold lettering of Mommsen's *History of Rome* and Balzac's complete works made football signals over his shoulder. The house was richly furnished and I didn't have to be asked to dinner to know that the cruet wouldn't be plastic.

On da Cunha's simple mahogany desk was a porcelain-and-gold pen set, a gold letter-opener, an elegant sealing-wax holder, a seal and half a dozen foolscap sheets of fine handwriting. They weren't held down by Coca-Cola caps either.

'I understand you to be attempting to locate a lost article by dredging the sea floor.'

It wasn't an exact description, but it wasn't a question either. I said nothing.

Da Cunha removed his gold-rimmed spectacles. There was a bright red mark on the side of his thin nose where they had rested. I wondered just how political you had to be to have a set-up like this.

'In the course of time this coast has attracted adventurers of all sorts. Not all of them have sought recently-lost treasure, and some of them have been far from successful. The town of Olhao was built entirely from the profits made by selling to both sides during the Cadiz affair.'

He said 'Cadiz affair' as though it had happened last week instead of the sixteenth century.

'However, in the case of your party I am of the opinion that the motives are not entirely honourable.'

He paused, and then said, 'I am hoping to provoke a reply.'

'Your English is excellent,' I said.

'I spent the years of 1934 and 1935 at Peterhouse College, but you avoid my question.'

'I'm not sure how your ideas of honour could be expected to key in with mine,' I said. 'You could buy a pair of shoes for every barefoot kid in Albufeira with that pen set.'

'Ten years ago I would have been tempted to explain why you are so wrong. Now, however ...' his voice trailed away.

The sun had disappeared over the hill now, leaving only a few fiery trees to mark its passage. Da Cunha hooked his spectacles over one ear and wriggled his nose into them.

'There is no discussion necessary. I am able to give you what you are looking for and I trust that then you will leave the Algarve and its people and not return.'

He walked slowly across to the corner of the room, the rich Persian carpet switching off the sound-track of his footfalls. He slid his hand into the shelf of loosely-packed books and removed about six between compressed palms. In the space behind the books was a brown-paper parcel about half the size of a cigar box. He tugged at a red velvet cord and then, bringing the parcel over to me, he put it on the mahogany desk.

I didn't touch it.

'I resent it,' da Cunha said, 'the whole manner of it, I resent it, tell your Mr Smith that, I resent it very much.'

I thought, 'I'll tell him all right – if I ever meet him.' Da Cunha offered me coffee, while I wondered who the ubiquitous Mr Smith was, and how he connected with this little gang of Portuguese pirates.

Coffee came in the only way it could travel in a house like that: in a silver pot attended by Limoges cups and saucers. On a side plate were soft marzipan cakes with a moist egg-yolk in the innermost centre. Da Cunha forced three of them on me in quick succession.

'I think of our Algarve as the secret garden of Europe,' he said as he poured the coffee. He flicked a finger towards the decimated plate of sweets.

'Almonds, figs, finest grapes in Europe, passable champagne. Wonderful olives, walnuts, oranges, tangerines, pomegranates; and lobster, squid, crab, eels, shrimps, sardines, cuttlefish, octopus; more than I can put my tongue to. Upon the upturned eaves of these houses (upturned to ward the evil eye away, as Portuguese sailors discovered in China) – upon these eaves sits the small nightingale so cherished by the Arab poet.'

'No fooling,' I said. I sipped my coffee and offered him a High Life cigarette – a cheap local brand. He declined and lit an oval Turkish which he discovered in a carved ivory box.

'There is a story told of the region,' da Cunha went on. 'It tells of a Moorish prince who married a Russian queen. She pined away thinking of her snow-covered northern home, until one February morning she awoke and looked from her window to see the white blossoms of the almond tree covering our whole land. You would love our Algarve in February.'

'I love it now in my own bourgeois way,' I told him, helping myself to another cheese of almond. He nodded.

With the second pot of coffee he told me of the São Marcos festival, when monks whip a calf on the church steps in order that all the cattle ills and troubles of the year fall upon that one poor calf. I drank the coffee and mused.

Mr Smith is somehow involved with the car following me down the A3. He has R.N. Signals Gibraltar doing a wire-tap job on me; when I get here his name is brandished on all sides, and now someone is giving me presents because they think he and I are pals. I knew how that calf felt.

With the smoked paprika-and-pork sausage da Cunha told me of the climb to the top of a hill on the day of São Vincente. If the flaming torch is blown out, preparations are made for a good year. If it stays alight, the farm-hands are sacked. Half a dozen cold beers later we were on to the witches' sabbath of St John's night, when boys and girls jump hand in hand over bonfires. The girl burns the flower of a purple thistle in the flames and plants the stalk. Only true love makes the stalk flower.

'Fascinating,' I said. Senhor Manuel Gambeta do Rosario da Cunha got up from the desk and walked to the door, where he had a whispered conversation. Then he told me briefly of the twelve grapes that must be eaten on New Year's Eve at midnight while drums, trumpets, and bells sound in every square in Portugal: only thus can twelve months of happiness be ensured. The door opened.

It was dark outside and Senhor da Cunha lit the little green-shaded brass lamp and cleared a space on the desk. The maid, in formal white cap and black dress, put a tray down on the desk. There was a lop-sided Portuguese loaf, butter, a red spider crab open and ready to eat, and a bowl of creamy fish soup floating with pink shrimps.

'The local cognac is good enough to follow such a small snack,' said da Cunha with Portuguese hospitalitity, 'and perhaps a little of the sweet anise liquor with a fresh pot of coffee.'

As I left he clicked his heels and said what a pleasure it was to talk with such an educated and cultured person. He wanted to send Maria through the garden with me to carry the lantern, but I insisted upon taking it myself. Halfway to the iron gate a gust of wind blew the wavering light out. There was a thin nail-paring of moon, and behind the house the dog began to bark again. Beyond the hydrangea flowers and the high wall, grey-blue in the moonlight, a two-stroke motor cycle started up.

I moved into the shadow of the wall and looked back towards the house. Only the light from the upstairs study shone across the garden. I hopped over a low wall and landed in the soft earth. I shook my head and tried to disperse the effect of the alcohol. I felt the bite of my pistol under the armpit. There was no one in sight; I walked along in the soft earth, quite happy at the idea of footmarks being discovered the next morning. Beyond the gate, where the motor-cycle tracks were still fresh, was an excavation. It was nearly seven feet long. I looked into it. It was three feet deep. It had another few feet to go before it could be called a well-made grave.

There was a simple wooden board at the head of it. It said, *Here lies the body of a petty officer of the German Navy, name unknown. Washed ashore May 2 1945. May his soul rest with God.*

I went back to where the car was parked high on the verge. I found the car key under a pocketful of almonds and walnuts and the motor buzzed calmly into life. What was that local saying that da Cunha had quoted – 'Italy, a place to be born, France, a place to live, and here is a place to die.'

Back at the house I had four small cups of coffee before I felt anything like sober and before anyone had summoned the courage to ask me what I had learned to my advantage.

'It won't be ready for me until tomorrow,' I said airily. I could hardly tell them that I had forgotten to bring it. 'Tomorrow,' I said to Joe MacIntosh, 'you and I both return to London.'

As I went to sleep that night the big grave was fresh in my mind, but the chisel marks on the headboard were even fresher.

18 Sad song

I was angry at myself. I went out to da Cunha's early next morning. His maidservant came to the door and said 'Bons dias.' She gave me da Cunha's engraved business card, on the back of which was written in neat writing, 'Your small package is quite safe. Please do me the honour of calling at 10 p.m. this evening to collect it. – Yours truly, M. G. R. da Cunha.'

She held out her hand for the card to be returned. I gave it to her, thanked her and returned to the car.

There was no diving that morning. The grey wind was breaking the points off the waves and white spray was thrashing the big rocks of the headland. We sat around doing nothing until H.K. invited us to his place for coffee. We went.

'Maria Teresa de Noronha,' H.K. was saying, 'the greatest little *fado* singer in Portugal.' A glass coffee machine was bubbling away on the blue-and-white tiled hearth and Charly, in her bronze toreador pants, was sitting cross-legged like some special sort of Buddha. Around her were scattered the brightly coloured record sleeves that are the folk art of the new world.

The walls were hung with brilliant striped local blankets and photos of H.K. standing with his gun underarm and his foot in the ear of various large quadrupeds.

Singleton and Joe were listening to H.K. doing a quick

rundown on Portugal (Joe had lived there over fifteen years). Giorgio was gazing across the balcony to the grey sea. I was looking at H.K.'s books, chest expander, the nicely kept 7-mm. Mauser sporting rifle and its beautiful Zeiss × 4 telescopic sight in a leather case. I looked at his modern lithographs and listened to the strange lament of the *fado* records. H.K. commented on each as he selected it. 'This is a song about a girl who rents a room in a house on the cliffs to watch her lover's return. One day the news comes that her lover is drowned at sea and will never return. So she sings to the old lady whose house it is. *"Faz um preço,"* she sings. *"Faz um preço mais barato para longa estadia?"'* H.K. said it in an impassioned and melancholy voice. Singleton nodded dolefully, Giorgio didn't even turn his face, but Charly clapped her hands and wore the sort of smile she wore when she was thinking about how the smile looked.

'Did you understand?' said Charly. 'It means, is there a lower price for a longer stay? It's what you hear the tourists in Lisbon saying all the time. You are a terrible tease, Mr Kondit.'

H.K. laughed. He poured big cups full of coffee and I took mine back to the shelves.

In them he had Fodor's *Spain and Portugal,* almost every D. H. Lawrence in print, including the Olympiad edition of *Lady Chatterley* and the Penguin book of the *Lady Chatterley* trial. There was Koestler's *Spanish Testament, A Guide to the World's Great Art Treasures for Children, Art Since 1945,* and a selection of books on modern painters illustrated in colour.

We made appreciative noises over the coffee and then Singleton said, 'What made you come to live in Europe, Mr Kondit?'

'Well,' said H.K., 'I was eating Milltown to sleep, Dexamyl to wake up and Seconal to get through to bed-time. Here I drink champagne all day and what's more, it's cheaper!' H.K. was lacing the coffee with Portuguese cognac. Joe declined.

'Yes,' he said, and he took a swig from the bottle before recorking it, 'there I was, you see, up to the back teeth in credit cards and Milltown, and worrying about what sort of season the Yankees were likely to have. How to break out of it? I knew there were jobs for Americans abroad but I was already too old for the big corporations, and Uncle Sam's got no job for an illiterate bum like me that don't involve an M.1 rifle. So one day I am standing in the bar car of the 5.11 out of Grand Central looking at all these commuting crums and thinking about how I would like the New Haven railroad not to play a part in my life-cycle every a.m. and p.m. and I think: what are all these narrow-lapelled nuts looking for that I could get them in exchange for money? And what do I conclude?'

He looked at his audience, picked up the Silex and poured coffee, enjoying the pause before answering.

'Culture.' He distributed the coffee and the sugar bowl. 'Now that handed a laugh to every crew-cut creep out in Flatbush where I was raised, because culture ain't something to put your arms into like an Abercrombie & Fitch overcoat.

'But me and a guy named Leo Williams-hyphen-Cohen, who was an old buddy of mine from way back and a would-be refugee from the sheet-music racket, had struck it rich with a couple of flags* at the beginning of the Korean War. I said it's now or never, "Wilco" baby – everybody calls him "Wilco" – we are going to snap out of being disorganization men and cut ourselves into the team tapped for the 1975 *Time* magazine covers.'

It was about 11.30 a.m.

---

* Patriotic songs.

I walked to where Giorgio was standing looking out of the balcony doors. There were occasional smacks of warm rain-drops on the balcony tile-work. On the beach two long lines of men were pulling at each end of a U-shaped net.

H.K. was saying, 'Nerts to the big-time art guys, I said, I'm for Mr Average Feller every time. And so we set up "Art for the Average Guy, Inc.", just a little stash on East 12th at first, with Wilco borrowing his brother-in-law's truck for deliveries once a week.'

'Harry, you are priceless,' said Charly, 'whatever were you delivering?'

'Well, we printed a little sheet called "Art for Aay-Gees"; Average Guys, see. We put it out to the coffee joints on McDougall and Bleecker and a few ads in the egg-head week-lies. We do all right – we don't have to buy vicuna coats for the Government – but we do all right. But one day my buddy Leo Williams-Cohen (with a hyphen) says to me, "Nerts to these Average Guys, Harry, they're just a set of peanut-circuit nogoodniks. What we need is a class angle." And he thinks of one there and then: "Art for Cognoscenti," he says.'

Harry Kondit walked across to the bookshelf and removed a pale-blue leather folder.

'It worked out?' Joe MacIntosh asked. He was still loung-ing back on the bright sofa holding an empty coffee cup on his knee.

Harry Kondit flipped open a copy of *Esquire* to a full-colour Modigliani nude. The caption read,

Art for Cognoscenti Club are honoured to present as 'Pic. of the Month' for January this fine colour reproduc-tion of one of the world's masterpieces. Join this month and receive two full-colour reproductions of famous nudes from the world's great works of art, each suitable for framing as exquisite decor for office, workshop, or den.

Receive each month a beautiful portrayal of unadorned womanhood, chosen by a panel of famous artists, teachers, and educationalists and accompanied by clear concise explanatory notes, criticism and description by Henri Zahn.

Charly started to clap her hands and Singleton, Giorgio, Joe and I all joined in. H.K. didn't take offence.

'But,' said Joe, 'how come you can live here in Albufeira?'

'Simple. I look through these here books …' H.K. grabbed three large books of art reproductions from the shelf, 'and choose the Pic. of the Month.'

The removal of the art books revealed three small ones that had fallen down the back of the row of books.

'But,' said Joe, 'it says …' Joe's face bloomed red in embarrassment. I quickly plucked out the books.

'Sure it says there's a panel of artists and jokers like that,' H.K. agreed.

One book was called *Formulae for the Physicist*, the next *Setting up a Lab.*

' … they choose it …' H.K. went on.

The third book was called *Molecular Structure*. I couldn't help thinking of the ice-melting theories. They rearranged molecular structure of water to make it ice.

' … but I, Henri Zahn, select it.' H.K. laughed a great boom of a laugh and smashed his thigh with his big hairy fist like he'd collapse in hysterics if he didn't beat himself serious quickly.

That Wednesday was one long wasted day as I look back on it. Giorgio and Singleton were to try a dive in the afternoon, but Giorgio's reducer was defective (which caused the air to blast into the demand valve instead of flowing). They turned back after only a few yards. I suppose I was a bit edgy, cursing myself for overlooking the package the night before and being a little too critical of everything, including the Borbigoes – large cockles – that Charly had cooked with hot paprika and smoked ham sausage for lunch. After lunch she disappeared back to H.K.'s and I had a talk about expenses and car hire with Joe MacIntosh, who was doing all the bookwork as well as being in charge of diving.

I was concerned about Giorgio. He had been so boisterous and effervescent until we began diving. Joe said all divers are like that after they begin a job.

'They mope around and worry about fresh-water currents and whether to remove a bulkhead door. He'll be O.K. when we complete diving.'

I looked at the diagram of the U-boat. Giorgio had cross-hatched the sections he had worked and there was a small red blob where the empty canister had been found under the control-room floor.

The marked area seemed very small compared with the size of the U-boat. I wondered how long it would be before we found the currency or log book, or London gave us permission to cease operations, or Mr Smith appeared on the scene.

It was when Joe was locking the plan of the submarine back into the writing-desk drawer that he noticed it.

We checked, sat down and thought about it, but Joe found the broken woodwork and then there was no doubt at all. The empty canister was exactly as we'd left it, still locked into the wardrobe, but someone had stolen the photos of it.

There is no alternative in situations like this. It wasn't

something that every young intelligence worker finds enthralling. It was a sordid little job of the sort that constitutes much of our work. Joe and I began to search everyone's room.

Apart from the usual personality insights that these searches always provide, there was only one remarkable thing. Among the several articles in Charly's room that a young single girl shouldn't know how to buy were twenty-five rounds of 7.65 parabellum ammunition.

Joe had called London and they brought a light civilian plane down to Algarve for me. It was a fine clear night when I went out to the airfield via da Cunha's house.

There were lights on, and outside the front door was a black Mercedes and a Seat car. Each had an E-plate and Madrid registration.* Farther along under the almond trees was H.K.'s little deux-chevaux. I knew that, as surely as a tickbird follows a rhino, a two-stroke motorcycle would be somewhere near by. It was. I remembered the Portuguese proverb that says, 'From Spain, neither fair wind nor good marriage.'

A bell jangled deep in the interior and echoed back like a belly laugh. I rang again. Finally da Cunha opened the door himself. A gold tooth glinted in the lamplight, and he passed me the package from under his velvet smoking jacket. It was still wrapped in brown paper and string and was as heavy as good advice. Joe had the motor running when I got back to the car.

The little villages were dark except for the doorways. Low-wattage bulbs shone yellow amid the black furniture and rough whitewashed walls. Here and there a sharp glint of light reflected from a bottle.

* Madrid numbers commence with an 'M'.

Inevitably there were the laden burros, bicycles, and unlit carts wobbling along the black roads. I drew up at the place marked on my map; palm leaves cut jagged pieces of darkness from the stars. The trees were heavy with olives and the warm night air held their aroma. From near by came the purr of a light aeroplane engine. I got the green canister from the boot and scrambled aboard.

We were skirting the Bilbao air traffic control zone before I discovered the note that da Cunha had tucked into the package. I showed it to Joe.

> *Dear Smith,*
> *During April 1945 the body of a German sailor was washed ashore a few kilometres to the west of here. I arranged that the body should be afforded a decent Christian burial and the accompanying package, which was the only thing found on the body, was buried with it. Since the fishermen who first discovered the body are now anxious that the package should be given to you, and since in my opinion the British Government has an obvious claim of ownership, I have pleasure in restoring it to you.*
> *Your obedient servant,*
> *DA CUNHA*

By 3 a.m. Gatwick airport was grudgingly clearing us for landing among all their big boys. In our little cabin the instruments glowed numbers and with a sudden leap the landing lights cut through the winter's rain. I began to worry whether Brown's Hotel would have a room for Joe.

19 Never say this

Dawlish picked it up and held it under the Anglepoise lamp. The burnished metal coruscated in the hard artificial light.

'Just gave it to you, did he?' said Dawlish. He flung me a fresh packet of Gauloises. 'Very good. A stroke of luck.'

The phone rang. Alice said she'd run out of coffee, would Nescafé do. It was 6.25 a.m. and Dawlish told her she'd better go home and get some sleep, but she brought it up for us.

'New cups and saucers, eh Alice,' I said. Her smile was like a shaft of Christmas-afternoon sunshine. Dawlish handed her the block of metal. It was eight inches by six and about two and a quarter inches thick. The arcs of milling shone as she twisted it in her bony hands.

A large hole was driven through the carbon steel block. Fitting exactly into the hole were three discs. Two of the discs were over an inch thick. Alice shook them into her open palm. The dies carried a fine intaglio design, on one a man on a prancing horse, on the other a portrait of Queen Victoria. Nestling between them was a shiny sovereign.

Alice studied each one carefully, and looked up at me and then at Dawlish.

'Isn't it just as I said, Mr Dawlish?'

'Yes, you were right, Alice,' said Dawlish. 'Excellent quality die for forging sovereigns.'

'But didn't I tell you that it would have Queen Victoria on it?' she asked Dawlish.

'All right, Alice,' I said, 'I was wrong, but we aren't through diving yet.'

Alice trotted off home at 6.45 a.m. and over our coffee Dawlish and I sat down and talked about staff changes and overseas finance and how many days to Christmas and it didn't seem like it and it doesn't interest us but Dawlish's kids liked it and the expense of it all; until Dawlish suddenly said, 'You never relax; it's getting you down, this job?'

It wasn't that he'd change it if it was, he just liked to know it all. Outside, dawn was bringing the sky to the colour of a mechanic's handkerchief.

'I can't make it fit together,' I said, 'and some things are too convenient.'

'Convenience is just a state of mind,' said Dawlish. 'It's understanding that's important. Understanding the symptoms you encounter will refer you to just one disease. You find a man with a pain in the foot and the finger and you wonder what he could possibly be suffering from with two such disparate symptoms. Then you find that while holding a nail one day he hit his finger with a hammer, then dropped it on to his toe.'

'O.K.,' I said, 'so much for Emergency Ward Ten. Now listen to my problems. First, I am signing contracts with these rebels who want to take over in Portugal, and since the Foreign Office want to help them along a little I have to dive into an old Nazi sub. to find counterfeit money. So far so good, but while I am doing that damned frogman course two cars follow me down the A3. Whose cars? Mr Elusive Smith, British Cabinet Minister. I ask to see a file about him but it never arrives ...'

'It will,' said Dawlish, 'it's delayed, that's all.'

I gave Dawlish the curly-lip treatment. 'O.K., then there's this man Butcher who sold us the ice-melting file.'

'And a lot of rubbish it was too,' said Dawlish.

'No one thought so at the time,' I said, 'and the department paid over six thousand pounds for it.'

'Five thousand seven hundred,' said Dawlish.

'So you looked it up,' I challenged. 'So you think it's dodgy too.'

'I wouldn't say that,' said Dawlish.

'No,' I agreed, 'you'd say "inconsistent with departmental precedent", but you'd *think* it was dodgy.'

Dawlish took out a handkerchief and lowered his nose into it, like he was going from a seventh-storey window into something held by eight firemen. He blew his nose loudly. 'Go on,' he said.

'Well, I am followed by this dark-blue job from Vernon and this man Butcher. When I get to Gib. they are going through our mail …'

'Oh, I wouldn't …'

'Well, I would,' I said loudly. 'And behind all three there is the paternal Mr Henry Smith. When we finally get something out of the submarine the canister is empty except for a piece of paper money. Out of this American clown's shirt comes another bill within a dozen serial numbers of it.'

'Yes, that *was* convenient,' said Dawlish.

'Convenient is the word,' I said, 'it stinks.'

'A …' Dawlish hesitated, ' … a frame-up,' he said very proudly.

'What's that mean?' I asked.

'It's an expression that American …' then he saw me grinning and he frowned. I went on, 'Then finally da Cunha gives me a long lecture about old Portuguese customs like he's the

Horizon Holidays man and this die, and says it's for a Mr Smith.'

'So what do you conclude?' asked Dawlish.

'I don't conclude anything,' I said, 'but if I see a man with a Union Jack in his buttonhole wearing a deerstalker I begin to wonder if he's trying to convince me about his national characteristics, and I wonder why.'

'What about the canister and the grave?' Dawlish asked.

'I'm hoping that the canister isn't as empty as it looks,' I said.

'And the grave?'

'Was never full,' I said, 'just a hole in the ground.'

'I trust you can tell a grave from a hole in the ground,' said Dawlish sardonically. He was staring out of the window. 'There's a new instruction about your diving,' he said without turning round. I said nothing. 'Foreign Office is not interested in the currency any more.' Outside on the window-sill a starling was getting itself a lungful of diesel smoke.

'O'Brien isn't interested in the money,' Dawlish said again.

'He's swinging with the syntax,' I said, 'but he's forcing the story line.'

Dawlish tried to touch his nose with his tongue. He said, 'If there are any containers that might hold scientific papers you are to send them to the Embassy people unopened.'

'How do I find out what's inside if I don't open them? Did they tell you that?'

'Unopened,' said Dawlish.

'So they *are* worried about the ice-melting stuff after all.'

'Ice-melting,' said Dawlish, 'who mentioned ice-melting? You've got ice-melting on the brain. The only ice-melting equipment that they are interested in is a glass of Johnny Walker.'

'All right,' I said, 'now try and see this from my point of view. The political people at Lisbon tell us that they'd like this job done and give it a BB8 requirement importance.* They tell us they've chosen us because it must be completely under-cover as far as the Portuguese Government are concerned; that means that I can't check properly on all these people: da Cunha, Harry Kondit and this small-time *éminence grise* Fernandes Tomas without risking a leak. You know what will happen the minute I ask 37† for a shred of information – every phone in Lisbon will ring.'

'Well,' said Dawlish, 'I can understand their point of view; they don't want to upset anyone.'

'Yes,' I said, 'exactly. Now that's the Embassy position as a rule, isn't it? Not to upset anyone. Don't upset all the good work we're doing – all that crap. Now doesn't it strike you as odd that the Embassy people at Lisbon not only egg us into this set-up and tell *us*, mark you, not to let the Portuguese know that we are doing anything down there, but they are all bright smiles and elevator shoes about it. Send us this Singleton character and this girl.'

'Well,' said Dawlish, 'what do you want me to do about Singleton?'

'Give him back to the Ovaltineys,' I said.

'Now then,' said Dawlish, 'don't start on that again. I know you don't believe it but I've checked those answers myself. Absolutely nothing. Singleton may be what you call "a jerk", but he's just a junior assistant to the naval attaché and he's as normal as income tax. Prep school, Dartmouth, good marks there too. Sea time with Mediterranean fleet. What else do you want me to do?'

---

* All jobs requested have R.I. codes and are then given D of C (Difficulty of Completion) code. A low R.I. (i.e. not very important job) will be attended to if it gets a low D of C (i.e. if it's easy to do). Similarly a high D of C job requires a high R.I. to get it approved for action.
† Rue Valéry: Interpol.

'Just one thing,' I asked, 'keep the wraps on that sovereign die find. Don't say a word about it to anyone without me okaying it. Let's keep it a nice cosy secret between the people in this office.'

'*And* Senhor da Cunha,' Dawlish said, so I knew he was agreeing to do so. (He would never promise to disobey regulations in so many words.) He continued as though I hadn't mentioned the die. 'The girl,' he said, 'Admiral's daughter, right schools, lives in Lisbon except when she goes to Naples with her father. Mediterranean holidays. You should think yourself lucky Lisbon are on their toes. You must admit it was a good idea. You couldn't have used local labour in the house, the security position being what it was. Why, you'd all have been standing around with damp dishcloths all day.'

I suppose I must have snorted.

20 Enemy

My flat in Southwark was cold when I got back there at 8 a.m. after the all-night discussion with Dawlish. I paid the cab and had difficulty getting the front door open because of the heap of mail on the front mat. There were the usual things. Red-printed ones from the rates office and a very patient one from Electrolux; thirteen pounds outstanding, I could almost hear the sigh. Advertisements for Lux, a postcard from Munich wishing I was there, a receipt from L.E.B., and the cistern was overflowing methodically.

I switched on the fan heater, boiled a kettle and ground coffee. While I was waiting for the coffee to drip through I phoned the office number, gave them the code word, then told the operator, 'If Mr MacIntosh phones, tell him to get a car and collect me at about five o'clock this afternoon. We have to go and collect my car from the airport. If he hasn't phoned in by noon get the message to him at Brown's Hotel.'

I poured a generous slug of Teacher's whisky into sweet black coffee and sipped it slowly. The night without sleep was beginning to thump me gently on the cranium. It was 8.45 a.m. I went to bed just as the next-door radio tuned in to Housewives' Choice. Upstairs the vacuum cleaner began its fiendish flagellation. I dozed.

* * *

I looked at my watch in the darkness. The doorbell was ringing. I had slept eight hours, and now Joe MacIntosh was at the door and eager to get to grips with the night-life of the Metropolis. He had one of the taxis from the car pool. They were specially tuned to do over ninety m.p.h. and MacIntosh was keen to find out how much over.

I took a tepid shower, which is my special way of entering the world of consciousness. Then I dressed in a manner suited to a Soho low-life tour – dark worsted and black woollen shirt, with a trench coat that can take home-brew alcohol splashes without flinching.

It was a pleasure to see Joe handle that souped-up cab. His huge shy hands stroked the controls and we slid through the traffic with an élan he never otherwise showed. 'Nowhere,' said Joe quietly as we ascended the Chiswick flyover, 'do Englishmen show a greater spirit of compromise than in straddling a traffic lane.' He nudged the horn, flicked the cab over to the fast lane and stabbed the speed up to seventy with an acceleration that almost fired me out of the jump seat. He moved through the crash gearbox that all these cabs had with a nerveless skill.

When we got to London Airport he parked behind the cab rank and put a glove over the flag in a very convincing way. My VW was tucked deeply into the Ministry of Aviation Priority pound; would I like Joe to get it for me?

It was only 6.30 p.m., but already it was dark and I felt fingers of rain tapping me on the shoulder. I gave him the key and went up to the bookstall for five minutes' browsing. The headlines read, 'No Capital Gains Tax this year – Official.' The Americans were planning a monkey ride to the moon, the new Wehrmacht wanted nuclear weapons, Lady Lewisham was complaining about dirty teacups and the Minister had said that old age pensions just couldn't be increased. I bought

Esquire and walked out into the drizzle. There were lights around the car pound and I saw that Joe had moved enough of the cars to provide a lane through which to bring mine.

A Viscount came down the GCA talkdown, its white, red and green lights peep-boing the traffic patterns. Full flap, throttle back. The dark shape passed overhead with a contrapuntal shriek. I heard the wheels hit the tarmac and the automatic control pull the blades into 'ground-fine' pitch. Joe was at the far end of the enclosure; he opened the door of my VW, got in and switched on the main lights. The rain tore little gashes through the long beams.

From inside the car came an intense light; each window was a clear white rectangle, and the door on Joe's side opened very quickly. It was then that the blast sent me across the wet pavement like a tiddly-wink.

'Walk not run,' I thought. I jammed my spectacles on to my nose and got to my feet. A cold current of air advised me of an eight-inch rent in my trouser leg. People ran past towards the car park. The explosion had fired the inflammable parts of an adjacent car. The flames lit up the neighbourhood and a bell began to ring close at hand. I heard the attendant shouting 'Two fellers went over there, two fellers.' I had my keys in my hand by the time I got back to the cab rank. I selected two. With the first I unlocked the anti-thief device on the gear lever. The second I plugged into the ignition, started up and pulled out of the rank. From the car park I heard another 'boom' and saw a flash as a petrol tank exploded. I drove round the roundabout. 'Other way, cabbie,' said an airport policeman. The grazed palms of my hands were throbbing and the steering wheel was wet with blood and sweat. I switched the radio to 'stand by' to warm the transmitting valves.

'What's going on over there, mate?' I asked him. 'Keep moving,' said the policeman. I was through the tunnel and away. Just to be on the safe side I turned left at the main road before using the two-way radio.

They answered promptly. 'Go ahead Oboe Seven. Over,' said the operator.

'Oboe Seven to Provisional. Message. Black London Airport Ministry of Aviation car park. One student: MacIntosh. Flat. Scissors.* Over.'

'Provisional to Oboe Seven. How are you proceeding? Over.'

'Oboe Seven. A4, approaching Slough. Over.'

'Thank you, Oboe Seven. Roger. Out. Provisional at stand by.'

When Dawlish came in on the radio telephone link he was touchingly concerned for my safety, but remembered first to ask for the name of my insurance company. He said, 'We can't afford to have them getting curious about how it happened before we send out the D notice.'†

I soon mastered the knack of double-declutching the crash gearbox.

* Code translation: Black: third of most urgent priority signals; Student: agent or employee; Flat: dead or presumed dead; Scissors: violence.

† D (Defence) notice: censorship directive to newspapers on various security matters.

21 Are the wages of this, that?

A great big sunny Friday in London, the policemen standing around like tourists. On Jermyn Street two old men edged crabwise past the calm cheeses of Paxton and Whitfield. On five-string banjo and accordion they whitewashed the sound of 'La vie en rose' across the brittle winter air. Jean was waiting for me at Wilton's restaurant. She wore a dark-brown Chanel suit. How did she manage it on her salary? A pale sherry awaited me and so did the news of the Strutton Report.

'O'Brien is forming one of his famous little committees,' she said.

'O lord,' I groaned, 'I know what that means.'

'You're well out of the way,' said Jean. 'Dawlish is sitting in on it at present. They will discuss chain of command.'

'Power,' I said. 'Lord Acton wasn't kidding.'

'Even the War House are trying to get into the act.'

'It can't possibly be anything to do with them,' I said.

'You know how it is,' said Jean. 'If they don't make at least a token play for the things they don't want, they'd have no bargaining gambits for the things they do want.'

'You are highly knowledgeable on the subject of inter-departmental committee work.'

Jean smiled and replied, 'I'm only telling you what every woman has always known.'

The waitress brought the famous Wilton menu that has no prices on it. I'd never been foolhardy enough to ask for anything but what the chef recommended and this was no day to start flexing my muscles.

The melon had gone, and the fresh salmon too, before Jean brought up the subject of the package that da Cunha had given me.

'Alice even predicted that the sovereign die would portray Queen Victoria – that was brilliant, wasn't it?'

'Brilliant.'

'How do you think she guessed?'

'No idea,' I said.

'You have too. Please tell me,' said Jean.

'For the simple reason that Queen Victoria is a woman.'

'*Was* a woman,' said Jean.

'Don't be smart,' I said, '*is* a woman where counterfeit sovereigns are concerned.'

'So?'

'Arab countries, or rather let's say Muslim countries, are very much in the market for sovereigns, right?'

'Right.'

'Muslims object to unveiled female face, therefore most counterfeit sovereigns depict a king. Therefore a Queen Victoria sovereign is unlikely to be counterfeit, therefore Nazis decide to make their super-duper authentic die in the likeness of Queen Victoria.'

'And it works?'

'When they thought of it it was a wow, but now it's been tumbled to for ages, but since counterfeit and genuine fetch the same price, who cares?'

'And Alice guessed that it would be of Nazi origin?'

'I radioed Dawlish and got diplomatic clearance for a

parcel of that size and weight. Alice jumped to a tentatively correct conclusion.'

'Tentatively?' Jean poured me some more coffee.

'Oh, it's dead right as far as it goes. But let's not jump to any conclusion. There are no markings on the mould, nothing to connect it with the U-boat or the Nazis or with anything, come to that.'

'I see,' said Jean, 'you mean that these people at Albufeira may have merely given it to you to get rid of you. In fact, as a straightforward bribe. That they didn't expect you to believe that it came straight from the sea.'

Jean paused. 'Or if they thought you were from this man Smith it could be a bribe to Smith,' she paused again, 'so he would do something.'

'Or not do something,' I prompted.

She looked up. 'Yes,' she said, speaking each word separately and slowly, 'discontinue the investigation?'

'Zen,' I said, 'you got it quicker than Dawlish.'

'Now let me see, this man da Cunha says it came from a German sailor's body that came out of a fishing net, but they don't do "bottom trawl" fishing anywhere near where the U-boat is, they do American-style closing circle fishing, don't they?'

'"Purse seine" style, yes, you're reading me loud and clear, and it didn't come from any German corpse either.'

Jean said, 'If it was a bribe, it would be a pretty good one, wouldn't it? I mean, worth a lot of money.'

'Yes, you can get about 50,000 coins from a good die and this is a good one. It certainly would be worth a lot of money, especially to someone involved with illegal movement of gold.'

'So that when you returned to London our people out there continued to dive on the wrecked U-boat. They realized that the bribe hadn't worked and so they planted dynamite in your car?'

'No,' I said, 'that explosion was a carefully planned venture. They find out that I always send my car to L.A.P., discover where it's parked, employ a specialist to do quite a complex wiring job, buy dynamite. I don't think that there is an immediate connexion between my getting the package from this man da Cunha and the bomb that killed Joe. The two things may be unrelated.'

'Then who is this man da Cunha?' Jean asked.

'Work it out for yourself,' I said. 'He speaks perfect Portuguese – syntax and inflection wonderful! He dresses like a Portuguese aristocrat should. I have had my knees under his table, I can tell you the food is authentic. As for Portuguese history and folklore, he is one of the greatest ear-benders in Western Europe.'

'You are going to prove that he isn't Portuguese,' Jean said, 'because he says he *is*.'

'I've got a hunch,' I said.

'What you've got is a pointed head,' Jean said rudely, 'but tell me what I have to do.'

'I want one of the movie people to go on holiday in Southern Portugal,' I said.

'Victor had better go,' said Jean, 'he has a genuine Swiss passport and he knows how to stay out of trouble.'

'That's good,' I said, 'we've had all the trouble we can use for the time being.'

Jean was quiet for a few moments, then she said softly, 'I'd just like to kill whoever murdered Joe.'

'I'll forget that you spoke.' I looked at her for a moment, then said, 'If you want to continue working in the department you'll never even *think* a thing like that, let alone say it. There is no room for heroics, vendettas and associated melodrama in an efficient shop. You stand up, get shot at, then carry on quietly. Suppose I'd been full of George-Cross-emotion and gone running back to Joe last night. I'd have got myself smothered in smoke, reporters, blisters and policemen. Act grown-up or I'll cut your security rating back.'

'I'm sorry,' she said.

'O.K., but don't ever hanker after tidiness. Don't ever think or hope that the great mess of investigation that we work on is suddenly going to resolve itself like the last chapter of a whodunnit: I've-got-all-gathered-together-in-the-room-where-the-murder-was-done kind of scene. After we're all dead and gone there will still be an office with all those manilla dust-traps tied in pink tape. So just knit quietly away and be thankful for the odd sock or even a lop-sided cardigan with one sleeve. Don't desire vengeance or think that if someone murders you tomorrow we will be tracking them down mercilessly. We won't. We'll all be strictly concerned with keeping out of the *News of the World* and the *Police Gazette*.'

Jean was determined to prove what a master of her emotions she was. 'The liaison officer at Scotland Yard sent pictures of your car over, did you see them?'

'Yes, they sent me a set of wet prints last night. By the way, thank Keightley for doing a good job; there's no mention in the dailies.'

'Yes,' said Jean, 'they were writing D notices like a literate traffic warden. There were four cars written off. If the Yard people are right in reconstructing the explosion points, it's almost as if they wanted the fire to spread.'

'Really? Where were they?'

'Under the bonnet, centre of the sunshine roof, behind the rear seat, between the front seats.' The black make-up around her eyes had smudged slightly. She pushed at her dark hair, sniffed and smiled at me. 'He brought me a green suede jacket,' she said.

I paid the bill and we walked up towards Piccadilly together. 'You always pump me when I'm dozily full of food and drink,' I teased. Jean gave me another weak little smile and I took her arm. 'I'm going back to Lisbon tonight. I want you to send that empty metal container up to F.S.L. at Cardiff.* They're very good at Cardiff. You've given me an idea, Jeannie. I think I know why my car was blown up now.'

I offered to get a cab for Jean but she declined. Outside Fortnum's I hugged her arm. 'It must have been absolutely instantaneous,' I said.

Jean blew her nose and continued to study her shoes.

* Home Office Forensic Science Laboratory, Cardiff.

22 Charly raises its head

Pow Pow Pow. The high-pitched note of a Continental car horn ripped the morning air. Harry Kondit's deux-chevaux was in the forecourt of Albufeira station.

'Hi there, Ace, climb into the sled. I told your boys I'd pick you up – they're diving and Charly's shopping.'

I wondered by what process of deduction H.K. had latched on to our diving so soon. Was it possible to keep such a thing secret in a town as small as this one? It made the whole job a little more dangerous. We sped down the sunny road. The fig trees had lost almost every leaf and stood bare and silver in the red fields.

'What's the good word, Harry?' I said. Perhaps I should tell London to prepare a new cover for us in case trouble blew up. We sped across the main road past the canning factories.

'I just got some new jazz records from the States, Ace. Pretty wiggy. Come around for drinks this evening. Get an earful of wax. Ha, ha, ha.' We were outside Number 12 by now. I said 'thank you' to H.K. and he bumped down the narrow cobbled street to his place. I went inside.

Unfortunately for Charly she was the first person I saw. She was cleaning fish in the kitchen. She wore a microscopic white bikini.

'Well hello, darling!' she said, putting a sustained accent on the final syllable of each word.

'Can the crap, Charly,' I said.

'Skilful alliteration, darling,' she said and wrinkled her nose. 'What's upset the chiefman?'

'First why is it too much trouble for anyone to meet me? Secondly I don't appreciate H.K. riding me back and telling me about how the diving is going.'

'How the diving is *going*? Admit it, lover, he didn't really tell you how the diving was *going*, did he?'

'No,' I said, 'he told me that the boys were diving. What sort of security do we have here? How much more information has he pumped out of you?'

'He's just done to us what he's done for you: mentioned the word "diving" to see what reaction he got. What would you prefer us to do, take him up on it and start playing "What's my line"?'

'I don't like it.'

'Well, you know, little us can't be expected to manage without big chiefman. You shouldn't leave us, darling.'

'Knock it off, Charlotte, and put some clothes on. So much flesh in the kitchen is revolting.'

'I've had no other complaints,' said Charly. She moved past me through the door, and paused, her nubile body brushing mine … 'so far,' she said, and leaned forward to touch the tip of my nose with her pointed tongue. 'You are breathing heavily, chiefman,' she said huskily just an inch or so from my mouth. 'Buzz off, Charly,' I said, 'I've got enough troubles already.' But I *was* breathing heavily.

'I hear you have a sexy little secretary tucked away in London, darling.'

'I wouldn't say sexy,' I said, 'she has two kids, three chins, and five per cent of the gross. She drinks like a fish and cooks the sort of food advertised on television.'

Charly gave a high-pitched giggle. 'You nasty old liar, you left a photo of her in your shirt last week, I know what she's like.'

'Do you wash *our* shirts, too?' I said.

'Well, of course I do, who do you think does your laundry? But don't change the subject. I've got the photo of your secretarial sex-bomb and what's more I can see the glint of matrimony at fifty paces.'

'Fifty paces from you is close enough,' I said.

'Then stop looking down my swimsuit,' said Charly.

'What swimsuit?'

There was a knock at the door. I backed away from her. It was a local urchin who went to the fish market for Charly sometimes. Would I like him to clean the car? Yes I would. I walked across to the Victor with him. We must be running up quite a bill with the hire company. He produced a bucket and cloth from nowhere and began to slop water over the windscreen. I sat inside the car and engaged this fourteen-year-old in conversation. Did he know H.K., da Cunha, Fernie Tomas? Yes, he knew them all. Was the tunny fish any good at present? It was all right but not like it is in July. Did he ever run errands for any of those people? No, they were too grand, he said. Would he care to do a small favour for me? But of course. And keep it secret? As secret as the grave. Did he know which barber Senhor Tomas went to? Augusto knew – the movement of the town was his pastime and career. He must get a small lock of Senhor Tomas's hair. A small piece of hair and no one must see. He and I would share this secret and further I would reward him to the extent of five escudos.

It would be for sending to the 'O país das fadas'? he asked. I thought of Charlotte Street. It would, I agreed, be for sending to the land of the fairies. I began to wonder how to tell them about Joe.

It would be for nothing to the YO park d sa fadas; he asked
I thought of Chafford Street. Itwould I agreed be for send
iny to the hand of the knitter. I began to wonder how to tell
them about Joe.

23 In the same one

Giorgio and Singleton got back at 3.30 for a late lunch of
grilled red gurnet and butter sauce in the Portuguese manner.
I didn't want to play the heavy father, but I suggested that
H.K. was coming too close to the family circle.

'You don't suspect him of being a Salazar police spy, do
you, sir?' asked Singleton.

'I suspect even you, Mr Singleton,' I said. There were no
grins behind the gurnet. They knew I wasn't kidding.

We continued to eat in silence. Then, as Charly collected
up the dishes, she said, 'H.K. has bought or borrowed a forty-
foot cabin cruiser.'

'No kidding,' I said. Charly had taken the used plates into
the kitchen. She called to us, 'It's coming into the bay now.' We
went out on to the balcony to watch. Down below, beating a wake
on the gleaming water, the big red-and-white launch cast a long
shadow in the afternoon sunlight. From the high wheelhouse a
cap, blue, soft, and nautical, peeked over the wrap-around windscreen. H.K.'s bronze face broke into a grin and his lips moved.
Charly put her flattened hand behind her ear and H.K. shouted
again, but the wind from the sea grabbed the words out of his
mouth and tossed them over his shoulder. He disappeared into
the inner confines of the launch, which kept just enough power
to hold its position without turning beam-to to the swell.

He reappeared with an electronic hailer.

'C'mon, landlubbers,' the metallic voice struck across the water. 'Get off your butts and get out here, kids.'

'He really is the most vulgar man,' said Charly.

'He is insufferable,' said Singleton.

'I only said he was vulgar,' said Charly. 'I didn't say I didn't like it.'

Giorgio blew on the lighted end of his cheroot. We all went down to the dinghy; the starter cartridge spat, and the outboard roared as we shot out towards the cabin cruiser.

'Are you sure we can feel quite safe with you, Mr Kondit?' asked Charly.

'Holy cow, how many times do I have to tell you to …'

'Harry.'

'Well, I'll tell you, Charly. These guys are safe. You – you aren't so safe,' and he pushed his yachting cap back and boomed his big laugh.

Inside the main cabin it was all mahogany veneer, bright curtains and soft music. Nautical procedures had gone overboard. Along the wall was a stainless sink and a refrigerator. In the corner was a seventeen-inch TV set. We sank into the armchairs while H.K. blended vodka and vermouth with ritualistic devotion.

'What's that all about, Harry?' Charly was looking at the mural of signal flags which decorated the cabin wall.

'It's kind of talk with flag, see, you haul them …'

'Yes, Harry, I understand the function of signal flags; what, I mean to ask, do they mean?'

'Sure, hon. They are international foreign code flags K.U.Z.I.G. and Y., nautical meaning …' H.K. leaned over close to Charly, '"Permission granted to lay alongside."'

Charly giggled. 'Oh, that's very nautical, Harry. I must commit it to memory.'

I noticed Singleton's lip curl, but whether at H.K.'s suggestiveness or seamanship I couldn't tell.

'Step up to the bridge,' said H.K. The record finished. The stereo player rumbled into a count-down for the next disc. Against the hull the water giggled and gurgled like a fool. I heard Singleton say, 'So this is the driver's seat?' H.K. replied, 'Yep.' I wondered how many of the jibes really bounced off H.K. and how many went deep under the skin like a chigger. Miles Davis began to pump the cabin full of sound.

From the forecastle overhead I heard Charly shouting, 'I'm falling, I'm falling,' in a not-very-convincing way, and the sound of Giorgio saving her in an embrace that suited them both. Just behind me on the bridge Singleton was admiring the R.D.F. and the electronic depth-gauge.

'Yes, sir,' H.K. said, 'a powered anchor; right here.' He pushed one of a series of brightly coloured buttons. There was a faint purr and I felt the big cruiser float free on the outgoing tide. 'Self-starter, a little choke.' The big motor suddenly battered the quiet bay. H.K. moved the gear lever, and the screw engaged the water. We slid forward.

H.K. held the steering wheel in firm proprietorial grip, bit on a large cigar and beamed at us all from his high stool. 'You British have had the monopoly of messing about in boats long enough; here, somebody else steer,' he said, and poured us all another round of cocktails from the big jug that featured a design of pirates dancing a hornpipe with the words 'splice the mainbrace me hearties' around the top. We made a scene as domestic as a beer ad.

110

24 Threads of a story

After dinner that evening Giorgio showed me on the diagram the proportion of the U-boat hull that had been searched. Charly made coffee and we sat around drinking the cheap local brandy.

An ocean-going U-boat is a very large piece of machinery. Over one thousand tons, over three hundred feet in length, it wasn't difficult to understand why such a small section of the diagram was cross-hatched to indicate that it had been searched. Giorgio had brought little up to the surface. There was one pair of spectacles with red lenses.* There was a tin marked 'Pervitin', which was the German Desoxyephedrine pep pill, and three German Admiralty charts of the Spanish coast. These interested me most. For, although they were of the standard German Admiralty pattern, there were figures on one corner in ballpoint writing. The number 127,342 was multiplied by 9,748 and the correct product inserted beneath.

Charts that are faded, tattered and corrugated by long immersion; charts that are dated 1940 and haven't seen the light of day since 1945 should not, I felt, have *anything* written on them in ballpoint writing.

---

* Red glasses were worn by lookouts to accustom their eyes to night vision before they went on watch.

The search had been completed on the port side of the control room and extended along the port side of the officers' quarters. The next compartment forward was the crew quarters, but before working on that we would begin to search the starboard side of the control room and work forward. Giorgio said that the starboard side promised to be more tricky. There had been a shift of the bulkhead that separated the control room and officers' quarters, resulting in a collapse of the port side of the floor on each side of that bulkhead. Exposed under the floor was a jumble of broken battery cases, dented compressed-air bottles and a thick oil sludge still clinging heavily inside the split fuel tanks. A complete search would entail delving, groping, and scouring through this tangle of dirty debris with bare, swollen hands tender from prolonged submersion. No wonder Giorgio had left it until last in the hope that we would have everything we required before beginning on the starboard side.

These days of working together had brought the three of them closer, and now I felt an outsider while they swopped stories and teased Charly, who skilfully kept them at bay.

' … is a millionaire this man,' Giorgio was relating, 'I teach him to swim underwater. You do not need all this, I say to him. But is of no use. He buy the American equipment, a rubber suit of bright red, flippers, depth-gauge, the magnificent underwater wrist-watch. Compass fit on the arm. An underwater gun with the arrow-head for fishing, which makes me very frightened I can tell you. He carries all this with him as well as his lung and a very pretty little blackboard and a mark that writes under the wet. I have to adjust his buoyancy for the weight of all this. He goes down with much breathing and blowing and when he is at the bottom another man join him there. All the other man have is the little bathing suit so small.' Giorgio measured it with his hands and gave

Charly a sly look. 'Is very small. Nothing else, no lung, no mask, no gun, no bright red rubber suit or the special wool suit from the Shetland. Nothing but a little pants. My millionaire friend go up to him and write on his little blackboard, "Hey, what you do here? I have the special equipment costing me the six hundred dollar and you come down here with the nothing; what you do, how dare?"'

The audience were gripped. Charly at last broke the silence. 'What did he say?' she asked.

'He say nothing,' Giorgio continued. 'You no speaking in the water. He take the little blackboard with the special mark for the undersea writing. He read the message from my friend the millionaire and he write, "Mama I drown."'

Charly said, 'No more coffee for you,' but I was beginning to notice that Giorgio wasn't worrying too much about coffee, he was hitting the brandy. It's not good for a diver to drink a lot. A Thermos of hot wine or a brandy to restore circulation after a prolonged dive was one thing; drinking yourself to sleep was another.

The talk went on over more coffee. Giorgio told us of his uncle. 'He wasn't happy in the water. He never take a bath because he say that he might slip and drown in the water, until one day my uncle is taking a bath. He has one of the big terracotta pots for the lemon trees, he fill up the hole in the bottom and put water inside and then he get inside the pot and take a bath but all the time in one hand he holds a hammer. He say that if he feel he is slip he smash the terracotta pot with the hammer before he drown.'

Then Giorgio told us about the diving ship *Artiglio* when it was trying to get the gold from the *Egypt*: how they all paraded twice a day and sang the Fascist anthem 'Giovanezza' – but somehow Giorgio glossed quickly over the war years, and there was even more coffee and Giorgio was on his second bottle of local brandy, and he and Singleton were discussing the techniques of diving, when there was a knock at the door.

Charly said, 'I'll go,' but I was nearest.

I guessed it might be the boy with a packet. It was. He had a small twist of newspaper in his hand. It contained a piece of Fernie's hair. I thanked him then sent him off again for a packet of cigarettes. Charly called, 'Who is it?'

'A kid,' I said. 'I asked him to bring me some fags around earlier today. He's finally got round to it and he brings me filter tips.'

'Have a cigar,' said Giorgio.

'No, I'm O.K. for cigarettes really, it's just that he pestered me for something to do.'

'I saw you chatting away like lost brothers,' said Charly, 'to the kid that hangs around that awful Fernie creature.'

'Hangs around Fernie,' I repeated, fighting back the hysteria. Out of all the kids in this town I choose that one for my mission.

Giorgio started talking about diving again and they both agreed that the air line made a difficult job almost impossible.

'An umbilical cord,' said Giorgio.

'My uncle used to say the goddess Atropos had her shears constantly poised against the air line.'

'Atropos – who was she?' said Charly.

Singleton said, 'One of the three Fates in Greek mythology. She carries a pair of shears and cuts the thread of life to decide man's destiny.' Giorgio said, 'Yes, each sharp edge of metal in a wreck represented the shears of Atropos, just as the flimsy pipe down which a diver's air comes is the thread of life.'

By the time we went to bed the wind was blowing a gale outside, and below on the beach, air, water, and sand thrashed together. Sometimes one could distinguish each separate wave; the roar, crash, confusion, and withdrawal. Often, however, the sound became just one long howl; rocking the window panes, vibrating against the metal bucket, flapping the deck-chair canvas, pounding into the head, filling the ears and spinning the mind into a whirl.

My room opened on to the balcony. Two or three miles out on the black ocean the lights of the cuttlefish boats were winking in the movement of the horizon. I imagined the misery of the open Atlantic at night, working for one per cent of the catch. I watched the black clouds move across the moon for a long time before going to bed. I tried to sleep, but the noise of the wind and the effect of the coffee kept me awake. At 3.30 a.m. I heard the kitchen door open. Someone else couldn't sleep; perhaps a cup of tea would be a good idea. The footsteps went across the kitchen tiles. I heard the far door open and the footsteps outside on the balcony. As I was climbing into some clothes I heard the rusty gate – half-way down the steps – creak open.

Looking over the balcony there was enough moonlight for me to see someone moving down the final flight. The figure turned and began to walk along the strand towards the west. I went down the staircase as quickly as I could. The wind cut me with an icy shiv and needle-points of spray penetrated my trousers and sweater. The metal of my pistol was cold against my hip. Twenty yards ahead of me the nocturnal stroller made no attempt to conceal himself. It was Giorgio. He walked well clear of the rocks that littered the foot of the cliff. He came to the base of the wide Guardi-like staircase which twisted like a lost ribbon between the beach and the high promenade.

To begin my ascent before he had completed his would be foolish. He had only to glance down to be certain of spotting me.

I gave him plenty of time to get to the top; then, keeping well to the inside of the staircase, began to walk up. I watched carefully for loose stones, although the roar of the sea would have swallowed the noise of anything less than an avalanche. I paused as I neared the top, took the Smith & Wesson out of my belt, breathed in and out very slowly and moved on to the promenade. If he was waiting for me, a lungful of air could make all the difference.

No one was waiting for me. To the right the narrow cobbled road was empty for half a mile or so. From the left came only the faint sound of a two-stroke motor cycle and the pandemonium of the sea. A little finger of grey cloud rubbed the tired eye of the moon. It seemed as though Giorgio had got a pillion ride. Who did we know with a two-stroke motor bike? I was losing friends faster than I could replace them.

25 Ready to jump?

The big droplets of rain dabbed at the grey slate windows. The bad weather had moved south from Lisbon as the radio forecast had predicted. The wind and rain gave no sign of relenting before tea-time, and we all sat around the house and moped. Albufeira was a town designed for the sun to shine upon. When rain came it looked confused and betrayed. In the market place rain dripped from the trees on to wet shiny vegetables and fruit, and in the café the proprietor whiled away the time playing draughts with his son and drinking his own coffee.

At Number 12 we had a late breakfast. Attention was now equally divided between devouring vast amounts of coffee and pancakes and watching Giorgio refolding his rubber suit in talc for the sixth time. He finally got it away into the polythene bag and dusted the surplus talcum from his cashmere sweater. Every day, whether he dived or not, Giorgio inspected his rubber suit, carefully pulling at the seams under each arm and leg where it had the most wear. Charly told me that he always did it with the same amount of care and professional attention, and each day his hands shook a little more than the day before.

Giorgio wasn't keen on the idea of my going down, as I had decided to do when the weather eased off. 'It will be too dark to see,' he said. Singleton disagreed. He said that since they were using large underwater torches powered by batteries in the boat, 'there's no reason why it shouldn't be better to dive at night than by day. We could go across the beach ready dressed. No one would notice what we were wearing even if anyone saw us.'

I watched him look towards Giorgio to see if he would veto it from a technical point of view. I forestalled that. 'I'm not putting it in the form of a resolution,' I said. 'If the weather eases at slack water – we dive.'

'Great,' said Charly; it was as sincere as a singing commercial, but it indicated that Charly, at least, would jump if I said 'jump'.

I continued: 'The first dive will be me and Giorgio. Then a dive by Singleton, then Giorgio and me again.'

Singleton said, 'Do you think it's wise? It's quite tricky to …' I fixed him with a malevolent eye. 'Yes sir,' he said. 'I've been very quiet lately, sonny,' I said to Singleton, 'but I've just been ruminating. Not mellowing.'

26 *The point of a pen*

Take the Atlantic ocean on a cold November night and keep a brisk and chilly wind striking across it from the north. Put a fourteen-foot dinghy somewhere between the heaving waves with the swell on its port quarter, and into it put a damaged echo-sounder, underwater lighting equipment, spare open-circuit bottles and five Thermos flasks of hot wine. Upon it, too, put a Portuguese fisherman with hands sore from trying to hold a heaving boat snagged against a submerged wreck. And standing clad in black rubber suits, complete with their own private arrangement for breathing, put three men: Singleton – a career naval officer anxious to demonstrate the bungling inadequacy of a civilian intelligence organization; a professional salvage free-diver anxious to collect a bribe for betraying his employer without betraying him; and a third man, who, thinking about scribbles on a U-boat chart, just can't forget that ballpoint pens were not on sale until after the war.

119

27 Gain this or lose it

The swell was enough to tip us down in the valleys between the waves at an alarming angle.

To the north I watched the coastline come into view from each wave crest. The scene was blue in the moonlight, and across the sea, like static, ran streaks of phosphorescence. The echo-sounder gave a shiver of noise and its needle began a steady metronome scratch across the roll of paper. From the bows came a momentary red glow as Giorgio tested each underwater lamp, pressing his hand over the thick glass as he did so.

I was already feeling the constriction of the tight rubber suit and began to wonder whether Singleton should wear his for another hour before diving. Giorgio gave me some last-minute words of advice. ' … Dolphin,' he said, 'knees together, that's the secret.' (The 'Dolphin' is a swimming movement like that of the crawl, except that legs move together instead of alternately.) I said I would remember. He patted my arm. After the waterproof lamps had been lowered overboard on their cables, Giorgio clambered over the side and I followed. The coldness of the water bit to the bone as I lowered myself in. I snapped the evil-tasting rubber mouthpiece between my teeth and pulled the rectangular face-piece down. A rivulet of salt water flowed from my thumb into the corner of my mouth. I wasn't to be rid of that salty taste for a long, long time. I pushed the flat of my hands against the soft, splintery side of the dinghy. A wave descended upon my shoulder-blades, and I found the boat resting upon my hands high above me like the world of Atlas.

I jack-knifed through the opaque water. Beneath the heaving surface the sea was green and without dimension. A white explosion of microscopic bubbles raced to my feet as I swam down towards the lamps, glowing redder and redder as I neared them. All was calm and soft. The water moved not at all. No longer green, the moonlit upper layer had given way to purple. To my right Giorgio was cleaving a phosphorescent wake. He adjusted the speed of his swimming to cater for my clumsy movement behind him. I watched him turn a somersault and touch his feet to the bottom with scarcely a movement of mud. I tried to do the same, but a tumble-weed of dirty water rose around my flippers. Giorgio handed me one of the big waterproof lamps, and as my eyes became adjusted to the purple darkness one vast portion of the sea bed grew darker than the rest. Fifty feet high, the huge pot belly of the sunken submarine loomed over us. Giorgio gave a hook-like motion with his free hand and climbed an invisible ladder on to the fore-deck. I followed him past the smooth convex swell of the main tanks. Here and there sections of the original paintwork were still in good condition. In spite of the slight list it was easy to imagine that this was a fully-manned submarine resting momentarily on the bottom before resuming a war patrol. We passed a big painted number on the conning-tower, and in the red glow of his lamp I saw Giorgio's silhouette as he pulled the hatch open. The big fuzzy glow of Giorgio's lamp suddenly became a sharp disc as he went inside.

I followed him. The soft paintwork shed its skin under my hand, the flakes spinning upward like perverse seeds. I dropped lightly on to the conning-tower platform, striking an ankle on the hatch cover.

Holding the side of the conning-tower ladder with one hand I controlled my drop into the small oval room beneath. I shone the big lamp around the interior. Red circles flashed from the walls as the glass-faced gauges reflected the light back. My lamp shone upon the hatch above my head. Floating between the piping and the periscope gland was a soft bundle in boiler suit and Draeger Gear.[*] I streamed out the lamp cable and moved carefully past the thin corpse of the coxswain, who gently tapped his head against the huge wheel of the hydroplane controls in deference to my movement through the water. Next to him the helmsman would spend eternity watching the dead face of the gyro compass repeater and waiting for an order that would never now come.

I kept to the port side of the cluttered interior. This was the side Giorgio had cleared and searched. The starboard side was choked with bundles of bedding, bunks, and clothing, among which bodies were barely distinguishable.

Above me broken piping hung like strange stalactites, while chairs and wooden stools danced against the ceiling. I imagined the final scene in this little space, crowded like a rush-hour tube train, all those years ago. I half walked, half swam past broken crates of food and smashed bottles. My light moved across dented metal. Thermos flasks and two photos of a woman still firmly stuck in the air-conditioning trunking, but almost faded away. My breathing became difficult. One bottle was empty. I turned the tap to let the full bottle 'equalize'. Breathing recommenced.

I could see the glow of Giorgio's lamp through the next bulkhead door. I moved on, noticing the pressure hull – well

[*] German version of Davis Escape Gear.

over an inch thick – it could withstand water pressures at over five hundred feet. I tapped it and the metal vibrated with a clang. The far side of the bulkhead was the torpedo stowage compartment. It was like looking at a baronial hall from the minstrels' gallery. The floor lay some ten feet below me down a ladder. On either side was rack after rack of inert torpedoes, greasy and silver like canned sardines. The mud had been washed gently through the torpedo stowage compartment by year after year of tides. Some of the lowest torpedoes and several bodies had almost disappeared into the silt. I began to check each warhead. Giorgio stood behind me holding both lamps. We both knew that it was not a job without its dangers. At the end of the war the Germans were experimenting with many different types of firing mechanisms or 'triggers'. There were acoustics, magnetics, electric eye, reflecting echo. It was not at all uncommon for a boat to have a mixed bag of weapons and we both knew that this was one of the most highly developed U-boats of the whole Nazi era.

'Fourteen,' I said to myself, chewing on the soft rubber mouthpiece. 'That's the lot.' I ran a forefinger across my throat and pointed upwards. Giorgio nodded. Fourteen torpedoes checked. None of the warheads could contain packages: they weren't hollow or full of currency; they were solid and deadly. I was disappointed; another theory had had a short life.

Giorgio gave me his electric lamp when we were back at the buckled bulkhead. He went up through the gun access trunking to the fore-deck. Giorgio's last task was to go round the hull exterior to check the bow tubes. I had to go out the way we came in because of the lamp leads. I looked at my underwater watch.

Through the conning-tower hatch and over the 37-mm. gun platforms: the ocean seemed vast after the U-boat interior. I swam gently down to the sea floor holding both lamps under one arm. I looked up at the huge hulk. Still Giorgio hadn't joined me. I floated easily through the dark water, using only my feet to propel me; I held the lamps to shine ahead. Dolphin: knees together. To be alone on the bed of the ocean at night was an unforgettable experience. The hull loomed over me, and I began to imagine that it was moving with the tide. My breathing starved again. I turned the tap to 'equalize', but now only half a bottle would pour into the empty bottle. Time was growing short. Where was Giorgio?

The electric light shone upon the grey metal, and fish and small crawling things scuttled out of the moving beam. I flipped a foot and glided forward past the three starboard bow caps. Around the bulbous snout the three tubes on the port side were closed. I stepped on to the deck. Above my head copious growths of weed swung from the jumping wire. I rested the rubber-clad lamps down in the mud in order to check my watch and compass.

There, inches away from my feet, was a flat, rectangular slab. The mud flurried around as I picked it up. It was a large, leather-bound log book. It was what we wanted more than anything, according to London. I must locate the anchor snag. It should be near the after hydroplane. I stuffed the log book under my harness and bent down to get the lamps.

The soles of Giorgio's rubber flippers were only three or four feet away from the lamps. His face-mask and rubber mouthpiece were dangling on his chest. One arm of his rubber suit was ripped into several separate shreds and above him rose a thin grey cloud of blood.

28 The boat gets one

I equalized again for the last time, before my air began to starve, and left the tap open. I would have no further warnings of air shortage, but now I would need both hands. At that moment both the lamps went out, and a second or so later the cables came thudding around me. It meant there was no decision to make. I lifted Giorgio's face and stuck the mouthpiece back into his mouth; he was unconscious, and it fell back on to his chest. I grabbed his armpit and gave a tentative shove off the sea bed with my foot. I pulled the ring on his harness to release the lead ballast and did the same with my own. Our heads broke through the ocean top. Wind ripped into my face like a blunt razor-blade. The splash of the waves broke the silence, and the cold biting into my head and shoulders made me suddenly aware of how frozen my body was in spite of the heavy woollen undersuit. I felt for the book and pushed it tighter under the straps. There was no sign of the boat. Whatever had caused them to jettison the lamps was serious and dangerous; but I had the log book.

Runnels of dirty white spume slipped down the waves, their black bulk leaned over us before butting us high on to their peaks. I turned Giorgio on his back and struck out towards the almost invisible shore-line. The sky was clear and star-filled. The Plough gave me more reliable bearings than did a glimpse of the coast from the crest of an occasional high wave. 'Atropos,' Giorgio suddenly shouted, and struck me a hard blow on the side of the neck with the edge of his palm. A wave, stronger than previous ones, shattered itself upon us and Giorgio wrenched himself free. He swam strongly southward for five or six strokes; then suddenly weakened and, as I grabbed for him, sank without any attempt to save himself. I got him about six feet under, and as we came up together it was hard to say who was nearer drowning. We spluttered and spat and finally I had him in tow again. Twice more he beat me about the head and shouted 'Atropos, Atropos,' and a gabble of Italian that I couldn't even begin to translate. His attacks on me had done wonders for his breathing. Had he not been taking in such a lot of sea water through his open mouth his breathing would probably have become normal, but the loss of blood was making him weaker with every yard we travelled.

The tips of the waves were trepanned by the sharp wind and suffused about our heads with a constant hiss. We had been in the Atlantic for perhaps one and a half hours. Every part of me ached. For the first time I began to doubt if we could reach the shore-line. I stopped swimming, and, holding Giorgio tightly, tried to see the boat. The waves flung us up and down like a trampoline. I shouted to Giorgio. He turned his brown face towards me. His eyes were wide open and his mouth moved. 'Atropos,' he said weakly, 'why is she putting the stars out?'

29 Entreaty

Giorgio's head floated on my chest. 'Hail Mary,' he said faintly, 'Hail Mary full of ...' – the sea smashed across his head like a beer bottle – ' ... grace the Lord is with ...' – he spluttered, coughed, and swallowed salt water – ' ... with thee. Blessed art thou among women ...' – Giorgio was lower in the water – ' ... and blessed is the fruit of thy womb ...' – so that I could hardly keep his head above the surface – ' ... Jesus. Holy Mary, Mother of God, pray for us ...' The beach was ahead – ' ... sinners now and at ...' – the waves became breakers – ' ... the hour of our death.'

We were both spun under the surface. I felt the beach under my foot. Lost it. Touched again. A wave knocked us full length into the surf. I climbed to my feet, caught Giorgio under the armpits and dragged him inch by inch up the beach until he was clear of the sea. I was so heavy. Giorgio was so heavy. I wanted to sleep. I knew I must pump air into those water-logged lungs.

I rolled him over on to his face. His dentures fell into the spume.

30 Grave trouble

They were all at the house. They were sitting in the dining-room, heads between knees, gazing at the floor, and concentrating all their attention upon breathing long, aching lungsful of air. No one looked up as I entered. Charly had made coffee and put blankets around them, but had the good sense to say nothing.

'Giorgio's on the beach,' I said, breathing between each syllable.

The old fisherman got slowly to his feet. 'I'll give you a hand,' he said in Portuguese.

'Have coffee first,' I said. 'Giorgio's in no hurry, he died as we got ashore.'

'Who tipped up the boat?' Singleton said, after a few minutes.

'Tell me,' I said.

'Well, either you or Giorgio tipped us over.'

I was finding it difficult not to get angry.

He added, 'It was someone in frogman dress.'

I said, 'Neither Giorgio nor I came to the surface before you capsized.' No one spoke. I eased the leather book from under my harness. A rivulet of water hit the floor. 'Besuchsliste', it said. I'd found the U-boat's visitors' book. It was not the log book. I threw it across the room with a clatter.

It took me ten minutes to dry off and change. I mixed black coffee and brandy in equal parts and poured it into my throat. I told Singleton and the old man to fetch Giorgio's body from the beach, strip it of its gear and put it on the balcony. Then I climbed into the car.

I jangled the bell at da Cunha's heavily and continuously until da Cunha himself came to answer it. He was fully dressed.

'I'll come in,' I said, and entered. Da Cunha made no protest. I said, 'One of my friends is dead.'

'Really,' said da Cunha calmly, but the oil lamp he was holding gave a little jump.

'Died under water,' I said.

'Drowned,' said da Cunha.

'I don't think so,' I said, 'but I would settle for that on the death certificate if it means a quiet funeral.' Da Cunha nodded but made no move.

'You are asking me to help you in some way?'

'I'm telling you to help, in *my* way.'

He said, 'That attitude won't get you very far.' He sounded just like Dawlish.

I said, 'I've got a piece of paper in my pocket. Inside it is a lock of Senhor Fernandes Tomas's hair.'

Da Cunha hadn't flinched.

'When London put it under a microscope, they will find that Fernie's black hair is ginger hair that has been dyed. Because ginger hair and blue eyes is about as English as you can get and far too conspicuous on a Portuguese. My subsequent orders might well concern you. Meanwhile a murdered corpse can cause you as much trouble as it can cause me, and I don't think Mr Smith can help you.'

'You are right,' he said. 'I shall arrange for a death

certificate immediately. Do you wish to bring it … him … er … here?'

'Why not?' I said. 'You have an unused empty grave.' Da Cunha moved his mouth around and finally said, 'Very well.'

31 From a friend

I came into London with my flaps well down. Giorgio had been murdered under the water. Joe had been blown to shreds. I had been only a few yards away at each event. Not that I thought that either had been unsuccessful attempts to finger me, but diligence brings more agents to pensionable age than bravery ever did. I decided to make a few inquiries on my own private grapevine, even if it did mean ignoring all the department's rules of procedure.

The icy wind carved up the Cromwell Road faster than the stockbrokers' Jags, and a cosmonaut on a 600-c.c. motor cycle came roaring past seeking cooperation in an act of suicide. I checked into one of those hotels near the West London air terminal. It was all chintz and dusty flowers. I wrote the name of Howard Craske into the register. The desk man asked for my passport.

'Did I cross the frontier?' I asked.

He took me up to a room on the third floor back. It had an antique gas-meter that looked hungry. I fed it some one-franc pieces. It liked them. The gas fire gave a sibilant hiss. I put on dry socks, raised my body temperature enough to get me back amongst the living, then went round the corner to the phone box. I had already decided to let a few hours pass before contacting Dawlish. I dialled a Bayswater number. The phone made the noises associated with making a phone call in England. It buzzed, clicked and purred; it had more tones than a chromatic scale. After two or three tries it even rang at the other end.

'Can I speak to Mr Davenport?' I said. He was my first ear to the ground.

'This phone is hot,' said the voice at the other end, 'and you are even hotter. Leave town.' He hung up. He wasn't a laconic man, but a tapped phone* affects some people that way. I rang another man who had an ear to the ground. This time I was a little more circumspect. I waited for Austin Butterworth to speak first. He spoke, then I said, 'Hello, Austin.'

'I recognize the voice of my old mate …' said Austin.

'You do,' I said before he could blab it across the phone.

'Are you in trouble?' he asked.

'I don't know, Austin; am I?' I heard him laugh like an engaged tone.

'Don't let's talk over this,' he said. He knew a thing or two about telephones.

'What about Leds in half an hour?'

'O.K.,' I said.

Leds is a dark-brown café near Old Compton Street. To enter it, you fight your way through Continental newspapers and movie magazines. Inside it's like an Aldermaston March mixing with the Chelsea Arts Ball. I heard someone saying ' … and thank you for a really lovely party.' It was mid-afternoon.

'Small black,' I said. Austin's skull shone through his thinning hair over a copy of *Corriere della Sera*.

'Hello, Ossie,' I said. He didn't look up. The girl behind the counter gave me the coffee and I bought some cigarettes and matches. She gave me my change; only then did Ossie murmur, 'Bring a tail?'

* See Appendix 1.

'Of course not,' I said. I had forgotten Ossie's mania. His years in prison had left him with a skilful technique in rolling cigarettes thinner than matchsticks, a mania about being followed and a lifelong aversion to porridge.

'Come right to the back so I can see who comes in.' We moved towards the rear and sat down at one of the glass-topped tables.

'Did you go round the block a couple of times to make sure?'

'Relax, Ossie.'

'You have to have rules,' said Ossie, 'only the mugs don't have rules and they get caught.'

'Rules,' I said, 'I didn't know that you were an advocate of rules.'

'Yes,' said Ossie, 'rules, you have got to know what to do in any situation, so that you can do it before you even think about it.'

'Sounds like something the chief screw at the Scrubs told you. What sort of rules, Ossie?'

'Depends. Like always jump off the high side of a sinking ship. That's a good rule, if you need it.'

I said, 'But I'm not expecting to be on a sinking ship in the near future.'

'Oh no?' said Ossie. He leaned forward. 'Well, I wouldn't be too sure about that, my old mate.' He gave me a Gilbert and Sullivan conspiratorial wink.

'What are you hearing then, Ossie?' I always found it difficult to believe that Ossie was a man who could keep a secret. He was such a transparent old rogue. But he had as many secrets as any man in London.* Ossie was the archetype professional burglar.

---

* See Appendix 2.

I ordered another small black for Ossie and myself.

'What am I hearing?' said Ossie, repeating my question. 'Well, I keep hearing about you all over.'

'Where, for instance?'

'Well, I am not free to reveal the source of my information as they say at the Yard, but I am able to state without no fear of contradiction that you are a hot potato as far as a certain gent is concerned.'

He paused, and I didn't press him as he is a man who hates to be hurried. I waited. He said, 'Little birdies 'ave it that you are hard on the track of a big bundle of a certain sort of merchandise as you and me once took a free sample of out of a high quality Chubb in Zürich.'

It's important to know when to be cagey and when to admit the truth. I nodded. Ossie was pleased to be right. He went on, 'If you was a gent making banging machinery for the government, machinery of all shapes and sizes, from the little ones that start the hundred yards free-style at Wembley to the big sort that features on the artwork of Civil Defence recruiting literature …' He looked at me quizzically.

'Yes,' I said doubtfully.

'And if you signed yourself a nice banging-machine contract that was big enough to give Birmingham City Council a smog problem for the next two years, and then suddenly you found that these Portuguese gents who had signed the perforated side of the contract were planning to pay you in Monopoly money: you'd be right cut up, wouldn't you?'

'If the Monopoly money came out of an old boat, you mean?'

'Yes, mate,' said Ossie. 'The bloke getting it out of the boat for the Portuguese blighters would suddenly become a spare benedick at a wedding. If you get my meaning.'

I got his meaning.

Ossie said, 'I wouldn't like to be quoted as to who finds you superfluous to requirements, but I wouldn't like to look his name up in a big telephone directory if I didn't know the initial.'

Ossie had confirmed what I suspected. At this stage I still had nothing with which to confront Mr Smith, but I knew where to find his stooge.

I left Ossie and walked along Compton and Brewer through Sackville Street to Piccadilly, and dropped in for a drink in the Ritz bar. Ivor Butcher was there. He's always there.

'Hi there, feller,' he said.

We dealt with him when we had to, but always one had the feeling that he was likely to pinch something off your desk if you took your eyes off him for a minute. He came across to me before the waiter could even take my order.

'Come downstairs, feller,' he said, 'it's quieter down there.' He had an accent like an announcer on Radio Luxembourg. Professional instinct prevailed over personal feeling. I accompanied him to the bar downstairs, where he insisted on giving me one of those sweet gin concoctions instead of sherry. He was wearing a Shepperton B-picture raincoat with the collar turned up at the back and kept one hand in his pocket as though any moment he might say 'reach for de sky youse guys'. He usually produced in me a feeling of merriment, but I was far from merry today.

'Nice vacation in Portugal?' He was always fishing around for stub ends of information that he could peddle. He squeezed a sector of lemon into his drink, gnawed at the yellow pulp and sucked the rind.

I said, 'What are you looking so happy about – did you just inherit Central Registry?'

'Say, that's rich,' he said, giving a brief laugh. He popped a cherry into his bright mouth. He had the pretty face of a rock singer; long shiny hair swept backwards over his head and struck his collar, while an artful wave fell forward across his forehead. 'You are looking great,' he said. Ivor Butcher was a congenital liar – he told lies outside working hours.

Forms of address among men who work together vary. There's the 'sir' or rank prefix by ones who don't wish to pursue their relationship, the nickname used to conceal affection or at least respect, the Christian names of friends and the surname form of address among men who think they are still at college. Only men like Ivor Butcher are called by their full name.

'What are you doing this afternoon? Wanna take a little ride down into Berkshire with me? I just bought myself a little country place, make a foursome, heh? Couple o' cute girls. Back in time for the late show at Murray's Club.'

'You are living it up,' I said, 'you've come quite a distance since 1956.'[*]

'Yeah,' he said, 'got me an E-type Jag: Cambridge blue – wire wheels – it's a gas.'

At the next table sat advertising executives with not enough chin and too much cuff. They were buying drinks with a generosity that an expense account brings. They prodded and discussed their product in low respectful tones. Sliced, sterilized and Cellophane-wrapped; a loaf. They talked about it like it was a cure for cancer.

[*] In 1956 Ivor Butcher had been a Home Office telephone tapper. He overheard some information which he promptly sold to three different embassies. He was fired from his job, but the laugh had been on the Home Office. In a way it was this incident that revived the Strutton Plan in my mind. Now Ivor Butcher lived by hanging around and offering hospitality to foolish people with access to secret, or semi-secret, information.

I sipped the cocktail and offered Ivor Butcher the geranium-coloured cherry from it. 'Mighty nice of you,' he said. He munched the cherry and spoke simultaneously. 'Could sell you a morsel of military dope you'd like I reckon.'

'The phone number of the War Museum?'

'Can it, Mac,' he said, 'this is real Zen stuff.'

'Zo,' I said.

He gave a one-decibel laugh and looked around furtively. 'Cost you a grand.'

'Just give me the sales talk,' I said, 'we'll get to the estimates later.'

'I get a call from a certain party in Maidenhead. This guy's a real high-class B & E man.* I've got all the B & E boys on my payroll. Anythin' they see unusual I get it pronto. Dig?'

'Dig.'

'This villain is doing a nice Cabinet Minister's home, also in Maidenhead, when he flips through the desk and finds a nice leather desk diary. Knowing I'm a collector he passes it across to me for half a grand. What I'm peddling to you is one page ...'

I signalled to the waiter over Ivor Butcher's shoulder and it amused me to see him spin round like the Special Branch boys were just about to lift him out of his coat.

I said, 'A Tio Pepe and another of whatever this gentleman is drinking, with two pieces of lemon and at least three cherries.'

Ivor Butcher smiled in relief and embarrassment.

He said, 'Gee, for a minute ...'

'Yes, quite.'

At the next table one of the ad-men said, ' ... but great copy slicewise.'

---

* Breaking and Entering, i.e. burglar.

137

'What do you think, then?' Ivor Butcher ran his tongue round his mouth to dislodge the particles of lemon and cherry.

'I didn't realize you did a bit of "black" on the side,' I said.

'We've got to live, haven't we, pal?' He would bleed an old-age pensioner or a set of hydraulic brakes with the same smiling self-righteousness.

'Want a second opinion?' I said.

'I haven't told you what's on the page yet.'

'You are going to tell and trust, are you?' It didn't seem like him.

'Naw. Just the first and last word.'

'O.K. One-two-three-go.'

'Word the first is "Venev"; word the last "W.O.O.C.(P)". Haw, thought that would make you stand up and sing "Rule Britannia", pal.' He sucked his teeth.

'I don't get the "Venev".'

'V.N.V.'

'What's that?'

'Don't kid me, pal; Portuguese underground.'

'We haven't even got a file on it.' I pretended to think deeply. 'There's a man called Jerry Hoskyn in the U.S. State Department. More their kind of thing, I'd say.'

'It's got your department right on the same page.'

'Don't shout at me,' I said irritably, 'I didn't write it.'

'Well,' said Ivor Butcher somewhat subdued. 'I was just trying to wise you up.'

'And very nice of you, but no sale.'

The drinks came. In Ivor Butcher's sugar-frosted glass were four bright-dyed cherries. Two wafers of lemon clung to the edge. He was radiant.

'I didn't think they'd bring them,' he said in a breathless voice, and to tell you the truth, nor did I.

I said, 'How big is it?' He raised his eyes to me and only

with difficulty remembered what we had been talking about. 'How big?' I said again.

'The diary? – this big.' He measured about four inches by five with his fingers.

'How thick?'

'Half an inch.'

'Doesn't sound like a grand's worth to anyone I know.'

'Garn, I'm only selling one page for a grand.'

'You are nuts,' I said.

'What you give me then?'

'Not a thing. I told you we have no file and I haven't the authority to open one.'

Ivor Butcher speared the cherries with a cocktail stick after chasing them around the bright yellow drink.

'Bring it to my place about seven. I'll have Dixon, the F.O.'s Portugal expert, with me. But I tell you now, I don't think there's a chance that they'll want it. Even if they do it will be with normal vouchered funds, so don't pay any super-tax in advance.'

The ad-man at the next table said, 'But bread *isn't* a luxury!'

Mr Henry Smith, the world-famous Cabinet Minister, lived in Maidenhead. Either Mr Ivor Butcher was double-crossing his boss or I was being set up.

When I got back to the hotel, the plastic flowers were heavy with the day's soot and the desk man was working his dentures over with an orange stick. I remembered the name I had given him. 'Craske,' I said. He reached back without looking, unhooked my room key and cracked it down on the desk-top without a pause in his dental hygiene curriculum.

'Visitor waiting for you,' he said with a heavy Central-European accent. He stabbed the frayed orange stick upward. 'In your room.'

I leaned forward till my face was closer to his. His razor had missed a section of face. 'Do you always let strangers into your guests' rooms?' I asked.

He removed the orange stick from his face – without haste. 'Ya, when I think they aren't likely to complain to the Hotel Proprietors' Association I do.'

I picked up my key and began to ascend the stairs. 'Ya,' I heard him say again.

I went up to the third. The light was on in my room. I switched off the hall light, put my ear to the door and heard nothing. I put the key in the door and turned it quickly. I flung the door open wide and moved through it stooped.

A man can go through his whole life making sure there is no light behind him when he enters a darkened room, unscrewing the base plate of a strange phone before using it, and checking the wiring before conducting a confidential conversation. All his life he can do these things and then on one occasion it is all worth while. However, this was not to be that occasion for me.

Spread-eagled full length on the rose-patterned Terylene bedspread was the seventeen-stone weight of 'Tinkle Bell'. A large and not clean grey felt hat was parked over his face.

32 For this game

'It's only me.' The words came muffled by the crown of the hat and the sentence ended in a chesty cough. All Tinkle Bell's sentences ended in a cough. A hand removed the hat from his face and an atomic cloud of smoke rose to the ceiling.

I straightened up, feeling a little foolish.

'What did you do to the doorman?' I asked.

'I showed him an old warrant card I hung on to from the war years.' Tinkle Bell stood up and produced a half-bottle of Teachers from his coat pocket. He poured a drink, using the two plastic glasses from the sink.

'Mud in your eye,' said Tinkle.

'Thanks,' I said.

By ingenious articulation of the finger joints he was able to smoke and drink virtually simultaneously. He coughed, smoked and drank for a few minutes.

'Surprised I found you?' he coughed. 'Astute, eh?' Some more coughing. 'Not really, y'know. Albufeira phoned this morning with a message. It wasn't difficult to sort through the plane passenger lists. You've used Craske once before, about a year ago.' He coughed again. 'Perhaps you're getting a bit old for this game.'

'We all are, Tinkle,' I said, 'we all are.' Tinkle nodded and continued to cough and drink.

'The old man would like to see you tomorrow morning, "10 a.m. if possible", he said.'

'Yes, he's always polite, you must give him that,' I said.

'He's all right, Dawlish,' said Tinkle, and poured us both another. 'Oh yes, and I'm to tell you that Jean is awaiting instructions. Perhaps you would phone her as soon as you can.'

He picked up his hat and downed his drink in one smooth motion.

'Anything I can do for you?' he said. 'I'm going back to the office.'

'Yes,' I said, 'mail interception.' I gave him Ivor Butcher's name and address.

'And phone?' asked Tinkle.

'Yes,' I said, and smiled at the thought, 'let's tap his phone.'

'Right, see you later,' he said, and I heard him coughing his way down the creaky stairs and out into the street as I began packing my bag again. Before I saw Dawlish at 10 a.m. I hoped to have something up my sleeve.

33 Jean when I find her

I got back to my flat about five thirty. I fixed coffee and started a large coal fire. Outside, lines of mud-spattered cars moved southward out of the city through a gauze of diesel fumes. The weather forecaster was worried about snow and I'll bet the six o'clock news didn't relax him any.

I erected a card table in the bedroom, dusted off the Nikon F and clipped it into the holder after loading it with fine resolution film. Over the baseboard four photoflood holders were directed downwards. I flipped the switch and a glare of tungsten light splashed around the walls. I left the bedroom and locked the door behind me.

I was drinking a second cup of Blue Mountain as Jean arrived. Her mouth was cold. We touched noses and exchanged hellos and 'isn't-it-turning-colds' and 'snow-before-Christmas-I-wouldn't-be-surpriseds', then I put her into the Ivor Butcher picture. Jean said, 'Buy it', but I didn't want to do that. If I showed any interest it would reveal more than I wanted to reveal, especially to Ivor Butcher. Jean said I was a paranoiac, but she hadn't been in the business long enough to develop that sixth sense that I was always telling myself I had.

Ivor Butcher sat in his blue Jag across the road for some time before coming to the front door. It was very professionally done. I took his coat and poured him a drink. We hung around waiting for my fictional man from the F.O. for twenty minutes. Ivor Butcher had the diary in a sealed manilla envelope. When the tension had built up a little I asked him if I could look at it. He passed the envelope across my desk and I tore the top off quickly and extracted a leather diary with gold-edged pages. The surface was scuffed and it didn't look any too new. Ivor Butcher was about to open his mouth to protest, but I kept the diary tightly shut and he kept his mouth the same way. I put it back into the envelope.

'Looks O.K.,' I said. Ivor Butcher nodded. I turned the envelope slowly around, passing it between fingers and thumbs. His eyes watched the envelope. I got up, walked across to him. I folded the torn envelope top and pushed it into the pocket of his shiny, synthetic fibre suit. He smiled sheepishly. 'I'll phone the F.O. man's office,' I said, and went to the extension phone in the bedroom.

It had been simple to drop the diary out of the torn end of the envelope into my lap and not too difficult to substitute an object of approximately the correct shape and size. Luckily Ivor Butcher's description of the dimensions had been fairly accurate, but I had two variations handy had it not been.

I clipped it on to the baseboard and switched on the bright lights. I pushed the shutter. *Kerlick* – the roller blind moved gently across the film. I turned the page and photoed the next one. Now everything depended upon Jean keeping Ivor Butcher occupied. She could reasonably ask him not to come within earshot of a conversation between me and the F.O., but if he got that envelope out of his pocket and found six coupons that would get him a bar of Fairy Soap fourpence cheaper, my photography was liable to be interrupted.

* * *

By 12.45 the last print was off the dryer and Ivor Butcher had long since departed, with his diary back once more in his pocket. I went into the lounge; Jean had slipped her shoes off and was dozing in front of the dying coal fire. I leaned over the back of the big leather chair and kissed her funny upside-down face. She awoke with a start.

'You were snoring,' I said.

'I don't snore.' She looked at me in the mirror.

'And you told me I was the only man in London in a position to know.' Jean ran her long fingers through her hair, dragging it high above her head.

'Do you think I should wear my hair up like this?'

'Don't wear any at all,' I said.

We were looking at each other in the mirror. She said, 'You are getting terribly fat. What are you going to do about it?'

'Not a thing,' I said, 'let's …'

At that moment the phone rang. Jean laughed, and although I let it ring for some time I finally went to get it.

'It's probably your Mr Butcher who has decided to come down to nine hundred,' said Jean. 'Poor Mr Butcher.'

'Thieves must learn to cry,' I said.

I answered the phone. It was Alice, who wasted not a word. 'Mr Dawlish says get along here right away, something urgent has turned up.'

'O.K., Alice,' I said.

34 Awakening

Sleet was falling as we arrived at Charlotte Street. A man in a shiny car threw a handful of sparks on to the wet road as he sped by us. We went up to Dawlish's office on the top floor. Things were hectic: Dawlish had taken his jacket off.

'Take that tea tray off the chair and sit down,' he said, and Alice poked her head round the door because she couldn't remember how many sugars I took.

'Terrible night,' said Dawlish. 'Sorry to drag you into this fracas. I've missed my Tuesday bridge game for the first time in nearly two years.'

'We must all make sacrifices,' I said.

'Yes, when our masters bid us jump,' said Dawlish.

'I understand,' I said. 'It wasn't my evening for playing anything, I'm afraid.' Jean shot me a glance.

'Strutton Plan, so it's all your doing,' said Dawlish in mock admonition. 'We now have permission to set up an Advisory Board' – he looked at the papers on his desk and read off the words – 'Strutton Plan Advisory Board'. He looked up and beamed. Behind the beam was a worried face.

'Subtle titling,' I said.

'Yes,' said Dawlish doubtfully, and then he · was away into the administration: this is what he was so good at – the tactics of bureaucracy – and don't ever imagine it's not important. 'The Board will appoint four specialized committees: Communications, Finance, Training, and a Control Structure Committee. Now we won't be able to control all of those, so what we do is this. Let the Ministry people grab anything they want, in fact we'll nominate a few of them, lavish compliments on their suitability. Incidentally,' Dawlish blew his nose loudly on a big handkerchief, 'don't overdo the compliments; they're beginning to suspect you of sarcasm over the other side.'

'No,' I said.

'Yes,' said Dawlish. 'Now; when they are committed up to the armpits you will suggest a fifth committee: a Compatibility Committee – for co-ordination …'

'Very neat,' I said, 'just as you did on the Dundee Report – you ended up in control – I've often wondered how you did it.'

'Mum's the word, old boy,' said Dawlish. 'I'd like to do it again before they tumble to it.'

'O.K.,' I said, 'but when does all this begin?'

'Well, you will be on the Board and I don't see who they can possibly suggest as Chairman of the Finance if it isn't you.'

'I follow you all right,' I said, 'between the two of us we'll have the situation well in hand; but what I meant was, when does it begin?'

Dawlish looked at his desk diary. 'Convened for Thursday at 3.30 p.m., Storey's Gate, for the first meeting anyway.'

'No, but look, I can't hang around here till next Thursday. The Albufeira situation is far too flexible.'

'Ah yes,' said Dawlish. 'I want to speak to you about that.' Dawlish walked across to the I.B.M. machine that correlated all his data. He fidgeted around with the controls. 'I want you to complete the report as soon as possible.' He kept his back towards me. I knew that this was what he really wanted to talk about, that the Strutton Report panic was a smokescreen. Dawlish came back to the desk and flipped a switch on his desk intercom. Alice answered; he said, 'Code name for the Albufeira operation?' Alice's voice squeezed through the tiny loudspeaker, 'Alforreca,' she said.

'Very erudite,' I said to Dawlish. It was the Portuguese name for the sea animal we call the 'Portuguese Man of War'. Dawlish smiled and flipped the key to tell Alice what I had said, then turned back to me.

'We're winding up "Alforreca",' he said. 'I'll need your report for the Minister in the morning. Special Cabinet instruction.'

'No dice,' I said.

'I don't think I follow you,' said Dawlish.

'I'm not through yet,' I said, 'I've a lot more to do.'

Dawlish was huffed. 'Possibly, but you won't be required to continue, completeness is just a state of mind.'

'So is high-level interference a state of mind; I'll go back there in my own time, I'll take my leave there.'

'Be reasonable,' said Dawlish. 'What's wrong?'

I brought the wad of photos from my pocket. Twenty-three pages from Mr Smith's private diary. Most of it used the uncrackable cipher of busy men – bad writing. There were cryptic lunch appointments and meticulous compilations of tax-deductible expenses. The reference to V.N.V. concerned sales of undefined goods and numerical nomenclature of Swiss bank accounts.

One page, however, contained something more specific. 'Tell K' he'd written,

BOARDABLE EXPAXIAL SASHERIES SUIST
COVERTLY BARONESS ZAYAT HORNPOCK

It was signed 'XYST'.

It wouldn't have meant a thing to me either if I hadn't noticed the words 'Moreing & Neal' on another page.

I had the research boys look up the Moreing & Neal commercial code while I put the prints on the dryer. Now I told Dawlish about it.

'It means "erection of chemical works", then "goods have been shipped", then "value of £7,100" and "deliver documents". The word BARONESS means "beware of" and HORNPOCK means "don't mention". ZAYAT and XYST are spare code-words for private use. XYST is obviously Smith's signature.'

I waited while Dawlish got the full import. He was swinging his tobacco pouch like a lariat.

I went on, 'It means Smith has sent K (that must be Kondit) seven thousand pounds' worth of laboratory gear (to do ice-melting experiments, I'd guess). "The documents" refers to the sovereign die (there is no closer codeword) and ZAYAT is me. Smith says to beware of me.'

'I know just how he feels,' said Dawlish. Solemnly he removed his spectacles, dabbed at his face with a huge white handkerchief, replaced his spectacles and read the whole thing through again. 'Alice,' he finally said into the squawk-box, 'you'd better come in right away.'

As Dawlish said, it *was* all a bit circumstantial. It didn't fit very neatly together. Why *would* Smith finance a laboratory in such an out-of-the-way place when it would be far less conspicuous in London? And Dawlish thought I was bending it a bit to interpret 'documents' as 'die'.

Dawlish's department was responsible directly to the Cabinet; you could see why the old man was so reluctant to cross a member of the Cabinet, a very powerful member of the Cabinet.

Finally, four Nescafés later, Dawlish leaned well back in his chair and said, 'I'm convinced that you are quite wrong.' The old man was staring at a corner of the ceiling. 'Convinced,' he said again. Alice caught my eye. 'And therefore it is only ...' he paused, ' ... ethical, to continue the investigation to protect Smith's name.'

That's what Dawlish said to the ceiling, and while he said it I lowered an eyelid slowly at Alice; and, do you know, she moved the corners of her mouth an eighth of an inch upward.

I got to my feet. 'Don't take advantage,' Dawlish said anxiously, 'I can only delay things a little while.' He turned back to the Strutton Plan papers. 'You'll overreach yourself one day,' I heard him grumbling to the filing cabinet as I left. I suppose he was fed up with talking to the ceiling.

35 At the door

Deep down in the lower basement of the Central Register building the air is warmed and filtered. Two armed policemen in their wooden office photographed me with a Polaroid camera and filed the photo. The big grey metal cabinets hum with the vibration of the air-conditioning fans, and on the far side of the wooden swing doors is yet another security check waiting. Perhaps this is the most secret place in the world. I asked for Mr Cassel and it took a little time to find him. He greeted me, signed for me, and took me into the inner sanctum. On both sides of us the cabinets rose ten feet high, and every few paces we dodged around stepladders on wheels, or around the serious-faced W.R.A.C. officers who service the records.

The ceiling was a complex grid of piping. Some pipes had pinholes in them, some, larger punctures; the fire precautions were delicate and comprehensive. We came to a low room that looked like a typing pool. In front of each clerk was an electric typewriter, a phone with a large number painted where the dial should be, and a machine like a typewriter-carriage.

Each document received from commercial espionage or government departments is retyped by the men in this room. When it is typed (in a typeface exclusive to these machines, on heat- and water-resistant paper), the supervising clerk compares the original with the newly typed summary, puts his stamp on the corner, and the typist feeds the original into the small machine which is a paper shredder. The destruction of the original protects the information source.

I watched as one typist stopped typing, picked up his phone and spoke into it. The supervisor walked across to him and together they compared the copy with the original. The typist explained what he had put in and why he had not bothered with other items. These 'clerks' are senior intelligence officials. The supervisor embossed the corner with a device like a pair of nail clippers, and they fed the original into the shredder. I noticed the care with which this was done. Both typist and supervisor held the paper above the shredder, and fed it in together. There was no feeling of hurry, it was a calm place.

Kevin Cassel's office was a glass-walled eyrie reached by a steep wooden staircase. From it we could see perhaps two acres of files. Here and there were brick columns on which hung red buckets and soda-lime fire-extinguishers.

'Hello, sailor,' said Kevin.

'Word gets around,' I said.

'Yes,' said Kevin, 'the Cabinet have promised us that we are the first people to be informed after the William Hickey column – you've put on weight, you old son of a gun.'

He motioned me into a battered green civil-service armchair. Kevin smiled expectantly; his moon-like face was much too large for his short, slim body, and was made even larger by a receding hair-line.

'First time you've been down to see us since Charlie Cavendish ...' He didn't finish the sentence. We had both liked Charlie.

Kevin looked at me for a minute without speaking before he said,

'Somebody put a firecracker under the Volkswagen, I hear.'

'Yes,' I said, 'someone from Rootes Group.'

'Take care,' said Kevin, 'they could get spiteful.'

I said, 'It was a metal canister they were after, not me.'

'Famous last words,' said Kevin. 'I'd wear the steel Y-fronts for the time being, just the same.'

He reached inside his green tweed jacket for his notebook and an old fountain pen.

'You wouldn't mind telling me something and then forgetting right afterwards.' In tacit agreement Kevin capped his pen, closed his notebook and replaced it.

'What do you want now?' said Kevin. 'Are you going to put a wall mike into 12 Downing Street or a sniper's rifle into the Press Gallery?'

'That's next week,' I said. 'I want to …' I paused.

'This will make you feel more comfy.' He swung a large neon tube down from the ceiling until it rested upon the desk between us; it would jam any known micro-transmitter, which is why agents always use a public phone that is near a neon sign if they have a chance. He switched the tube on. It flickered before underlighting Kevin's face with a blank blue glare.

It took Kevin only a few minutes to produce the documents I wanted to see. I glanced through the medical 'flimsy'. It was a clinical description of physical being: height, weight, scars, moles, birthmarks, blood group, reflexes and a blow-by-blow description of teeth and medical treatment from the age of eleven.

I turned to the card.

SMITH, Henry J. B. *This file renewal cycle:* six months.
Birth:
    Born 1900.
    White Caucasian. British National of British Birth.
    U.N. passport. U.K. passport.
Background:

Eton/New/Horse Guards/Stockbroking. Married P.F. Hamilton (q.v.) 1 child.

Property:

Maidenhead. Albany. Ayrshire.

Assets: (cash)

Westminster: Green Park br. = £19,004 dep., £783 current.

Shares: (See p.k.9.)

Interests:

Horticulture. Collects 1st editions of horticulture books, also flower prints. (A dwarf form of scarlet-flowered pomegranate named after him.)

Art: Owns 3 Bonnards, 2 Monets, 5 Degas, 5 Bratbys.

Pressures: rh. 139 wh. 12 gh. 190 gh. 980.

Shooting: Grouse shooting – fair shot.

Bentley Continental/Mini Cooper. Cessna aeroplane. 320 Skyknight.

Personal:

Mistress (see gh.980).

Teetotal. Vegetarian.

Extra-curricular:

Member of, Celebrite/Eve/Nell Gwynne under name of Murray.

Keeps small current account in name of Murray.

Clubs: White's, Traveller's.

No recorded homosexual tendency. In Sept. 1952 the (deleted) department of (deleted) arranged for homosexual overtures to be made to him to gain evidence for (Case 1952/kebs/832). There was no response.

Travel:

Extensive (see ah.40).

Photos:

aa/1424/77671.

36 Sort of Secrets

Kevin walked across to the *Country Life* calendar, stared at it and turned before answering my question.

'What's he like?' he repeated. 'It's hard to say in a few words. He was made a Fellow of All Souls before he was thirty. Which means he is no fool. They say that when he was up for election,' Kevin paused, 'it's probably not true but I'll tell you anyway. Candidates are invited to stay to dinner to see if they tuck their napkin into their collar or drink from the finger bowl.' I nodded. 'Smith was served with a cherry tart to see how he got rid of the pips. But he fooled them by swallowing the cherries, pips and all. I don't know if it's true but it's in character.

'All Souls is C. P. Snowland. These are the boys who tell the Government what to do. At weekends all the Fellows and a crowd of the "quondams" – men who used to be Fellows – get together for a big gutbash and a cosy yarn – they're the sort of people who have devoted a lot of time and expensive training to detecting the difference between Russian and Iranian caviare. He has about ninety thousand a year.' I whistled softly. Kevin repeated, 'Ninety thousand pounds a year. He pays tax on some of it, and sits on ten or twelve boards who like to have a representative on the old-boy network. Smith's big contribution is that he can influence affairs abroad with as much aplomb as he can move them here. He can afford to lay off every bet by backing the other side. He paid Germany and Italy for planes, tanks and guns that they were sending to Franco in 1936. He also quietly financed a Loyalist division. When Franco won, his reward was holdings in Spanish breweries and steel works. When he went to Spain in 1947 there was a Spanish Army guard of honour flashing swords around at the airport. Smith was embarrassed and told Franco never to do it again. In South America he has always been quick to put a few thousand into the hands of a discontented general. He's persona grata with Fidel Castro. It's gambling without risk.'

The red phone rang. 'Cassel.' Kevin pinched his nose. 'Complicated diagram?' He pinched the bridge of his nose again. 'Just photostat it in the normal way, show the engineering people before you destroy the original.' He listened again. 'Well, just show them the part that hasn't got the name on.' He put the handpiece down. ''Struth,' he said, 'they'll be asking me if they can go to the lavatory next.

'Where was I?'

'I wanted to ask you about shipping investment,' I said. 'Isn't that how he first made his fortune?'

'Of course, the fiscal side; I always forget that you are the money expert.'

'Try and tell my bank manager,' I said. Kevin lit cigarettes for us, then spent several minutes removing a shred of tobacco from his lip.

'The wartime government insurance of shipping. You know about that?'

I said, 'The British Government insured all ships carrying cargoes to U.K. during the war, didn't they?'

'Yes,' said Kevin. 'Overseas suppliers wanted money before the goods left the wharfside at Sydney or Halifax;

what happened after that was purely a private arrangement between us and the Germans.'

He smiled, 'Like your insurance policies and mine the insurances for shipping in 1939 were carrying six-point type saying "except for Acts of War". It was *possible* to get insured against U-boat attack in the North Atlantic, but the actuaries had little experience and the assessors were apt to be pessimistic. So H.M.G. decided to do their own insurance. Shipowners bringing goods to the U.K. would be insured against sinking. It didn't take long for the wide boys of the shipping industry to see the opportunity, and there are some really fly boys in the shipping industry between here and Piraeus. To get rich all you had to do was to buy some rusty, derelict old ruin, register it in Panama where anything goes as far as crew, pay, seaworthiness and experience are concerned, then trundle it off to hobble a North Atlantic convoy to six knots and make enough smoke to alert every U-boat in the vicinity.

'If it got to Liverpool you were rich, if it sank you were richer.' Kevin smiled. 'That's how Smith got richer.'

The phone rang. 'Phone me back, I'm busy,' said Kevin and hung up immediately. He turned back to the card, asking: 'You understand the pressure column?'

'Well, I'm no expert,' I said, 'but I gather they're filed items of human weaknesses like drink, women, or membership of the Tory Party Central Committee.'

'That's right,' said Kevin.

'I know, for example, that references commencing "mh" are sex things.'

'Feminine complications,' said Kevin.

'What a nice way of putting it,' I said.

'Makes you cynical though,' said Kevin, 'if you work here.' He smiled.

I read from the card I held: 'There's a "gh."'

'Accessory after an illegal act,' said Kevin quick as a shot.

'Does that mean something he has been prosecuted for?' I said.

'Good lord no,' said Kevin, in an astounded voice. 'He's never been in a law court. No, for anything about which the Mets* know anything it's another sort of card altogether – it's a "j" card.'

'Spare me the details,' I said, 'What about a "wh"?'

'Bribery of a public servant,' said Kevin.

'Again not prosecuted?'

'No, I told you,' said Kevin, 'it has a "j" suffix if it's been made public. It would be a "wj" card if he had been *accused* of bribing a public servant.'

'And "rh"?' I said.

'Illegal selling,' said Kevin. Now I was beginning to understand the system and I'd found the item I wanted.

---

* Mets (slang): Metropolitan Police.

37 Two readings

After I'd had Jean show me the revised notes of the Strutton Plan and I had torn them into small, bite-sized pieces and scattered them into the waste-paper basket like pantomime snow, and after we'd been all through it again, and she'd typed it, I thought some more about Smith. Two items about him were still fuzzy. I phoned Kevin, scrambled, and said, 'That matter I spoke of this morning.'

'Yes?' said Kevin.

'War service?' I asked.

'Ah,' said Kevin, 'his mother did very well. Too young for Number 1 and too old for Number 2.'

'O.K.,' I said, 'second question: why did you have his file card so handy on your desk?'

'Simple, old bean,' said Kevin, 'he'd sent for your card only that morning.'

'That's just great,' I said, and I heard Kevin chuckle as he hung up. He could just be kidding, I thought. No one in W.O.O.C.(P) had a card on file at Central Register; but I didn't chuckle.

38 Chin wag

The butler led me along soft corridors, men in red coats and tight trousers looked quietly down from the dark paintings lost in a penumbra of coach varnish. Mr Smith was seated behind a table polished like a guardsman's boot.

A slim eighteenth-century clock with frail marquetry panels paced out the silence, and from the Adam fireplace a coal fire ran pink fingers across the moulded ceiling. On Smith's table a lampshade marshalled the light on to heaps of papers and newspaper clippings. Only the crown of his head was visible. He spared me the embarrassment of interrupting his private study. The butler motioned me to a hostile Sheraton chair.

Smith ran a finger across the open book and scribbled in the margin of one of the typewritten sheets with a gold fountain pen. He turned up a corner of the page, ran a finger-nail along the crease and closed the leather cover.

'Smoke.' There was no trace of query in his voice. He pushed the box across the table with the back of his hand, recapped the pen and clipped it into his waistcoat pocket. He picked up his cigarette, put it into his mouth, drew on it without releasing his grasp on its battered tarnished shape, mashed it into the ashtray with controlled violence, disembowelling the shreds of tobacco from the lacerated paper with his long pink nails. He thumped the ash from his waistcoat.

'You wanted to see me?' he said.

I produced a bent blue packet of Gauloises. I lit one with a flick of the thumb-nail against a Swan match. I tossed the dead match towards the ashtray, allowing the trajectory to carry it on to Smith's pristine paperwork. He carefully picked it up and placed it in the ashtray. I drew on the harsh tobacco. 'No,' I said, denuding my voice of interest, 'not much.'

'You are discreet – that's good.' He picked up a battered filing card, held it under the light and quietly read from it a potted description of my career in Intelligence.

'I don't know what you're talking about,' I said.

'Good, good,' said Smith, not at all discouraged. 'The report goes on, "inclined to pursue developments beyond requirements out of curiosity. He must be made to understand that curiosity is a dangerous failing in an agent."'

'Is that what you wanted to do,' I asked, 'to tell me about curiosity being dangerous?'

'Not "dangerous",' said Smith. He leaned forward to select a new victim from his ivory cigarette box. The light fell momentarily across his face. It was a hard bony face, and it shone in the electric light like the expressionless busts of Roman emperors in the British Museum. Lips, eyebrows, and the hair on his temples were all colourless. He looked up. 'Fatal.' He took a white cigarette and put it into his white face. He lit the cigarette.

'In wartime soldiers are shot for refusing to obey even the smallest commands,' said Smith in his most gritty voice.

'They shouldn't be.'

'Why not?' His drawl had gone.

'Oppenheim's *International Law*, sixth edition: only lawful commands need be obeyed.'

It was not the reply that Smith was expecting and he flushed with anger. 'You are demanding that an investigation in Portugal be continued. The Cabinet have instructed that it be closed. We should never have sanctioned such an operation in the first place. Your refusal is impertinence and unless you change your attitude I shall recommend that severe measures be taken against you.'

He pronounced the personal pronoun with discreet reverence.

'No one owns a spy, mister,' I told him, 'they just pay his salary. I work for the government because I think this is a good place to live, but that doesn't mean that I'll be used as a serf by a self-centred millionaire. What's more,' I said, 'don't give me that "fatal" stuff because I've taken a postgraduate course in fatality.'

Smith blinked and leaned back into the Louis Quatorze chair. 'So,' he said, finally, 'that's it, is it? The truth is that you think *you* should be as powerful as a Cabinet Minister?' He rearranged his pen set.

'Power is like a fried egg,' I told him, 'no matter how equally you try to divide it someone is sure to get most.'

Smith leaned forward and said, 'You think that because I hold a controlling interest in companies that make jet engines and automatic weapons it precludes me from having a say in the control of my country.' He held up a hand in an admonishing attitude. 'No, it is now *my* turn to lecture *you*. You are a spy; I do not impugn your motives as a spy but you feel free to impugn mine as a manufacturer. You say that you work for the government. What *is* the government you speak of? You mean as each political party is elected to power all the intelligence groups are disbanded and new ones formed? No, you don't mean that, you mean that you work for the country, for its prosperity, for its power, for its prestige, for its standard of living, for its health scheme, for its high rate of employment. You work for all those things, to keep them and to improve them, just as the motor-car manufacturer does. If there is a way for me to sell, for instance, an extra fifteen thousand vehicles next year, my duty is to do so.

'You might say: it's my duty to increase the prosperity of every Englishman living. That is why it is your duty to do as I say in these matters. Your orders come to you through the legitimate line of command because all your superiors understand these things. If, in order to sell my fifteen thousand vehicles I need your help, you will provide it …' He paused for a moment before adding, 'without questions.

'Your job is an extension of mine. Your job is to provide success at *any* price. By means of bribes, by means of theft or by means of murder itself. Men like you are in the dark, subconscious recesses of the nation's brain. You do things that are done and forgotten quickly. The things I've mentioned are the realities of this world. No one deliberately chooses that this should be so. No historian is asked to account for the evil of the world. No man who writes a medical encyclopedia is responsible for the diseases he catalogues. And so it is with you. You are a cipher – you are no more than the ink with which History is written.'

'I'm a stoker in the ship of state?' I asked humbly.

Smith gave a cold smile. 'You are worth less than a substantial foreign contract for Clydeside. You sit here talking of ethics as though you were employed to make ethical decisions. You are *nothing* in the scheme. You will complete your tasks as ordered: no more, no less. You will be paid a just amount. There is nothing to discuss.' He leaned back in his chair again. It creaked with the shift of weight. His bony hand clamped around the red silk rope that hung beside the curtain.

In my pocket with my keys and some parking-meter sixpences I could feel a smooth polished surface. My fingers closed around it as the butler opened the big panelled doors.

'Show the gentleman out, Laker,' said Smith. I made no move except to put the gleaming silver-coloured metal on his mahogany table. Smith watched it, puzzled and fascinated. I bunched my fingers and flipped it. It scampered across the mahogany surface, clattering against its own bright reflection.

'What's the meaning of this?' said Smith.

'It's a gift for the man who has everything,' I said. I watched Smith's face. 'It's a die for making gold sovereigns.' I watched the butler out of the corner of my eye; he was hanging on to every word. Perhaps he was planning his memoirs for the Sunday papers.

Smith flicked a tongue across his drying lips like a hungry python. 'Wait downstairs, Laker,' he said, 'I'll ring again.' The butler had withdrawn to his notebook before Smith spoke again. 'What has this to do with me?' he said.

'I'll tell you,' I said, and lit another Gauloise while Smith fidgeted with his guilt feelings. This time he left the dead match where it had landed.

'I know of some gear for wolfram-mining that goes to India in regular consignments. I'll tell you, those people in India must be inefficient because they have received tons of it and yet *there is no wolfram in the whole Indian subcontinent*! You can hardly blame them when they try to resell to – someone just a few miles north.'

Smith's cigarette lay inert in the ashtray and quietly turned to ash.

'There are people in Chungking who will take as much as the Indians send. Of course, it wouldn't be kosher if an English company sold strategic goods to Red China, and the Americans would blacklist them, but what with all this muddle in India everyone ends up happy.' I paused. The clock ticked on like a mechanical heart.

'As a way of moving gold there's nothing to beat …'

'You are just guessing,' said Smith.

I thought of the diary that Smith's confidant Butcher had made available to me and how easy it had made my subsequent guesses, 'I am just guessing,' I agreed.

'Very well,' said Smith in a resigned but businesslike voice, 'how much?'

'I've not come to blackmail you,' I said, 'I just want to press on with my job of stoking without interference from the bridge. I'm not pursuing you. I'm not interested in doing anything beyond my job. But I want you to remember this: *I* am the responsible person in this investigation, not my boss or anyone else in the department. *I'll* be responsible for what happens to you, whether it's good or bad. Now ring your bell for Laker, I'm leaving before I vomit over your beautiful Kashan carpet.'

39 Inside a cabinet

When I got to Charlotte Street on Tuesday morning, Alice was sitting alongside the switchboard operator comparing knitting patterns and drinking coffee. When she saw me she crooked a bony finger and I followed her into the office that Dawlish had recently given her. It was stacked to the ceiling with directories, gazetteers, *Who's Who*s and cardboard folders of newspaper clippings. She sat down behind the tiny table she used as a desk. I helped her move the two-pound bag of sugar, an electric kettle, two laced and lead-sealed secret files and a Nescafé tin with a hole cut in the top in which contributions to the office tea swindle were kept. She turned the pages of a file.

'You've had coffee?' said Alice.

'Yes,' I said.

'Alforreca is on,' said Alice, 'officially I mean, word came from the top.'

'Oh good,' I said.

'Don't try that "oh good" stuff with me,' she said. 'I know what you've been up to.'

'Smoke?' I said. I offered her a Gauloise.

'No,' said Alice, 'and I don't want you spreading a lot of fumes through this room either.'

'O.K., Alice,' I said and I put the cigarette back in the packet.

'Clings for days,' said Alice, 'that French tobacco.'

'Yes,' I said, 'I suppose it does.'

'That's all,' said Alice. It seemed odd that Alice should invite me into her office for the first time just to say that. As I got up Alice said, 'Try to look a little bit surprised when Dawlish tells you. The poor man doesn't know you as I do.'

'Thank you, Alice,' I said.

'Don't thank me,' said Alice, 'I just want him to keep his pathetic illusions, that's all.'

'Yes,' I said, 'but thanks anyway.' I turned to go. Alice called, 'There *is* one more thing. Jennifer,' she said.

'Jennifer,' I repeated dumbly, mentally riffling through all the code names I knew.

'Jennifer in the cashier's department; she's getting married.'

I felt no guilt or jealousy. 'I don't even know who you are talking about,' I said.

'We've put you down for two pounds,' said Alice irritably, 'towards a present.'

In the office I found Jean (who had put her hair up after all), thirty letters to sign and a great mass of abstracts to read: American State Department, Counter-Intelligence Corps and Defence reports as well as the pink foolscap translations from *Red Flag, People's Daily* and *M.V.D. Information*. I put the whole bundle into my briefcase. The snow was still threatening and the heavy grey clouds hung across the sky like a false ceiling. Wardens were licking their pencil stubs and policemen with a huge tray of keys were unlocking double-parkers and driving them to the pound. I looked into Dawlish's office. He was hammering panel pins into the wall.

'Hello, what do you think of this?' he said. It was a framed coloured print of the Iron Duke seated upon a rotund horse, doffing his hat with one hand and waving a sword with the other. Under the print in a fine copperplate it said:

All the business of war,
And indeed all the business of life,
Is to endeavour to find out
What you don't know by what you do.

'Very handsome,' I said.

'Present from my son. He's very fond of quotations by Wellington. Each year on the anniversary of the Battle of Waterloo we have a little party, and all the guests have to have an anecdote or quotation ready.'

'Yes,' I said, 'I do the same thing every time I pull on my Wellington boots.' Dawlish slid me a narrowed glance.

I offered him a cigarette to break the tension.

'You intend to pursue the Alforreca operation?'

'I want to know why Smith sent Harry Kondit a seven-thousand-pound laboratory to a backwater of Portugal.'

'You think that will explain everything?' said Dawlish. He smacked the metal hammer-head into the palm of his hand.

'I don't know,' I said, 'perhaps I'll be able to tell you better after I've talked to the man who's been examining the canister. I think the explosives in my car were placed so as to destroy that rather than the driver.'

Dawlish nodded. 'Have a nice trip to Cardiff,' he said, and began hammering. I said, 'Don't hit your finger and drop the hammer on your toe.' He nodded again and continued hammering.

I leaned upon the gravy-stained tablecloth as Paddington slid past. Soot-caked dwellings pressed together like pleats in a concertina. Grey laundry flapped in the breeze. Past Ladbroke Grove the small gardens suffocated under choking debris, only corrugated iron and rusty wire remained of things collapsed.

'Soup,' said the attendant. He set a chipped cup before me. A girl across the aisle applied cosmetics in three primary colours to her blotchy face. I wrote the word STURGEON into the crossword. That would make 23 down MULGA. The clue for 2 across was 'old solution': SISTRUM, because I knew the last four letters were TRUM.

I was a long way out on a thin plank over a deep sea. I had blocked Smith at least for the time being, but I had done it at the expense of making a V.I.P. enemy. It wasn't something one could do too frequently without uncomfortable consequences. Perhaps it was something one couldn't do *once* without uncomfortable consequences. I wrote NOSTRUM to replace SISTRUM.

I was beginning to get it now.

Up here the snow had gathered into light grey clumps in the corners of brown fields. Cows snorted white puffs and huddled together in the dells under bare trees splattered with blots of birds.

I crossed STURGEON through and made it STALLION; this gave me MAQUI as 23 down, instead of MULGA.

The train wheels chattered across a junction and my warm chicken-leg made concentric waves in the thin gravy. I wondered how many people in Albufeira had connexions with Smith. Who had stolen the photographs and to whom were they delivered? Why had either Fernie or the sound of a two-stroke motor cycle been everywhere at once? The blonde girl with the painted face was putting pink acetate on her finger-nails; the acrid smell assailed my taste-buds as I chewed the chicken – it was better than no taste at all.

Past the City Hall the Cardiff traffic was as thick as Welsh rarebit. The clock struck five thirty as we turned on to the A469. The moorland was bleak and wind-scoured. Through the twilight 'our man in Cardiff' lifted a finger at the crooked castle of Caerphilly. Under the dark sky the stone houses squinted yellow light through the lacework. The shops had been tightly shut since lunch-time. I had no matches.

The Cardiff man spoke in a mocking Celtic treble.

'I thought you London men could afford lighters.'

'And I thought you Cardiff men could afford car-heaters.' I blew on my hands and received a wizened glance of amusement from under a stained bowler hat. The Welsh are gourmets at the feast of insults.

Beyond the ruins of Caerphilly Castle stunted trees grew hunchbacked against the wind.

We pulled off the road, the loose surface shuffled and the eggshell crack of ice splintered under the wheels. The wind was screaming through the car's radio antenna as a bald man in a roll-neck sweater opened the door of a small stone house. Inside, the cool green light of an oil lamp described circles on the table and ceiling. Draught made the fire flare, a soot-caked kettle buzzed with boiling water, and almost before we were seated a large bowl of sweet dark tea was warming the palms of our hands. I lit a cigarette with a stick from the wood fire. Our man from Cardiff rapidly sank his scalding tea and pulled on his dirty knitted gloves and bowler hat.

'I'll be pushing along then,' he said. I didn't mean to look pleased. He said, 'Ah, you develop a strong sense of knowing when you are not wanted here in Glamorgan.' I grinned.

He said, 'You can phone when you want to be collected. Would you want me to arrange a room at the Angel for you? American Bar and television they have there. It will be just like you were still in London.'

Their singing voices argued the pros and cons of my travel arrangements, and finally my host in the roll-neck sweater offered to let me stay the night.

'On a "Put-U-up", you know; nothing fancy.' I agreed, and watched the small, heatless car rumble down the rough road and turn back towards Cardiff.

We sat quietly making toast in front of the fire and Glynn would every now and then get up to fix the back door, draw an extra can of water from the outdoor pump or attend to something for the pigs. Finally, he lit a filthy old pipe and said, 'You had my report all right? Your canister contained traces of crude morphine. The young lady was most anxious that it didn't go astray.' The man in the sweater was also on a small retainer from W.O.O.C.(P) and a smaller one from the Home Office Forensic Science Lab. in Cardiff.

'It was fine,' I said, 'but I decided to come down to see you because I know so little about dangerous drugs.'

'Ah,' he said, 'well, what do you want to know?'

'Everything,' I said. 'Just talk about drugs so I'll know my way around.'

40 H without an H

'I'll tell you all about drugs,' said Glynn, 'like I tell the young-sters that come to work in the lab. There are three kinds of dangerous drugs. First there is the coca bush, this is what cocaine is made from.'

I said, 'That isn't such a problem, cocaine, is it?'

'Don't ever think that, man. It just depends where you are. There are about a million and a half addicts in Peru alone. In South America it has been a part of the diet since the Incas used it as a pep pill. You can sniff it into the mucous mem-brane. The poor swines take it because it mutes their hunger and because it's the only way they can face hellish hard work in conditions a lot worse than my pigs have. They chew it mixed with ash. You're right, though, from a European view-point it's one of the lesser problems. The second is what we call cannabis.'

'Hashish,' I said.

'Hashish in the Middle East, kif in Morocco, bhang in Kenya. Called Indian hemp, marijuana …'

I interrupted, 'These are all the same?'

'Roughly. It's easy to grow, the flowers and leaves are made into cigarettes, while the resin is dried into a slab which is smoked in a pipe – that is hashish.'

'Where is it grown?' I asked.

'Almost any damn where. There are some trade routes that come out of Jordan south to Sinai through Negev into Egypt. There's the route out of Syria to Sharm-el-Sheik, at the tip of Sinai, through Saudi Arabia. And there is the sea route from Tyre to Gaza …'

'O.K.,' I said, 'I get it. Now what about opium?'

'Well, that's the third drug. It's a very different story from the others.'

'Tell me about opium,' I said.

The kettle had been singing for five minutes and he turned the wick of the oil lamp up a little to give him light to make tea. I wielded the bent wire toasting-fork and put a dish of Welsh butter nearer to the fire to soften it. Outside the wind moaned around the small windows. 'Opium,' said Glynn as he warmed the teapot.

'Difficult to grow, therefore sought after. The basis of narcotic smuggling, grows anywhere up to a latitude of 56°. The oriental poppy or the common poppy is of no interest to the narcotic trader, only the P.S.L. (the *Papavar somniferum Linnaeus*) gives opium. They are sown in May for the August crop and in August for the April crop.'

'It's like painting the Forth Bridge,' I said.

'Yes, it's year-round employment,' said Glynn. 'To get it … you want to know?'

'Sure.'

'Little incisions are cut into the green capsules of the poppy before the seeds ripen. White latex appears and you wait ten to fifteen hours for the latex to harden and turn brown. The evening they do this you can smell the aroma for miles.'

'Are there various strains of poppy?'

'Yes, from purple-black to white, but I don't know which strain is the best.' Glynn made the tea and I traded a thick piece of toast with him.

'Why do Home Office do sample tests?'

'Oh, I see what you mean. What we can do is make a fair guess at whereabouts a batch came from, by analysis. But it's seldom needed; they come packaged with trade marks and even signs saying "Beware of Imitations". You must know that.'

'Yes, I have seen some of those packs,' I admitted. 'But where is it grown? You haven't said where.'

'Chiengrai in Northern Siam is said to be the world trading centre, but whether that is true or not, we can say that it is the Yunnan-Kwang-si area. Or let's generalize and say Burma, Laos, Siam, and Korea. The Americans say that the Chinese Government support the traffic to undermine U.S. moral fibre. It tends to move towards the U.S.A. anyway, because that's where it commands the best prices. Mind you, I've been talking about illegal cultivation, but Yugoslavia, Greece, Japan, and Bulgaria grow it legally, as well as India, Turkey, and Russia. The U.K. produces forty-five legal kilos a year.'

'And there's the processing too?'

'Oh yes,' said Glynn, 'the latex from the P.S.L. poppy isn't much good as it is. It has to be made into morphine base, and then that has to be made into diacetyl-morphine. Which is what you would call "heroin", or "H", or "horse" I believe, in some circles.'

'Do you need a big place to do that?'

'It's the drainage, man,' Glynn said, 'that's the problem. There is a tremendous amount of acetic acid to get rid of. If you start floating it down the public drains it's likely to excite attention. You know what acetic acid is like?'

'Yes,' I said, 'it's the stuff my local supermarket sells as vinegar.'

'Supermarket,' said Glynn, pronouncing each syllable separately, 'yes, they would do that in London.'

We talked on into the lonely Welsh night, eating sandwiches and toast and drinking strong tea with goat's milk in it.

Dawn crawled red-eyed over the horizon before we finished talking. Glynn dozed in his huge wing armchair. I could get no further with the crossword.

I lifted the latch gently and stepped outside into the damp Welsh mists.

On the horizon bare branches grew across the grey skyline like cracks in a sheet of ice. Foraging around the snow patches rooks fluttered and flopped until my arrival sent them climbing into the moist air, their black wings richly pink in the light.

I thought about my talk with Glynn as my shoes built up a rim of loam. So the green canister had contained traces of crude morphine. I was right about the explosives in my car. Someone wanted to destroy the evidence. Where had it come from, how much had there been, who had moved it, to where? My investigation at Albufeira was no nearer to completion than my crossword, in which I had made STALLION into STARLING. The clue to 19 down was 'Bright red'. I wrote down BALAS – a red ruby.

'Bright red,' I thought; perhaps I should write TOMAS; he had bright red hair which he dyed. Why did he dye it? Was he bright red in the political sense? H.K. said he had fought in Spain. Would H.K. know, and if he did would he tell me the truth? It was alarming that so few people told me the truth. Fought in Spain, I thought. I wonder how many Englishmen fought in Spain? The Home Office keeps a file devoted to Englishmen who fought in Spain. I would ask Jean to study it.

41 It's moving

Jean met me at Paddington. She was still driving Dawlish's old Riley.

'What is it you do to Dawlish, that he lends his pride and joy?'

'You have a disgusting mind.' She gave me a girlish smile.

'No kidding, how do you get him to trust you with it? He sends the doorman out to watch me when I park near it – let alone trust me inside when the wheels are moving.'

'Well, I'll tell you,' said Jean. 'I *compliment* him about it. It's something you've never heard about, but among civilized people compliments are all the rage. Try, some day.'

'My compliments tend to oversteer,' I told her, 'and I end up in a ditch backwards.'

'You should try a touch of brake before changing direction.'

'You win,' I said. She always wins.

The Admiralty is next door to the Whitehall Theatre, where they get paid for farce. The policeman spotted Dawlish's motor and let us pull across Whitehall into the courtyard among the official cars, their smooth black contours heavy with wax and crowded with reflection. Under the porch hung an old lantern, and brasswork was burnished to an illegible sheen. Inside the entrance a vast grate of incandescent coals flickered electric light through its artful plastic embers. A doorman in a braided frockcoat directed me past a life-size Nelson in a red niche who stared down with two blind eyes of stone.

The cinema projector and screen had been set up in one of the upstairs rooms. One of our own people from Charlotte Street was threading it up and opening and closing little boxes of blinding light. There were three senior officers there when we arrived, and we all shook hands after a sailor on the door was persuaded to allow us in.

The first minutes were hilarious. There was this boy Victor from the Swiss section, dressed up in long shorts with the elastic of his underpants grappling with his belly. But the serious stuff was well done. An old black Ford threaded its way over the uneven Portuguese cobblestones, stopped, and an old gentleman climbed out. The tall thin figure walked up a flight of steps and disappeared into the black maw of a church portal.

Another shot, same man, medium close-up moving across camera. He turned towards the camera. The gold spectacles glinted in the sun. Our photographer had probably complained that he was blocking the view, for da Cunha walked a little more quickly out of the frame. There were fifteen minutes of film of da Cunha. He was the same imperious gaunt figure that had given me a brown-paper parcel on a night that seemed so long ago. Without warning the screen flashed white and the film spool sang a note of release.

The three naval men got to their feet, but Jean asked them to stay a moment longer to see something else. A still picture flashed on the screen. It was an old creased snapshot. A group of army and naval officers were sitting, arms folded and heads erect. Jean said, 'This photograph was taken at Portsmouth in 1938. Commander Andrews sorted it out for us.' I nodded to

Commander Andrews across the darkened room. Jean went on, 'Commander Andrews is third from the left, front row. At the end of the front row there is a German naval officer – Lieutenant Knobel.'

'Yes,' I said.

The operator changed the slide. It was a part of the same picture enlarged, a big close-up of the young German sailor's face. The projector-operator went to the screen with an ink marker. He drew spectacles on Lieutenant Knobel. The picture was very light in tone and now he drew in a new hairline on the plastic screen. He drew a darkened eye-socket.

'O.K.,' I said. It was da Cunha as a young man.

42 Hidden within treason

BRITISH NAVAL OFFICER FACES GRAVE CHARGES
BEARING ARMS AGAINST COMRADES
SIX CHARGES OF TREACHERY

The 1945 press cuttings that Jean had photostated for me lay on the dusty table in the Admiralty Library. The dates on the cuttings helped me to locate the file I wanted to see. It had a grey cover with a reference number. The pages were fastened together with three star-shaped clips and numbered to prevent loss of one of them.[*]

Out of the medical envelope slid cards, flimsies and reports. Here it was, the clincher:

O/E Bernard Thomas Peterson
Red-haired man. Complexion white c̄ freckles
Eyes: light-blue. Height 5′ 9″
Weight: 9 stone 10 lb. Attentive→excitable
Birthmark: scar right ear-lobe. Intelligent.

This was Fernie Tomas. Jean's search of the Spanish Civil War files at the Home Office had found a name curiously like

[*] See Appendix 6 for more detail.

Fernie Tomas – Bernie Thomas: otherwise Bernard Thomas Peterson.

So Fernie was an expert frogman, a renegade R.N. officer. I remembered the two-stroke cycle that gave Giorgio a ride in the night, the capsizing of the boat 'by a frogman' and Giorgio's voice as he told me that the stars were going out. And da Cunha had been a German naval officer; they made quite a pair.

My hands were black with dust. I borrowed the soap from the bent tin and used the small stiff towel that was kept for visitors to the Admiralty Library.

'Don't forget your pass,' someone called, 'you'll never get out of the building without it.'

180

43 Friday on a Portuguese calendar

To wake up in the sun in Albufeira is to be reborn. I lay in the no-man's-land of half-asleep and hugged the crater of bedclothes, afraid to advance into the gunfire of wide-awake. The sound of the town dripped into my consciousness; the tinkle and clink of bell-laden bridles; the hoof taps, and the rumble of tall wheels over the cobblestones; the high note as trucks came up the hill in bottom gear; the crackle of water dropping from overflow pipes on to the beach below, and the squawk of cats exchanging blows and fur. I lit a Gauloise and eased my toes into the daylight beyond the blankets. From the beach came the rhythmic chanting of men heaving at the sardine net, and from the seagulls hoarse cries as they slid down the onshore wind to pounce upon discarded slivers of fish.

I stepped on to the balcony. The stone floor was hot underfoot, and on the grey wooden chairs sat Buddha-like cats squinting into the sunlight. Charly was fixing coffee and toast in the kitchen, holding the front of her silk housecoat closed. I am pleased to tell you that a lot of the coffee-making was a two-handed job. She stood against the light of the window and I began to realize for the first time what every male in the region had known since she arrived; she was five feet ten inches tall and every inch was soft and delicious.

The deaths of Joe and Giorgio had curtailed the diving

181

operation. Each day Singleton went out to the sunken submarine and continued the search, but I had long since concluded that what I was looking for was on dry land.

After lunch Singleton said that he must drive to Lisbon to recharge the air bottles. How long could he stay there, he said. I looked at Charly and she looked at me. 'Have two or three days there,' I said. Singleton was pleased.

I walked along the beach trying to arrange the facts I had access to. As I look back on it I had enough information then to tell me what I wanted to know. But at that time I didn't know *what* I wanted to know. I was just letting my sense of direction guide me through the maze of motives.

It was clear to me that Smith was connected with this town in some way or other, legal or illegal. Fernie was a frogman and Giorgio had been killed under water. The canister from the U-boat had contained heroin and someone had emptied it recently (or how had the ballpoint writing got inside?). Smith had sent £7,100-worth of equipment to K (Kondit begins with a K, but so does the real name of da Cunha – Knobel).

Did Smith have a say in Giorgio's death or in Joe's? Did da Cunha want Smith to have the sovereign die when he gave it to me, and why had he invented a mythical dead sailor and manufactured a grave?

I met Charly in the main square.

The scrawny old houses stared red-eyed into the sunset. Two or three cafés – houses with a public front room – opened their doors, pale-green colour-washed walls were punctuated with calendar art, and crippled chairs leaned against the walls for support. In the evening the young bloods came to operate the juke box. A small man in a suede jacket poured thimble-size drinks from large unlabelled medicine bottles under the counter. Behind him green bottles of 'Gas-soda' and 'Fru-soda' grew old and dusty.

It grew darker and juke-box music scalded the soft night air. Between the strident rock vocals came the occasional *fado*. Brazilian jungle melodies, transposed for Lisbon slums, they sounded curiously right in a Moorish land. I sipped brandy and chewed the dried-cuttlefish appetizers – rubbery and strong-tasting.

'Medronho,' said the man behind the counter, pointing to my glass. It is made from the medronho berry from the mountains. 'Good?' he asked with his sole word of English.

'Medonho,' I said, and he laughed. I had made a Portuguese joke; 'medonho' means 'frightful'. Above the noise Charly was saying, 'You speak Portuguese?'

'A little,' I said.

'You cunning old bastard,' said Charly in her clear Girton voice, 'you understood every word I've said for weeks.'

'No,' I said, 'I only have a smattering.' But she wasn't to be placated.

We went to the Jul-Bar for dinner. The place was full of men doing Toto-Bola football pools and the seventeen-inch TV was cutting us in on the secrets of Tide and Alka-Seltzer. Our table was set with a tablecloth and cutlery and a flask of wine. The meal was simple and the drink relaxing, and by 11 p.m. I wanted to go to bed, but Charly suggested a swim.

The water was cool and moonlight trickled across it like cream spilt on a black velvet dress. The night and the water reminded me of the night Giorgio died. Charly's blonde hair shone in the light and her body was phosphorescent in the clear black water. She swam near to me and pretended to have cramp. I grabbed her as I was intended to do. Her skin was warm and her mouth was salty and the clear white brandy had done things to my better judgement.

What a short journey it is to any bedroom. How difficult to remove a wet swimsuit. She was a considerate and inventive lover, and afterwards we talked with the soft, kind truth that only new lovers have.

Her voice was low and close; she had discarded the banter with her clothes.

'Women always want love affairs to go on for ever and ever,' Charly said. 'Why aren't we clever enough just to enjoy it on a day-to-day basis?'

'Love is just a state of mind,' I said, using Dawlish's slogan and grinning to myself in the darkness.

There was a note of alarm in Charly's voice. 'It *has* to be more than that,' she said.

I held the cigarette against her lips. 'A mortal's attempt to define infinity,' I said.

She inhaled and the red glow lit her face for an instant. She said, 'Sometimes two people see each other just for an instant, perhaps from a moving train and there's a rapport. It's not sex, it's not love, it's a sort of magical fourth dimension of living. You never saw him before, you'll never see him again; you don't even intend to try because it doesn't matter. Everything that is wise, I mean, that is good, that is understanding and profound, in the two of you becomes real at that instant.'

'My old man gave me two pieces of advice,' I said, 'don't ride a hard-mouthed horse or go to bed with a woman who keeps a diary. You are beginning to make noises like a diary-keeper. It's time I faded.' But I made no move.

'There's one thing I'd like to know,' said Charly.

The church clock clanked one o'clock and there was a sudden scurry of cats across the balcony.

'Why are you really so interested in this submarine?' Charly asked. I suppose I must have snapped awake, for she added, 'Don't tell me if it's a big man's secret and I'm not allowed to know.'

I didn't answer.

'What is it that you are trying to find out here? Why do you stay here after two men have died? You know as well as I do that there is nothing in the submarine. Who is it that you are so interested in? I would like to think it's me, but I know it isn't.'

'You sound like you have a theory,' I said. 'What do you think?'

'I think you are investigating yourself,' she said.

She waited for a comment, but I made none. 'Are you?' she said.

I said, 'There's a law held inviolate by the people among whom I work: *truth varies in inverse proportion to the influence of the person concerned.* I'm going to break that law.'

'Must you do it alone?' Charly said.

'Look,' I said, 'everyone *is* alone, born alone, live alone, get sick alone, die alone, everything alone. Making love is a way for people to pretend they aren't alone. But they are. And everyone in this business is even more so, alone and aching with a lot of untellable truths in his brain-box. You're groping in the dark through the Hampton Court maze with a hundred people shouting different directions at you. So you grope on; striking matches, grabbing handfuls of privet and occasionally getting mud on your knees. You *are* alone and so am I. Just try getting used to it or you'll wind up telling people that your husband doesn't understand you.'

'I'm still single,' Charly said. 'I'll make a lot of men miserable on the day I get married.'

'No kidding,' I said. 'How many men are you going to marry?' She gave me a spiteful punch in the ribs and tried to make me jealous by talking about H.K.

'Harry has a canning factory,' Charly said; she lit two cigarettes and passed me one. 'He's very proud of it. Practically built it with his bare hands, according to him.' I grunted. We smoked cigarettes and outside the sea that had caused it all kicked the shore in delinquent spite.

'What does H.K. can at this canning factory?' I asked.

'Tuna in the season, sardines, pilchards. Anything that's a good buy. All the canning factories mix their products. Harry does pickled things too, I think.'

'Yes?' I said.

'Oh yes,' said Charly, 'as we drove past his laboratory tonight the smell of vinegar was as strong as anything. It almost choked me.'

There is a tremendous amount of acetic acid to get rid of ... Boardable ... erection of chemical works ...

I thought about it all for a minute. Then I said, 'Get dressed, Charly; let's take a look at H.K.'s laboratory right now.' She wasn't keen to go but we went.

44 *W.H.O. is part of this not me*

We left the old Citroën down the road and walked the rest of the way. Our feet sank into the dry red earth as we moved around the rear of the low building. A light was on at the far end and the sound of water gulping down a drain was loud in the night. Above us hydrangea flowers walked along the walls, and from the lit window came the atonal, knife-edge sound of a *fado*. I raised my head slowly above the sill. I saw a grimy room with long lines of machinery teetering away into the darkness. A draught of hot air was coming from the heater fans. It seemed a strange luxury in this sub-tropical night. Nearer to me an electric vacuum pump was pounding gently. Harry Kondit walked across the room, his white T-shirt marked with bright yellow stains. The smell of vinegar was almost overwhelming. I felt Charly's hand on my back as she looked over my shoulder and heard her swallow to avoid coughing on the acrid fumes. H.K. went across to the little electric pulverizer and pulled the switch. The sound of the motor almost obliterated the music from the gramophone, so H.K. turned up the volume and the *fado* added to the din.

This was no ice-melting experiment, and this lab. hadn't cost anything like seven thousand pounds. This was a small morphine-processing factory: pulverizer, vacuum pump, drying-room, everything to turn morphine into heroin before it was sealed into sardine-tins for export. Harry Kondit, I thought; Conduit – a channel or pipe through which supplies travel. I leaned through the open window, raised the pistol and aimed with care. The Smith & Wesson kicked in my hand and the sound thrashed around inside the walls. The gramophone record exploded into a thousand sharp black knives.

'Switch off the pump and the pulverizer, Harry, or I will,' I said. For a moment H.K. stared, then he did so and silence descended like a candle-snuffer.

'Now walk slowly across to that door and open it.'

'But I …'

'And don't say a word,' I said. 'I haven't forgotten that you killed Joe with dynamite.' H.K. turned to me to explain but decided not to. He went to the door and slipped the bolt. I gave Charly the pistol and she walked around the building to the door. While I was saying, 'Just stay as you are, Harry, and I won't blast any of the expensive machinery …' H.K. was biding his time, waiting until I had to move away from the window, but when Charly put the barrel of the .38 against his belly-button he realized that he had been fooled. Charly moved H.K. back at a professional range. I joined her, closed the door behind me and bolted it again.

The three of us stood there in silence until H.K. said, 'Welcome to the dream factory, fans.'

We said nothing.

'So you were a cop after all,' said H.K.

'You mean you weren't sure when you bombed my car and killed Giorgio out on the U-boat.'

'You got it all wrong, Ace,' said H.K. He was tanned darker than ever, and the skin where his watch had been was like a white bangle. His shallow forehead wrinkled like a washboard and he wet his lips with a large pink tongue. 'It's no use to explain,' he continued, 'I thought you were an O.K. guy. No hard feelings. When winter comes you know which trees are the evergreens.'

'It's going to be a long, hard winter, Harry,' I said. He looked at me and gave a rueful smile.

He said, 'You're using a thirty-foot voice for an eighteen-inch conversation.' He was as calm as the Serpentine in June.

'How did you get into this racket?' I asked him quietly.

'Can I sit down?' he asked.

I nodded, but took my pistol from Charly and kept it handy.

'We all got problems, Ace,' said H.K. as he sat down heavily, 'and problems obey the laws of perspective; they look big close-to.' I threw him a cigarette and a box of matches. He took his time lighting up.

'You don't have to worry about telling me more than I know, Harry. I know a lot,' I said.

'F'r instance?'

'I know that I've been given the run-around by the phoniest set-up this side of Disneyland. I traced a red-haired Englishman who fought in the Spanish Civil War (we have files on all of them) and I find he's a black-haired man who stays out of the sun for fear of getting some English-style freckles.' I paused before adding, 'Fernie Tomas was in a good position to know things about sunken U-boats; like that a certain one would be full of heroin.'

'Yeah, full of horse, you are right,' said H.K. reflectively, and he nodded and suddenly began to talk.

'That green canister was just crammed with old heroin that some Nazi was scramming with. Fernie Tomas brought it to me and said did I know anyone who would handle it. I suppose you could say that neither of us was very keen about it, but that canister was worth a lot of dough. I couldn't afford to pass it up. My pal Harry Williams-Cohen was on a tax rap at the time and it looked like he was going up the river for a telephone number. * We got enough on that horse to pay off his tax and penalties. Then Fernie and I decided to plough our money into this factory which was just going to close.'

'Brooklyn boy saves Portuguese fish factory,' I said, 'with U.S. know-how and a couple of kilos of diacetyl-morphine.'

'Be smart,' H.K. pleaded, 'go home and see what someone paid into your bank account.'

'Thanks, Harry,' I said, 'but no.'

H.K. drew on the cigarette I had given him and waved it gently in the air. His initial burst of nervous talking had passed and now his speech was slower and more cautious. 'Listen,' he said. 'In another five years the government are going to legalize the import of reefers. I know for sure. Then the big business boys will take over; there'll be tastefully designed packs, and colour ads in *Life* magazine with two ritzy models saying, "I never knew smoking could be FUN until I got hooked".'

I said, 'But this is now, Harry, and people who break the law and make money out of it are often misunderstood.'

'You're such a wise guy,' Harry said. 'O.K. So I did it for money and as I got it so I spent it. You know how money is.'

'No, I don't,' I said. 'How is it?'

'It's as tricky as uranium but ten times more dangerous. It disappears like youth or multiplies like enemies.'

'You have a fair share of those,' I said.

'Yeah, it took me a lot of time and talent to make those enemies.'

'And Fernie Tomas is one of them?'

Harry grinned. 'I know him too well to be a friend,' he said.

I waited while he fooled with his cigarette. I knew he'd have something to say about Tomas.

* Large numbers (of years in prison).

190

'You think Fernie's a really subtle character-study, don't you? Young naval officer hero goes over to the enemy – all that stuff. You can't figure out anything like that, you government men. Real puzzling it must be.'

He threw the cigarettes back for me to catch. But you can't teach an old dog new tricks. I kept the .38 aimed at H.K.'s T-shirt, the cigarettes fell against the pistol and splayed across the floor. H.K. made a move towards my feet to pick them up, but seeing the gun-barrel move a fraction of an inch he thought better of it and sank back into his chair. We looked at each other; I shook my head, and H.K. smiled.

'No hits, no runs, no errors,' he said.

'Just tell me how us government men can stop being puzzled about Tomas,' I said.

'He's a malcontent,' said H.K. '"Whatever it is, I'm against it" is Fernie's motto. The only reason we didn't come to a knock-down, drag-out fight once a week was because I'm such an easy-going sort of slob. He plants an old twenty-dollar bill into the green canister just so that if anyone steps out of line he can put one from the same batch where it can do the most damage. He's a nut.'

I nodded. I thought that the twenty in H.K.'s shirt was too convenient to be true. I said, 'Everyone's against you, Harry, and yet you are such a nice guy at heart,' and I smiled. I was thinking of Joe, but I smiled at H.K.

'Round outside means a soft centre,' H.K. said with a grin.

He pointed to a cigarette near his foot. I nodded and he picked it up and lit it from his stub. 'This man isn't a martyr, idealist or intellectual. He thinks with his muscle. Guys like him work themselves into an early grave organizing wildcat strikes or breaking up political meetings. In wars they get V.C.s or court martials. Sometimes both. Fernie said he had been recommended for a D.S.A. at the time of his capture.'

'A D.S.O.,' I said.

'Well, there you are. Like I told you, no sex, no drink, no politics, a dedicated malcontent and maybe the best underwater man in Europe.'

'The best now, maybe,' I said, 'but until there was a fatal accident out on the ocean floor not too long ago, he was number two.'

H.K.'s face tightened like a clenched fist. He said, 'Fernie would never do that. I don't like the guy but he would never kill in cold blood, believe me.'

'All right,' I said, 'we'll leave that for a minute. Tell me how da Cunha fits into the picture. And before you start: I'm not a cop; my directions don't include bringing you in. I'm here for information: set up the facts and then you can fade as far as I'm concerned.'

Charly rose to her feet.

'Fade?' said Charly. 'Do you know what sort of filthy business this man is in?' She moved in on the equipment like a Luddite and swept some of it to the floor with a crash of disintegrating glass and dented tin.

I said nothing.

H.K. said, 'Sure he does, sweetheart, he's just too smart to mention it before he has all the info. he can get.'

Charly froze. She said to me, 'I'm sorry,' and sat down.

'I'm not kidding, Harry,' I said, 'I'll break you up as far as staying in Europe is concerned but I'll give you a chance to get clear.'

'I'll sing,' said H.K., 'what do you want to know?'

'Who is da Cunha?' I asked.

'Boy, you're really skipping the easy ones,' he said. 'Da Cunha; they think a lot of him hereabouts. He says he's the V.N.V. agent for the district. He says that when the revolution comes he will be the Governor of the district.'

'But you don't believe him.'

'One Fascist bastard is much like another as far as I'm concerned.'

'Meaning?'

'Meaning that I have paid him a sum of three hundred dollars per month via a New York bank in exchange for a promise that the new government won't snoop too close around here.'

'Insurance?'

'Yes, that's it. I could afford to throw him a little dough on the off-chance – a load of good it did me, eh?'

'Don't be bitter, Harry,' I said. He kneaded his brown face with a hairy hand, and as his eyes and nose emerged from the open fingers he smiled a humourless smile.

'And Fernie,' I said, 'how did he get along with da Cunha?'

'O.K. Nothing special. Just O.K. is all.'

'Did you ever go into a room and hear a snatch of conversation between them that you weren't supposed to hear? Any scientific talk, for instance?'

'Loads of times, but it was never anything special.'

'That's all,' I said, 'we'll play it your way. You think you're the blue paper in my potato crisps, but I can work you over my way and still have enough left to shovel up for the Lagos cops.'

'F'r instance,' said H.K., but his voice was a little hoarse.

'Well, I'll tell you, Harry, if we can't have a gentlemanly chat I'll warm up a nice big dessertspoonful of warm water and lactose and give you a generous ten per cent dose of the stuff in that pulverizer over there …'

'Just try,' said H.K.

'You've got me mixed up with those weedy accents that play policemen on English TV, Harry,' I said. 'I *will* try.'

There was a short sharp silence.

'I'm not a hop-head,' said H.K. His tan had disappeared now. 'A ten per cent dose will kill me.' He folded his arms tightly.

'You may swell a little but you'll survive for the second dose and the others until I hand you over to the cops. Then you can rest until I call back for you in a week's time. You'll talk, Harry, believe me. Just look upon it as sales research – it's probably tax-deductible.'

Harry's head sank forward and he rocked gently in his seat as he tried to wake up in a morning in which I did not exist.

When he continued to speak it was in an impersonal monotone, like an announcer with a weather report which he didn't believe. 'Fernie worked for da Cunha. Fernie had a great respect for him. Even after we had enough money not to worry, Fernie would continue to say "sir" to him. Fernie had contacts all over the world, and they all liked him. Maybe you find that hard to believe, but it's true. Fernie had only to whisper about something he wanted done and, bingo, it was done. Fernie arranged the supplies of the morphine base, I processed and arranged sales.'

'How did the morphine base arrive?' I asked.

'By ship once a month. The ships didn't stop. Only an expert frogman could do it. We went out in the boat and then Fernie used his frogman gear and a powered undersea sled to get under the hull of the moving ship and remove the container that was held on the bilge keel by magnetic clamps. We processed the stuff here and sealed it into sardine-cans. Then Fernie fixed the consignment to a ship heading Stateside. I notified my contacts in New York. They gave the ship time to clear customs, then had a frogman go under it while it was at the quayside and prise the horse loose. Easy. How am I doing?'

'You are doing O.K.,' I said. 'Your boat; did Fernie ever use that?'

'Sure, he was a mile better sailor than I'll ever be. He borrowed it whenever he wanted to. It was da Cunha borrowing it that made me sore. I'd never trust the old guy alone, I don't care if he was an *admiral* in the Kraut navy.'

'Did they always use a similar amount of fuel?'

'Yeah,' said H.K., 'I checked on that out of curiosity. They went up the coast about twelve miles, give a little, take a little.'

'Tell me more about da Cunha,' I said.

'Da Cunha rides around the town in that old 1935 Ford like it was a Thunderbird. Thinks he owns the town. He closes his eyes; it's night. When he sends Tomas along to borrow the boat it's like he's doing me a favour. Da Cunha; wise guy. One day I get here; he's loading himself a crate of sardines. "I've gotcha red-handed," I say, smiling like I might be joking. "Better the red face than the black heart, Mister Kondit," he says – an old Portuguese saying it is, he says. "So who cares?" I say. "I do," he says, "and I'm the only one," and off he drives with the sardines.

'He's in deep with the local church, and last week there was a gang of business tycoons down from Madrid. Whatever he intends to do for Portugal it certainly won't include moving the average wage up from four dollars a week.' H.K. raised his head and said, 'You're not kidding me about letting me scram, are you? Because if I'm shooting my mouth off for nothing …'

'No,' I said, 'you can talk your way out as far as I'm concerned.'

'Boat and all?' asked H.K.

'Boat and all,' I said.

'I bet that da Cunha's V.N.V. is a local branch office of the Young Europe machine. You know what I'm talking about?'

'Talk on,' I said.

'It's a network of Fascists throughout Europe, Rabat to Narvik. The O.A.S. in France, the Belgian M.A.C. As far as these boys are concerned the present régime here in Portugal is Socialist.'

'What can you offer as proof?'

'Not a thing, pal. I wish I had something, it's been my big dream to iron him out.'

'Looks like you're too late now,' I said.

'The Fascists will tumble; historically it's all part of the class struggle.'

'Class struggle,' I said, 'that's hilarious, coming from you. You are the spokesman for the Hopheads and General Narcotic Dealers' Union?'

'Yeah, the dope outfit – I'm the chief dope,' said H.K.

H.K.'s eyes held mine. I decided to try a bluff. 'The English visitor,' I coaxed gently, 'don't forget the English visitor, Harry.'

'Pal of Fernie's,' H.K. said. 'Nice little guy, great sense of fun.'

'His name?'

'Ivor Butcher,' said H.K., 'great sense of fun.'

'*Great* sense of fun,' I said. Now it was shuffling its way together. Ivor Butcher knew Fernie. A messenger? A courier? Did Smith tell Fernie what to do or was it the other way round? In either case: why?

I looked around at the darkened factory: the oily machinery, the great piles of tins.

'Harry,' I said, 'I want Fernie Tomas here; get him here and you can go.'

H.K. sucked his cheeks in and snorted a laugh down his nose. 'You can get him as easily as I can,' he said, 'you don't have to rub my face in the dirt.' He walked across to the sink and washed his hands with the strange flecked Portuguese soap that looks like Roquefort cheese, dried them, put on his wrist-watch and turned to face us. 'You did the hero bit already, pal. Now I'm walking out of here, hardware or no hardware.'

'You think so,' I said, but I did nothing as he walked across to the chair and picked up his cashmere cardigan, and nothing as he walked down between the machines towards the door. He looked back once to see how I was reacting. I put my gun into my jacket pocket and he looked reassured. It was then that a flash roared across the tension and echoed through the piles of empty tins like a *piranha* in a goldfish bowl. Charly had fished a pistol out of her handbag and let fly at H.K. I saw him spin around and fall forward against the pressing machine. I reached out to take the gun from her. The gun crashed again and the heat bent the hairs on the back of my hand. The bullet nicked the machinery with a clang and whined off into the darkness. My hand closed over the barrel to drag it from her, but it was hot enough to burn me and I dropped it with a crash. I flung my arm around Charly and held her captive.

From behind the machinery H.K.'s voice asked, 'Where did that loony dame get a gun?'

I looked at the old Italian Victoria 7.65 automatic on the floor. 'Out of a Christmas cracker by the look of it,' I said. 'Now beat it, fade, before I change my mind.'

Charly beat her fists against my button-down madras and yelled, 'Don't let him go – he killed your friend!' over and over again. She stopped to draw breath. 'You just aren't human,' she said quietly. I held her tightly while H.K. limped away with a big red hand clamped across his forearm.

I sat Charly down. Finally she blew her nose into my hand-kerchief and told me that she worked for the Federal Bureau of Narcotics, Washington, and that I had just messed everything up. It was her damaged esprit de corps she was crying about as she sat in Harry Kondit's dream house.

'Then you knew that the smell of vinegar was acetic acid and would be coming from the processing of morphine. Why didn't you tell me the real story?'

She blew her nose again. 'Because a good operator lets other law-enforcement agencies spearhead his actions,' she quoted between sniffs.

At that precise moment we heard H.K. start the engine. 'He's taking *our* car,' said Charly, 'we're going to be left here.' She began to giggle.

It was a little over three kilometres to Albufeira. We skirted the huge plantation of fig trees and smelt the olive crop ready for the press. Charly took her shoes off after one kilometre and stopped sniffing after two. For the fiftieth time she said, 'You've let him get away. I must phone the police.'

'Look,' I finally said, 'I don't know what they teach you in the Treasury Department,* but if you think your prestige there depends on putting the iron bangles across H.K. you are quite nutty. Let him go spread panic among his pals. If he goes to the end of the world you can be there in a day or phone there in an hour. This is a strictly cerebral business and just because I wave an old war-souvenir pistol around to impress you, it doesn't mean you have to go off your trolley. You might hurt him.'

This last remark stung Charly into a fury and she said I was just as bad as H.K. As for hurting H.K., if it hadn't been for me getting in the way she would have killed him and a good thing too.

You can't help envying these narcotics sleuths. The governments of the world are all so keen to prove themselves blameless that, far from asking awkward questions about firearms,

---

* Treasury Department, U.S.A., controls Narcotics Bureau and Secret Service. In 1959 in Naples, where she lived with her parents (her father was R.N. attached to NATO), she had been recruited into the department. The endless round of parties she attended made her a useful ear for the Narcotics Bureau.

they will steady up your gun elbow while you're firing. I couldn't afford luxuries like remembering that H.K.'s desire to remove the evidence had certainly killed Joe MacIntosh.

My position wasn't quite so pretty. I couldn't have Charly phoning up the police and attracting attention to our enterprise. At least not before I contacted Singleton, folded up the equipment and faded out. I began to be aware of a silence and realized that Charly had asked me a question. 'Umm,' I said, as though I was considering it carefully.

'It's so confusing, isn't it?' Charly said.

'Confusing,' I replied, 'of course it's confusing. You involve yourself in industrial espionage and then you complain about it being confusing.'

'What do you mean?' said Charly. 'I'm not involved with industrial espionage.'

'Aren't you?' I said. 'Narcotics is a multi-million-dollar industry. Half of that industry is devoted to making money, the other half to making you confused.' There was a silence. 'In one way or another,' I added.

'Just exactly what does that last crack mean?'

'It means authority can be confused in many ways, by bribes, codes, camouflage, false informers or even by pressures so powerful that the law can be changed to suit the lawbreaker. But the most confusing thing of all is old-fashioned lying by old liars: like H.K.'

'Why, was a lot of what he said untrue?' She stopped in the centre of the road and pulled her shoes on again.

'Yes,' I said, 'but like all first-class lies it had a firm foundation of truth, like margarine with twelve and a half per cent butter.'

'What did he say that was true?' asked Charly.

'Well, suppose you get those smart boys at the Treasury Department to work it out for you. I'll just say he didn't leave us in any doubt about the way our investigations should continue. Providing that we want it tailored one hundred per cent to the convenience of Harry Kondit.'

'Yes,' said Charly obediently, and she hugged my arm. I wish I had listened to my last remark more closely.

45 Man and boy are this

It was damn nice of H.K. to leave the car outside Number 12 Praca Miguel Bombarda. Charly said that it looked as though we had collected a parking fine. Which was Charly's idea of a joke; the white envelope under the wiper was a note from H.K.:

> Sorry to hijack the sled but when you got to go, you got to go. I didn't think you were levelling with me when you promised; but like I said, when winter comes you find which trees are the evergreens!
>
> Al Content [obviously H.K.'s guarded way of naming Fernie] is moving like a scalded cat. What you said I could take I ain't taking but you can bet Charly's pants that Al wants it instead. [This could only mean the power boat.]
>
> What I didn't tell you is that Al has the sweetest blackmail set-up of all time and do I mean all time. If the name Weiss List means anything to you you'll know I ain't kidding.
>
> Watch what I ain't taking and you will get your file closed – AND HOW!!
>
> Yours in a million years,
>
> HARRY

Singleton was not expected back from Lisbon for another twenty-four hours. Anything to be done had to be done alone. I went into Joe's old room and prised up a floorboard with one of the kitchen knives.

'What are you doing?' asked Charly. I told her to buzz off and fix some strong tea. I was feeling very tired what with one thing and another.

From under the floorboard I got the small radio transmitter with which Joe had contacted London. I set it to transmit, raised the antenna and set the cipher numbers on the Kurier.* I cranked the handle at twenty-three minutes past the hour (as our arrangement with R.N. Gibraltar demanded) and then put the apparatus away.

Charly brought tea. I told her I had sent a signal to London and she was now free to take any action she wished in respect of the narcotics processing. I also cautioned her that under the Official Secrets Act any mention of the operation in which we had been engaged at Albufeira was actionable, and that if there was any reason to suspect her of indiscretion in this respect her employment by the Federal Narcotics Bureau in the U.S.A. made her liable for trial as an agent of a foreign power. I thanked her for the tea and gave her a reassuring and not too brotherly kiss.

'You must row me out to H.K.'s boat,' I said. I was dog-tired.

Charly brought the dinghy alongside the forty-foot cabin cruiser with skill befitting an admiral's daughter. I scrambled on to the teak-laid deck in my stockinged feet – I couldn't risk leaving wet footmarks across it. Charly spun the dinghy round and rowed back to the cove. I watched the cliff-top and willed

* See Appendix 5.

Fernie Tomas not to appear until she was over the headland by the steep high path. Then I walked across the bridge and got into the big stowage locker under one of the extra bunks. It was a bit coffin-like, but I jammed a pencil under the lid, which gave me air, although not enough to dispel the smell of tar and mothballs. I waited.

Something struck the side of the boat with a thud. It wasn't very Royal Navy and I began to wonder whether it was Fernie Tomas. Perhaps H.K. had lured me into a trap. I flushed with sudden fear at the thought of this locker really becoming a coffin.

A woman's voice – Fernie's wife – gabbled in Portuguese, the dinghy was drifting away. Hold the rope. Couldn't he help her. Take the suitcase. There is water in the bottom of the boat. An oar has slipped into the water. The conversation went the way it does when women are in boats.

I heard Fernie's voice telling her to hurry in rapid Portuguese. Reassuring and direct. I realized why he had been so taciturn when I had seen him before. His Portuguese had a strong English accent. There were splashes and thumps, and then a third voice, rather higher than Fernie's, which spoke least of the three. They seemed to be an age getting aboard, and then I heard the woman's voice, this time from some way off. She was returning to the shore in the dinghy. There was a click as someone switched on the small light over the controls. If I held my face horizontal, with my ear pressed against the cold locker-lid, my left eye had a narrow range of vision that included the top half of the person at the controls.

I could see Fernie in profile – the egg-shaped head with its black domed moustache hanging over the mouth. Upon his head was the black trilby hat of the peasant. The anchor came up like a curtain and the motors beat a drum-roll as we began the last act at Albufeira. Fernie engaged the screws and I felt the water thrash under the hull. The light above his head threw his eye sockets in black piratical patches. His hands moved across the controls, articulate and smooth, his head watched the beams, the compass, the rev. counters. This was a Fernie I had never seen, Fernie at sea, Fernie the sailor. From the seat at the controls he couldn't see the ship's clock. Every few moments he would call to the boy with him, 'What time is it?' and the boy would tell him.

He moved the throttles as far forward as they could go and at 3,000 r.p.m. the hull began hammering against the water like a pneumatic drill. When he was satisfied with the course, Fernie told the boy to hold the wheel steady. I heard the clicks of a suitcase being unlocked. I pushed my ear harder against the lid of the locker and raised it two inches. The boy was staring into the dark, while Fernie crouched on the floor over a radio chassis into which he was pushing small valves. Then his footsteps clattered down the saloon staircase and he reappeared with a black cable from the 24-volt supply to which he connected the radio machinery. He shouted, 'Port – keep the lubber line on 240.' The boy he had brought aboard was Augusto, who had secured a lock of Fernie's hair for me.

Augusto sat on the high stool like a child at a tea-party, holding the wheel tightly between his small grubby hands. Fernie spoke in Portuguese about 'the strong American at the railway station'; it must have been a question, for Augusto said that 'the strong American' (which was what the local people called H.K.) had unloaded a crate of sardines at the station to be put on the morning train to Lisbon.

There was a click and Augusto was bathed in reflected light as Tomas moved the beam of the big searchlight out across the waves. Slivers of rain and water droplets snipped at Augusto's halo as the boat slammed into the swell and the sound of shipped water rushed along the deck outside. The little radio had warmed up and emitted a high-pitched note like a badly adjusted TV set. Tomas reappeared; his hand was on the radio. He tuned it. 'Make it 245,' he shouted above the noise.

I felt the boat vibrate as it turned at high speed. So far, and then it straightened again.

Tomas's hand came into my view and he moved the radio. The signal it was receiving became stronger. '250,' he shouted, and in his excitement broke into a gabble of Portuguese as he demanded that Augusto should give it more throttle. Augusto said it was as far advanced as it could get, and he pushed at the big levers with his child's hands in order to prove it. Suddenly from the radio came a sound like 'The Flight of the Bumble Bee' played at double speed on a flute. Tomas put the set down roughly and moved out of my sight. Augusto's head was one moment illuminated by an intense light-beam and the next moment drawn in dark silhouette against the bright heaving water.

Tomas was sweeping the ocean, looking for something in the roaring foam. The something was a metal container.

The flute-like sounds of the high-speed Morse stopped and the steady whistle replaced it. There was a cracking sound, and for some minutes I puzzled over it. It was difficult to imagine an ex-R.N. officer slapping his own face in Latin excitement and anger. 'Too late!' he shouted to Augusto, 'too late, too late, too late, it's down again to the sea bed.' He snatched the wheel from Augusto and spun it viciously. The boat slid sideways, uncontrolled, the propellers screaming to get a hold on the water as the deck heeled over towards the dark sea.

It was unfortunate that I chose that moment to emerge. I fell forward, sprawling across the deck with my knees still trapped in the locker. My face walloped against the starboard bunk, my arm twisted under me, and I heard my Smith & Wesson pistol slide forward and drop with a crash into the saloon. 'Steady amidships,' I heard Fernie call, and the deck came level.

'Get on your feet,' Fernie said, like something out of a Greyfriars school story. I wasn't too keen to get on my feet if it meant I was to be knocked down. On the other hand, lying there could earn me a slam on the kisser too.

'I don't want to fight you, Fernie,' I said.

'I'm going to kill you,' said Fernie. He didn't say it like a killer but like a prefect about to administer a thrashing.

'You are making a mistake, Fernie,' I said. But it was no use; when a man has fitted into the system as badly as Fernie had done, he has stock-piled spite and sadness, rage and revenge, until violence has built up under the surface like boiling lava.

Augusto had the boat on an even keel; he throttled back slightly. Fernie faced me across the bridge. He advanced slowly, keeping an even balance. His eyes stared into mine, sizing me up and judging my probable actions. We were an arm's length apart when his hands moved slowly and easily upward. He put his hands higher than his waist and I detected a very slight turn of the shoulders. It told me what I wanted to know. Punching fighters hold themselves in a boxing stance, one hand and one foot slightly advanced. Judo fighters stand flat. Fernie was a left-handed puncher.

A rivulet of sea-water meandered across the deck, caught the light and became a scimitar under Fernie's feet. I opened my left hand and advanced it in a protective, flinching manner across my chest and towards his rocksteady advanced right fist.

I watched his eyes deciding that I was going to be a push-over. He decided to clip me with a short left jab. My body was wide open. My fingers closed upon his advanced cuff, as my left toe kicked his right ankle under him. Fernie grabbed at my extended left knee to spin me to the ground. It was the correct counter but he was slow, far too slow. Before I had pulled his sleeve more than an inch to the left he'd lost balance. A man off balance thinks of nothing but getting balanced again; aggression disappears. He began to fall. My left hand pulled and continued to pull as I turned to my left. Right hand high. My turn was complete, right armpit clamped upper arm, left hand threatened his ulnar and radius bones. I heard a sharp intake of breath against my ear, and saw Augusto's face turn towards us, his eyes like Belisha beacons.

Even at that instant Fernie did not allow the pain to influence him. He kicked. The radio set slid across the deck slowly, and gently fell over the side. There was a flash as the cable from the batteries shorted and a thud as the radio swung against the hull. At a slower speed, perhaps the radio would still have been plugged on the end when we hauled the cable in.

He was a character, this Fernie. He fell away and sat on the floor rubbing the arm I had so nearly broken. He said, 'You know I could just throw you overboard – and no one could ask any questions?'

'Sure,' I said, 'but there is just the chance that I'll wring your neck while you're trying.'

The electric cable had wrapped around the port screw, Augusto said. I heaved Fernie below into the cabin and into a bunk – he was too old for this sort of caper, he was badly shook up. I told Augusto to head back to Albufeira, using only the starboard motor. It would be a slow journey and the wind was backing against the dawn sun. This floating Cadillac was no sort of boat to face bad weather in. I retrieved my pistol, put it away and went across to Tomas.

'I've got a Portuguese passport,' Tomas said.

'When you are in Tarrafal* you might wish you had some other sort of passport.'

'I've served my time in prison; I don't have to put up with the British Gestapo around my neck for the rest of my life.'

'That doesn't have to be too long,' I said. 'If you peddle narcotics across the world you must expect to attract a little attention. It's captious to complain afterwards.'

'Save your lies for when you write your report,' said Tomas. 'You aren't interested in narcotics.'

'No? What am I interested in, then?'

'You're interested in the "Weiss List", the item I nearly tugged out of the ocean a few minutes ago.'

'That's exactly right,' I told him, 'I am.'

'It's lost,' he said, 'lost for all time. You can never get it.'

'But you know what it consisted of?' Tomas's face went grey – he was frightened and he didn't take fright easily.

'Let me help you remember,' I said. 'I'll tell you one name that was on it.' I named Smith. Tomas said nothing. 'The man that you and your friend Ivor Butcher decided to blackmail,' I prompted.

'You know about Butcher,' said Tomas. 'Leave him out of it. He's just a nice little fellow trying to help me. He's not to blame.'

'He's not, eh?' I said, but I didn't disillusion him.

I sat down. I was as limp as a Dali watch.

Fernie tugged at his moustache, paused and then said, 'I was the only survivor from the U-boat. I thought at first …'

'Look, Fernie,' I said, 'I seldom interrupt people when they're talking; especially when they are inventing complicated

* A Portuguese political prison on the equatorial island, Santiago, 300 miles off the coast of Africa.

lies, because they are often far more interesting than the truth. However, for you I'll make an exception; start telling the truth or I'll sling you over the side.'

'Very well,' said Fernie affably, 'where shall I start?'

'You can forget all that fairy-story stuff about dead sailors washed up with sovereign dies and digging graves to prove it. Also forget any nonsense about your career in the U-boat. Unless you know what caused it to sink.'

'No,' said Fernie, 'I don't know that.'

'Did your friend da Cunha deliberately open the valves before he rowed ashore with the "Weiss List"?'

'No,' said Fernie quietly, 'he would never do anything like that. He is a man of great honour.'

'Sure,' I said, 'you all are; you, Kondit and da Cunha. An honourable bunch of thugs. Look, Peterson' – it was the first time I had used his English name – 'you're just trying to kick a step out of a moving staircase. Behind me is another agent, behind him another. I'm a soft touch compared with some of the yahoos that are going to descend on you in any part of the world you go. All they want back in Whitehall is a nice clean file with the word "Closed" written across the front so that they can put it in the cellar. Try to be a bit sensible and I'll write a little note about what a help you have been. You never know when a little billet doux like that could be useful.'

'What do you want to know?' he said.

'I don't know what it is that's missing until I hear it; if there are any bits you don't want to tell me, miss them out.'

'Very cunning,' said Tomas, 'the gaps tell you more than the story in between.'

'Sure,' I said, 'I'm the Attorney-General travelling incognito with a Japanese tape-recorder under my toupee. Or it could just be that you are a little on the paranoiac side.'

Fernie sipped at the big glass of whisky I had given him.

He said, 'Do you remember the Spanish Civil War? Do you remember the newsreels? Dead horses, wounded babies.' He removed a fleck of tobacco from his lip. 'Frightened, I was so frightened. People like you don't understand. Do you?' he said. He wanted a reply.

I said, 'As long as you don't say it's my lack of imagination.'

He went on staring into space and smoking. 'That was this same Spanish Civil War that H.K. said you were a hero of?' I said.

Fernie Tomas nodded. For a moment I thought he was going to smile.

'Yes, I was there. There are times you're so frightened of something that you have to make it happen sooner. I was just someone who wanted to come to grips with my trauma. Everyone I knew who had volunteered had gone to fight for the government; so I went to fight for Franco just to be different. They posted me to an Italian unit. I was with General Queipo de Llano's second division at the fall of Malaga. Kondit thought I was *defending* Malaga. He liked it that way so I never disillusioned him.'

'You didn't like it?' I said.

'Yes. I used to lie on the beach watching the cruisers *Canarias*, *Almirante Cervera* and *Baleares* come up to bombard Malaga. It was just like an exercise, a crash and a puff of smoke and then after a couple of hours they would clear off down the coast again for dinner. It was pretty. Nice clean boats. Nice impersonal fight. No view of what you are hitting. No one trying to hit you. It was a gentleman's war. When we got into Malaga … well, you've seen a town after bombardment.'

'Who hasn't nowadays?' I said.

'That's right,' said Tomas. 'I remember …', but he didn't go on. It was as though he were dragging it out of a crystal ball.

'I remember,' he said again, 'the last time I saw my old lady. I got compassionate leave because our house was bombed. The old man died of his injuries and my mother was living in the kitchen with a tarpaulin rigged across the ceiling. She didn't want to go to a rest centre because of "all the happy times she'd had there".'

'Happy times.' He shook his head as he remembered. 'It was a slum, and she'd worked herself half to death there. She kept saying that they'd taken the old man to a hospital in "a proper ambulance, not one of these A.R.P. things", she said, "it was a proper ambulance". Well, that's what Malaga was like; dead, swollen horses and a smell of brick-dust and drains.'

I could see that in some curious way the destruction in Malaga and London had fused into one, and he wouldn't be able to sort them out. I remembered how, when he was arrested, he had said that it was all the same war. I wondered about that.

'When I came back I joined the British Fascist Movement. I met Mosley in person. He's a much misunderstood man, that Mosley, dynamic and honest. All the really Machiavellian supporters of the B.U.F. had seen the war coming for years and they buried themselves deep in the Conservative Party. Half the boys that give you your orders from Whitehall and gave us all those rousing anti-Nazi speeches were kicking themselves rotten that they didn't have a nice big armament factory in Germany. But we were simple-minded idealists. Later, the war, and more especially the Molotov-Ribbentrop Pact, had changed our minds. I stopped trying to understand it. I went into the Navy as a telegraphist and then got a commission …'

'Was that difficult for you?' I asked.

'No,' said Tomas, 'anyone who bought a pipe, a pair of

pyjamas and walked around with Penguin books about Paul Nash was singled out as officer material.'

'No, I meant difficult on account of your having been so political.'

'If they'd kept out the politicals in 1940 there wouldn't have been enough recruits to man a dinghy. The only English people who knew the slightest thing about fighting a modern war were the people who had been in Spain.'

'Yes, I suppose you are right,' I said.

'I went to *Prince Arthur* at Brighton and became a naval officer in four months. I loved it. You spend a long time with the same people inside a small ship. You get to know every nut and bolt of the ship and every nut and bolt of the crew. When the boat is sunk it's worse than being divorced after a happy marriage. You lose your home, your personal gear, your friends are dead, wounded or posted. You have nothing left. After the second time in the drink I wandered around the London pubs for twelve days hoping to see a face I recognized. I decided that I couldn't go through that again. I volunteered for the submarine service. If you get sunk there you stay down. But before I ever got near a submarine I found myself in Scotland, messing around with frogman gear.'

Tomas asked for a cigarette. After lighting it he said, 'You don't want to hear about frogman training?'

'Just tell me what you think is interesting.'

'You are a funny sort of bastard.'

'*Touché*,' I said.

'I had orders to report to the depot. Everything had gone wrong that Thursday; the bank manager was gunning me for a lousy £12 and the MG had plug-trouble on the Great North Road – you remember what motor spares were like during the war – and this fat swine in the garage where I stopped was fiddling some petrol for two blokes with Boston haircuts and a van full of tinned fruit. I hung around fuming, but he told me I should be grateful for one of his precious spark plugs. "I reckon it all goes to you blokes in the services nowadays," he said, as though we were living on the fat of the land. "Yes," I said to him, "it must be a tough war back home, listening to Itma and knitting socks," and then these other two got nasty and after some words he said he didn't want any money for the plug, so I left. I can remember every minute.

'It was from that time that I began to feel afraid of the deep water. I was quite O.K. diving in daylight or near the surface, but I couldn't bear working with the thought that under me there was just darker and darker depths of water until you were just swallowed up.'

Fernie Tomas shouted to Augusto to make sure he didn't forget the engine temperature, and Augusto said he wouldn't.

'You don't know what it's like on a midget,' said Tomas. It was a plain statement of fact. I didn't. 'Imagine that you've crossed the North Sea inside the bonnet of a motorcar, jammed against the engine. You dress yourself in underwater gear. Much more incredible and inefficient than modern equipment. You dress in a space much smaller than a telephone booth, and then clamber through the flooding chamber, which has a nasty habit of going wrong and leaving you jammed in a tight-fitting coffin. But you may be lucky; the hatch cover isn't jammed or fouled so you can crawl out into the ocean. You walk along the top of the midget submarine – it's not much wider than a plank and getting narrower and narrower as you move forward. The pointed bow upon which you are finally balancing is bumping with great metallic crashes against a vast anti-submarine net which stretches as far as you can see in every direction. The rungs of the net are nearly as big as a steering wheel and you hold on to one to

213

steady yourself as you wield the cutting tool. All the time the skipper keeps the motor running so that the bow will continue to nudge the net, but the deck grinds and grates and perhaps a flow of fresh water throws the buoyancy out, or rain makes it even darker than before. Your metal boots slip off the tight-rope you are on.'

Tomas rubbed his arm and shivered. 'I had a recurring nightmare in which I slipped off the deck and fell into the bottom of the sea.' He shivered again. 'So of course it happened. I grabbed the net as the submarine slid to one side. The motor had failed and the current swept it back out of control. I was alone in the sea hanging on to the net.'

Tomas rubbed his forehead and took a stiff drink. I poured him another. He said nothing until I said, 'What did you do?'

'I climbed up the net rung by rung.' Tomas's white hands clasped the blanket. 'I held on to the top of the net until a German boat came along in the morning to check it. They told me afterwards that they had to prise my fingers away from the metal to get me into the boat. I was the only survivor of the force that attacked. They gave me food and I slept the clock round in the local navy barracks. I could only speak schoolboy German, but it was enough to hold a conversation. On the second day I had dinner in the German officers' mess, and I supposed I'd had a few extra drinks to celebrate being alive. In the normal way I would have been sent to a P.O.W. camp and there the matter would have ended, except for something one of the officers said at dinner that night.

'Two bodies had floated up under the port screws of the big cruiser. They had tried to move them but there was no diving unit within a hundred miles. He said there was no option but to run the screws. He hoped I'd understand. It wasn't a thing a sailor liked to do, he said.'

Tomas sniffed and swirled his whisky around in his glass. 'I said that if they would give me my equipment back and recharge the oxygen cylinder I'd have them up in a jiffy. Everyone in the mess said what a sense of comradeship that showed – that I would do that to retrieve my friends' bodies for a ceremonial burial, which the German Navy would be honoured to give them.'

Tomas looked up at me; I hadn't smiled.

'It's easy to be cynical now and see it as a put-up job, but at that time the propaganda pundits had got us all acting like the cast of a British film. You know what I mean?'

'Don't I just,' I said.

'Anyway, they had a couple of Kriegsmarine officers accompany me and they said could they use the apparatus. I wasn't keen about that. They didn't press it. They were professionals, just as you're a professional. They knew what sort of process getting information really is.'

'Yes,' I said, 'collecting information is like making cream cheese from sour milk. If you squeeze the muslin bag to force it – it's ruined.'

'Yes, that's the way it went; they collected their information drip by drip, and all the while I was living in their officers' quarters and had a servant and good food and they were telling me not to hurry and perhaps I would like to be sure that there were no other bodies near by. After they'd had a big funeral with lots of stuff about fellow-sailors challenging the mighty ocean deep and all that, I was sent down to Cuxhaven to a P.O.W. unit. The food was ghastly and I was treated like a convict. One night, when I was feeling as low as it's possible to get, one of the German officers that I'd stayed with in Norway visited me, together with a man named Loveless.'

'Graham Loveless?' I asked. It was Smith's nephew.

'Yes,' said Tomas. 'I told them that I had been a member of the British Union of Fascists. They said that if I joined the Legion of Saint George (what was later called the Britische Freikorps) they could arrange that I lived with German naval officers. They said that I would only be called upon to use the underwater equipment to save life or property or against our mutual enemy – the sea.'

Tomas looked at me and shrugged.

'And you fell for it?' I said.

'I fell for it,' said Tomas.

'Then you met Giorgio Olivettini?'

Tomas didn't fall into the trap; he walked into it slowly and deliberately. He looked at me and said, 'Yes, I saw him soon after that. He told you?'

I tried a simple lie. 'I guessed,' I said, 'when I saw you on the U-boat the night Giorgio died.'

'That was you, was it?' said Tomas. 'Yes, I sometimes did a night swim for pleasure.'

I knew he was lying. He had obviously been out doing his heroin-delivery service that night, but I said nothing.

I poured a drink for both of us; the whisky helped Tomas to relax. He finally said, 'It was a Moray eel.'

I offered him some ice from the refrigerator. 'It was a Moray,' he said again. I put a cube into his glass and two cubes into my own. 'It was a Moray,' Tomas screamed as loud as he could scream, 'a Moray, do you hear?'

'O.K.,' I said.

'They tear you to pieces. Huge Moray eels as big as pigs, they have teeth like razors. They terrify me. There are thousands along this coast, many of them eight feet long. They live in the rocks as a rule, but these were living in the cracked pressure hull.'

I remembered the gashes across Giorgio's body. Perhaps it

was true. Tomas began to speak quickly. 'He was a lieutenant when I first met him. The Wehrmacht had a pretty low opinion of the Italian armed forces, but these frogmen were different. Everyone hung on their every word. It was funny really. Giorgio was the only person that understood what a farce the whole bloody war was. We both fought on both sides. He had a German medal and an American medal.'

'I didn't know that,' I said.

'Yes, I saw him presented with a German Eagle Order of Merit with star.'

He picked up his drink and sipped at it. 'He was a fabulous underwater man.' He drank some more. 'Kill him, I couldn't have killed him. You can't imagine a trapeze man pushing another trapeze man off the wire, could you? Well, it's like that.'

'Tell me about the period immediately before V.E. Day,' I asked him.

'You know my real name, so you have read the court martial?' asked Tomas.

'It doesn't give a clear idea,' I said.

'Loveless was a big man with the Germans,' Tomas said. 'People said that when the Germans won the war they'd make Loveless the Prime Minister of England. When Loveless said to me that it was all up, I knew it was all up. It was his idea to go to Hanover. I wanted to go farther south to the sector where the Americans were advancing, but Loveless said if we went to Hanover we wouldn't have to worry any more, so I went. There was a Wehrmacht Archive Unit in Hanover and Loveless had got permission to examine certain of the documents.

'He went to the Archives and photographed the "Weiss List".' I nodded, hoping that Tomas would explain further.

'It was about the size and shape of a paper-back novel. It

had thick grey card covers. Inside were the names of British Nationals and their addresses. They were in alphabetical order. Between each section there were plain pages with pink ruled lines for additions. Each name was that of a person who would actively assist the Germans when they invaded Britain.'

I said, 'Did Loveless think that these people would be best to negotiate a German surrender through?'

'Perhaps you are not following the story,' said Tomas. 'Loveless didn't give a damn about the Germans and the sort of surrender that they were likely to get.'

Outside it was blowing a Force 5 and in the warm, well-lit cabin it was easy to think that we were back again in that world of 1945.

Tomas poured himself another drink and shouted to Augusto to cut the engine revs, and told me that we were just wasting fuel. We agreed that Augusto was a bright boy and that the Portuguese were natural sailors, and Tomas took a generous throatful of H.K.'s firewater and continued.

'Loveless photographed the "Weiss List" (it was called that as an antonym for black list) and buried the prints in a garden in a badly bombed part of Hanover. We were held in a German prison for some time. The lights were on all the time, day and night, everything was white, tiles shining like false teeth and slamming doors that would echo like a thunderclap and the constant jangle of bunches of keys that the warders carried. Now and then the spyhole in the cell would flip open and the psychiatrist or the quack would be spying on you and you knew he was writing everything down and attributing reasons. They thought everyone was nuts except themselves. Apart from the odd eyeball the prisoners seldom saw a sign of any other human life. But now and again I would hear Loveless's voice asking the guard some foolish question in order to let me know that he was still there. I finally got a chance for a short talk with Loveless when the R.N. sent two C.P.O.s to escort us back to the U.K. He was a Commander R.N.; they were very impressed and got us cabins on the Harwich ferry. Loveless told me that he intended to go into the witness box and reel off the name of every Englishman on the "Weiss List".'

'That must have made him popular,' I said.

'They didn't want that at *any* price. They told him that if he would quietly plead guilty to the five charges they would do a deal with him.'

'A deal?' I said.

'That's right,' said Tomas. 'He was told that if he pleaded guilty he would be sentenced to death but that it wouldn't be carried out. They would declare him mentally sick.'

'Why did he believe that?'

'That's what I asked him,' said Tomas. 'I make it a point of honour never to trust anyone.' If he intended it as a joke he gave no sign; I nodded. 'After sentence,' Tomas went on, 'the President of the court martial signs the sentence of death, seals it and it's conveyed to the prisoner. But before sentence can be carried out the confirming officer examines the proceeds of the trial and ensures that no irregularities or illegalities have occurred. As you know a court martial isn't like a civil trial. Most of the people present have never had legal training or even seen a trial before. It's a shambles.'

'Luckily I'm in no position to contradict your first-hand experience,' I said, 'but continue about this deal.'

Tomas said, 'One of the things the confirming officer checks is the mental health of the prisoner. Under Section Four of the Lunacy Act of 1890, a J.P. and two medical certificates are all a confirming officer requires to *remove the record of the conviction* and send the prisoner to a civil mental hospital. Admiralty Instructions are that after one month the Admiralty shall discharge him from the service.'

'And Loveless believed that this would happen to him if he pleaded guilty?'

'He did; you see, someone brought his daily medical reports and let him burn them. He was told that they would post-date others to show a symptom of mental trouble.'

'You didn't ask for the same treatment?' I asked.

'No,' said Tomas, 'the officer preparing my summary of evidence before the trial mentioned the "Weiss List", but I pretended that I didn't know what he was talking about.'

'Was Loveless tried before you?' I asked.

'Yes, he pleaded guilty, was sentenced to death and came down to his cell. They weren't ready to start my hearing, but next day they began. Then that night, the night of the first day of my trial, it happened.'

'What happened?' I asked.

Tomas wiped his hands on a handkerchief with a dozen darns in it, sipped his drink and eased his shoulders back on the pillow as though about to doze off. I went closer and leaned across him.

'What happened?' I said again. Tomas had his eyes closed, he winced from the pain either of arm or memory.

He said very quietly, 'I heard Loveless screaming, he was shouting, "help me Bernie, help me," and then there were the footsteps and jangle of a guard running and I heard a low voice that I think was the chaplain, I couldn't hear what he said. Then I heard Graham's voice again. It was high-pitched and more distinct than the others. "They're going to hang me, Bernie," he shouted, then he shouted "help me" again. There was a jangle of keys and a door clanged and it was all quiet.'

'Did you shout to him?' I asked.

'No,' said Tomas. 'I've thought about it, perhaps every day

of my life since. But what could I say – "I told you so", or "hold on I'm coming", or "it's all for the best" – what could I have shouted at him?'

'That's right,' I said, 'there wasn't much you could say, they hanged him anyway.'

Somehow I knew it was all true.

46 Little else to give

Tomas and I sat looking at each other for a long time. When I finally said it I let it come as casual as can be. 'So when you came out of prison you took a trip to a suburb in Hanover and bought a spade?'

'I'd have needed more than a spade,' said Tomas. 'When I got back there I went to the house where Loveless had buried the "Weiss List". The whole place was one great twelve-storey block of workers' flats.'

'So how did you get it?'

'You make me laugh,' said Tomas. I found it difficult to believe. 'Don't you realize even now that we have been outsmarted by a man who is cleverer than both of us put together?'

'Go on,' I said.

'One man has access to that "Weiss List", to the only copy that remains in existence. One man went to a lot of trouble to get it and even more to putting it somewhere where only he can get it.' He paused; after a long silence he said, 'The papers are inside a German Naval meteorological buoy* on

---

* These buoys were dropped into the ocean by German ships and planes during World War 2. Every twelve hours they came to the surface and transmitted a radio message. The message was a reading from the meteorological gear inside it. In this way the German met. service prepared forecasts based upon a large number of weather reports without sending ships or aircraft anywhere near.

the sea bed. To service the buoy one needed to have a radio *recall* unit which "called" the buoy to the surface by transmitting a radio signal to it.'

'And that's what you were trying to do just now.'

'No,' said Fernie, 'that unit that da Cunha gave me was only a *listening* unit. We heard the buoy on the surface just as Senhor da Cunha heard it and gloated over it every evening. He had given me the *listening* unit.' Tomas's voice went very quiet. 'He'd tricked me again.' He looked up at me sharply. 'It's back on the bottom of the ocean now!'

I nodded. 'Tell me about Smith,' I said.

'Smith was only *one*,' Tomas went on, 'da Cunha forced a lot of people on the "Weiss List" to send him money or gifts.'

'But *you* soon got the idea,' I supplemented, '*you* told Smith to arrange supplies of morphine so that your little partnership with Kondit would flourish.'

'It wasn't hard to guess, I suppose.' Tomas nodded.

I said, 'What did da Cunha do with the money?' There was no reply. I said, 'Did he finance the Young Europe Movement? Did it all go to present-day Fascist groups?'

Tomas closed his eyes, 'Yes,' he said, 'I'm still a believer.'

'And to finance his ice-melting laboratory experiments?'

'Like many great men,' said Tomas, 'Senhor da Cunha has some childish weaknesses. His ice-melting machine is one of them.' His eyes were still closed.

Augusto's voice from the wheelhouse sounded above the beat of the sea. We were nearing the coast.

'I'll come up,' said Tomas. As he said it there was a thump like a heavy hammer being swung against the hull. 'A piece of flotsam,' said Tomas. Augusto had brought the throttles back to half-speed. Again there was a thump and a third immediately after. Augusto coughed and then fell down the ladder into the cabin. I caught him. Augusto was limp as he slid to the floor. The front of my suit was soaked in blood. Augusto's blood.

Tomas and I stood motionless as we processed the possibilities through our brains. I was thinking of nautical mishaps, but Tomas had a more practical bent. He knew the person concerned.

'It's Harry Kondit,' he said. The boat purred gently towards the shore.

'Where?' I said.

'Firing his target rifle from the cliff-top,' said Tomas. There were two more thumps and now, listening for it, I heard the gun crack a long way away. The floor was slippery with blood.

Tomas was as calm as a Camembert. He said, 'If we go up to the wheelhouse we get shot. If we stay here the boat heaves itself on to the cliff at Tristos and we drown.' The boat lurched against the swell.

'Can we get to the rudder control without going across the deck?'

'Too slow, in this sort of sea we have to do something quick.'

Without Augusto at the helm the boat was slopping and slipping beam-on to the sea. It was a plywood boat. I imagined it hitting the rocks and changing to firewood at one swipe. Augusto had stuffed a signal flag into his mouth. He bit on it hard instead of screaming through his punctured lung.

Tomas was carrying the little refrigerator across the cabin, and up the four steps. How he lifted it I have no idea. It thumped into the wheelhouse and then Tomas climbed to the bridge, using it as a shield. He pushed it forward and I heard a great echoing clang as one of Harry Kondit's bullets glanced off the metal. Tomas was lying full-length on the deck by now, with the lowest part of the control wheel in his hand. He pulled it and the boat began to answer. Through the port-hole I could see the rocks. They were very close, and after each great wave the water ran off the jagged fangs like a drooling monster awaiting its prey.

The boat was well into the turn now. I shouted to Tomas to come back in; he yelled, 'Do you want to go round and round in a bloody circle?' He stayed where he was. Again there was a slam of metal hitting metal. The door of the refrigerator fell open and coke bottles, ice and smoked salmon came sliding down into the cabin.

As soon as we were round far enough Tomas jammed a footstool into the wheel. He began to crawl back, but he had left it too late. The change of course that had reprieved the boat sentenced Tomas to death. The refrigerator was no longer a shield. H.K. pumped bullet after bullet into him; but with those Zeiss $\times$ 4 telescopic sights, one would have been enough.

47 Relinquish

A dozen spent 7-mm. rimless cartridge shells on the cliff-top was the only trace of H.K. in the vicinity by the time we had anchored the power boat. The weather had dragged the cloud base and the barometer well down, the fishermen were working on nets scattered along the strand like huge discarded nylons.

I went up the beach to get Charly. Augusto needed a doctor quickly. When I reached the top of the steps I looked down from the high balcony. Augusto was still on the boat with eyes unseeing and his mind in neutral; he was holding Fernie Tomas's hand very tightly. He wouldn't let go.

Charly was at the café with two plain-clothes pidemen.[*] She took the death of Fernie Tomas in her stride and wrote it into the narcotics investigation smoothly enough to allow me to escape entanglement.

After what Fernie had told me, a lot of the unrelated ends began to tie themselves together. Not all of them did, of course, but that was too much to expect. There would always be unexplainable actions by unpredictable people, but the motives began to show. I knew, for instance, what we would find up at da Cunha's house, but I went anyway.

[*] P.I.D.E.: Internal Police for the Defence of the State, i.e. Secret Police.

The furniture was shrouded and my footfalls echoed and creaked round the bookless shelves. Some of the big chandeliers were burning bloodshot in the bright daylight. I went upstairs, searching for the sort of room that I knew must be there. I had to break the lock in order to open it. The heavy oak door moved grudgingly. It was a long room, painted white. Fluorescent lights hung over the benches and a lot of equipment remained, showing that it had been a well-equipped laboratory.

This wasn't a hasty hole-in-a-corner pharmacy like the one H.K. had assembled in a spare corner of his factory. It was a large air-conditioned research lab. of the type that pharmaceutical companies build instead of paying income tax. I moved along the benches, looking at the meters, test-tubes, and electric vibrators. I examined the radiant-heat machinery and the complex array of thermometers for measuring conductivity of liquids. I didn't find Senhor Manuel Gambeta do Rosario da Cunha, because he had been gone for a long time.

Clive Singleton had returned from Lisbon in time to be told to pack everything up and head right back again.

I told him that he had the most important task of all. He would be returning the underwater gear to London. It would cost me more than I cared to think about if anything happened to it. Charly was enjoying her performance as the narcotics investigator and Clive Singleton was more than ever her devoted slave.

I phoned London on the open line. I told them to have Ivor Butcher shadowed. Use Tinkle Bell, I told them. They said he wasn't very good as a tail, but I told them that we all have to learn. 'Suppose Butcher tries to leave the country?' London said.

'Take him in on a holding charge,' I told them patiently.

'What charge?' they asked.

'Try the Street Offences Act,' I said, and hung up irritably.

48 Ivor Butcher entertains

I stepped through the aeroplane door at London Airport and watched the rain swirling across the shiny apron. The mainplanes shed little niagaras, and the ground hostess clamped her collar in her fist and screwed up her face in the teeth of the rainstorm. Jean was waiting for me in the lounge with a heavy briefcase.

It was the beginning of a week of hard work; we had the first meeting of the Strutton Committee. It went as all first meetings go; people requiring definitions, and asking for copies of memos that had long since been lost. Dawlish and I made a good team; I turned the major objections into minor objections and Dawlish's speciality was ironing out minor objections. As these combined committees go, it was successful enough but I could see that O'Brien was going to make trouble for us. He insisted upon all kinds of procedural rigmarole hoping that Dawlish would get flustered or annoyed or both. But Dawlish had been weaned on this sort of thing. He let O'Brien talk himself to a standstill and then paused a long time before saying, 'Oh yes?' as though he wasn't sure that O'Brien had made his point. Then Dawlish made *his* point all over again in careful measured syntax as though speaking to a child. Dawlish would rather split his trousers than an infinitive. I tell you it was a pleasure to watch him handle it.

*   *   *

Bernhard was a new, intelligent youth that Charlotte Street had recruited in my absence. He was a tall, good-looking boy who wore woollen shirts, went to see films with writing on them and was apt to use one long word where eight short ones would do. I told him to start investigating all Smith's holdings. Smith employed a legal staff to wrap up his companies in holding companies, and other holding companies' companies. It would be a long task.

On Thursday morning Ivor Butcher phoned. He used one of the outside phones which was listed as a Detective Agency in the G.P.O. list. Jean said that I would see him at an S.W.7 address at 8.30 p.m.

I was busy all that afternoon. At 7.30 I closed and locked the I.B.M. machine which we used to correlate most of the secret information we held in the building. Without it our file cards were meaningless collections of street numbers, road names, photos, and data.

I'd submitted a superficial report of the Albufeira situation; I marked the Alforreca file 'closed' and submitted it to Dawlish for initialling. He chiselled his signature into the little manilla rectangle without comment, then gave the file to Alice, but his eyes never left mine.

Number 37 Little Charton Mews is one of a labyrinth of cobbled cul-de-sacs in that section of Kensington where having a garage as a living-room is celebrated by planting a rose bush in a painted barrel. Outside, two men in short lambswool coats poured whisky from a hip-flask into glasses. I tapped lightly on the brass-plated doorknocker and a man in a rubber gorilla mask opened the door. 'Come one come all,' he said. His voice vibrated and boomed inside the thin rubber.

'Popsies to the right, booze straight on.' He smelled of Algerian wine.

There was a dense scrum of party-goers – men with regimental ties and girls with velvet gloves up to the armpit.

Someone behind me was using words like 'quasi-humanist' and 'empirical' and a man who was using two hands to drink his beer said, ' ... so what; does Picasso understand *me*?'

I reached the big table at the far end. Behind it was a man with a paisley scarf inside an open-neck shirt.

He said, 'There's only gin, beer, tonic, and ...' he shook a bottle of sherry viciously, ' ... sherry.' He held it up to what light there was and said 'sherry' again. A girl with a long ivory cigarette-holder said, 'But I like my body better than I like yours.'

I took my drink and wandered off through a doorway into a tiny kitchen. A girl with smudged mascara was eating pilchards out of a tin and sobbing. I turned round. The girl who liked her body was talking about automatic chokes.

Nowhere did I see Ivor Butcher. It was just as crowded upstairs except for a small room at the end of the passage. Inside were three young men in jeans and thick sweaters. The blue TV set had its controls set to give a narrow distorted image and its sound turned down. The soft music of Mingus came from the gramophone. They turned their heads slowly towards me. One face removed its dark glasses, 'You're standing there like it's another channel, dad.'

'Sorry fellers,' I said, and closed the door on the gentle fug of reefer smoke. I finally found Ivor Butcher downstairs. In the centre of the crush half a dozen couples danced very slowly so as not to get their clothes slashed by diamond rings. Ivor Butcher was dancing rather unsteadily with a short girl who had green eyes, a large body and a small evening gown.

'Great to see you pal,' Ivor Butcher said in a slurred voice. 'Swell party?'

'Fascinating,' I said. He grew with pride and I decided that hyperbole had outlived its usefulness as a means of communication. After his dance Ivor Butcher wanted a word with me. He went out to my car with uncertain steps. The man in the gorilla mask was holding the shoulders of a girl who was being spectacularly ill.

49 *And again*

'Do you know what?' said Ivor Butcher once we were seated in the car. He was looking around the dashboard anxiously. I pointed to the second knob from the left. He pulled it and the windscreen wipers started. He nodded. Windscreen-wiper motors mar tape recordings.

'What's the trouble?' I asked.

'I'm being followed,' he said.

'Really,' I said.

'Straight up,' he said, 'I wasn't sure until today. Then I phoned you.'

'I don't know why you phoned *me*,' I said. 'There's nothing *I* can do.' I paused. 'It's gone too far for me to interfere.'

'Too far?' said Ivor Butcher. 'What's gone too far?'

'I don't know anything about it,' I said, like I'd said too much already.

'You mean the Portuguese business? The Spanish bloke and all that?'

'What do you think?' I said. 'You've been dabbling in pretty big stuff. Can't Smith help you?'

'He *says* he can't. What's going to happen now?'

I tapped him on the shoulder and said, 'You know I could get into a lot of trouble just talking to you.'

Ivor Butcher said, 'Yeah,' in varying permutations about

twelve times. At what I considered the appropriate interval I said, 'It was because you gave us false information that things really came to a head. You know,' I said casually, 'became treason.'

Ivor Butcher repeated the word treason a few times, changing it from a statement to an interrogative, transcribing it to a minor key and pitching it an octave higher each time. 'You mean that I could be shot?'

'No,' I said, 'this is England after all. We don't do things like that. No. You'll be hanged.'

'No.' Ivor Butcher's voice came back like an echo and he leaned heavily against the passenger door. He had fainted. The man with the gorilla mask left his friend and asked if he could help. 'My friend isn't very well,' I told him. 'It's all that heat and noise and strong drink. Perhaps a glass of water would help.' It took gorilla-head a long time to push his way through to the kitchen. In the meantime Ivor Butcher shook his head and breathed heavily.

'I'm sorry,' he said, 'you must think I'm a terrible neddie.'

'It's all right,' I told him, 'I know exactly how you feel.' I knew.

'You're a good sort, you are,' he said. 'Do you think I should make a proper statement? Smith paid me practically nothing for what I did. I'm just small fry.' He closed his eyes at the thought.

I said to make a proper statement would be a sensible idea. Then gorilla-head came back with a jam-jar of water.

'There aren't any glasses left in the kitchen,' he said in his echoing voice.

He offered the water to Ivor Butcher, who said, 'He's the one,' in a shrill, frightened voice and lost consciousness again.

'Is that girl with the smudged mascara still in the kitchen?' I asked.

'Yes,' said gorilla-face. 'She says Elvis Presley is a square.' His voice echoed.

'Why don't you go and see if you can't talk her round?' I said, 'because you needn't continue with this surveillance any longer.'

'Very good, sir,' he said.

'And Tinkle Bell,' I said, 'take that mask off, it makes your voice echo.'

50 *One named* OSTRA *has no number*

If you ever get clear away from a difficult situation by abandoning a large part of your personal belongings, you may feel an urgent need of certain articles you have left behind, like a Locarte fluorimeter that has an eight-month delivery time. Don't *send* for them; because that's how we traced da Cunha.

I asked Alice for a manilla cover and wrote 'Ostra' on the front. Into that I put certified copies of all Ivor Butcher's mail. I added six foolscap sheets of his statement, laced the file and locked it back into the top drawer of my desk. So far it had no file number. It was my special secret contribution to the nation's security. I looked at the map. The Ford station-wagon with da Cunha's laboratory equipment was moving north and looked as though it would cross the Spanish border near Badajoz.

Dawlish called me up for a drink that evening. He had been so busy building the administrative side of the Strutton Committee that I had seen little of him. I knew that O'Brien was still making things difficult for us. O'Brien, unmarried, propped up the corner of the downstairs bar at the Travellers' Club, twenty-four hours a day. What he was giving up in food he was gaining in influence. O'Brien was trying to get Foreign Office people on all the subcommittees with executive power. Dawlish said that, at the meeting I had missed, he had taken the liberty of putting me up as convening chairman of the training structure sub-committee. I told him that I might be away for a few days. Dawlish said he thought that might be the case. He blew his nose loudly and smiled drily from behind his big handkerchief. 'I'll convene the meeting and you delegate your vote to me. It will be all right.'

'Thank you very much, sir,' I said, and I drank to his success. Dawlish came from behind his desk and stood near the gas fire, which was popping and spluttering as they always do about 5 p.m.

'Did you check with the Sc.Ad.C.* about the molecular ice-melting theory?' I asked him.

Dawlish gave a histrionic sigh. 'Don't you *ever* give up?' he said. 'It is *impossible* to rearrange molecules as a way of changing ice to water.' We stared at each other for a minute or so. 'Very well, my boy, I'll ask him.' He closed his eyes, gulped down his claret and leaned against the wall like a worn-out roll of lino.

He said, 'Keightley was on the phone today.' (Keightley was the liaison officer at Scotland Yard.) 'You can't keep this man Butcher available for questioning unless you are preferring charges.'

'I'll clear that in a few days,' I said, 'he'll make no complaint; he *wants* to be in custody.'

Dawlish said, 'I'm feeling a certain amount of pressure in respect of the Alforreca business.'

'Look,' I said, 'I didn't ask you to hold the door open. But don't start closing it now that I'm half-way through.'

Dawlish produced another handkerchief with the aplomb of a tea-party conjurer. 'Careful not to slam it on my fingers,' he told me, 'there's a good boy. Oh, I know that you have a

---

* Sc.Ad.C.: Scientific Adviser to the Cabinet.

thousand reasons for not slipping up, but remember that the man who fell off the Empire State Building said to a resident on the first floor as he fell past him, "So far so good".'

Dawlish smiled blankly.

'Thank you for those words of encouragement,' I said. Dawlish walked across to the drink cupboard. He spoke over his shoulder. 'There are certain things which if I know about I must act upon. As it is I'm happy enough to leave them. But if you go wrong I'll tear you to shreds and anyone you try to protect will be torn up with you.'

'What about another drink?' I said.

'It's a good thing you like Tio Pepe,' replied Dawlish self-consciously.

Dawlish thought I was heading for where the sherry comes from.

51 Where I shine

The brown tilled earth of the Castilian steppe surrounds Madrid like a brim around a stone hat. The northern section of the stone crown has crumbled to produce the Cuatro Caminos where thousands of *productores* live in the rubble. Along the streets which lie deep between pink-brown buildings only the blue-shirted Falangists go jacket-less. Traffic cops wear flashing white cross-straps on their uniforms and cite, pass and dedicate the brave blue two-decker buses, while between the densely packed riflemen there is scarcely room to pry a peasant. They stand, eyes focused on long ago, lining the route of a procession that never comes.

Café la Vega is a bright, stainless, espresso temple. Cups clatter, machines hiss and high heels click across the white marble floor. An elderly American couple argued about pasteurized milk and Felix the Cat tripped happily through the TV screen in a city where TV is something to go *out* to. From the Super Mercado across the street there is a continual flash of red neon, and an advertisement for sherry balances on a skyline of tiles.

I sat near the door where I could see the street. I ordered some hot chocolate and watched a bald-headed man shining a pair of two-tone shoes. I sipped the sweet cinnamon-chocolate for which Madrid used to be famous. The shoe-shine man's box was studded with brass studs; inside the lid were pin-ups of movie stars. He delved amongst the bottles, tins, brushes, and cloths and offered a last flick to the toes. From the upper extremities of the two-tones a large hand descended with paper money.

A young army officer in a grey, immaculate uniform, hung around with aiguillettes, tapped his saucer to summon the shoe-shine. The high black boots were a long and careful operation. It was 7.30 p.m. I looked at the menu. I was worried in case something might have gone wrong. This was a country where it is easy to go wrong.

The shoe-shine man was kneeling at my feet. He placed small pieces of paper inside the shoe to prevent polish soiling my sock. After he had finished polishing, one piece of paper remained there. I could have shouted or tapped my saucer in the Spanish manner, or I could have merely pulled the paper out and thrown it away; but I went to the toilet and read it. On the paper it said, 'Calle de Atocha and Paseo del Prado. Corner. 8.10.' Both the Army officer and the two-tones were gone by the time I returned to my table.

The wind whistled down the Paseo del Prado and the night was suddenly cold, the way it goes in Madrid's fickle climate. A new Chev. rolled down on me like the day of judgement, all headlights and flashing signals with chrome and enamel poured over it like cranberry sauce. I sank into the pink upholstery, the hood dipped, and we purred south towards the river.

Cats sat around with their hands in their pockets and stared insolently back into the headlight beams. The driver parked the car with meticulous care and killed the lights. He opened a wrought-iron gate for me and conducted me to a first-floor front. A man silhouetted in the narrow rectangle of window was studying the café opposite with an enormous pair of binoculars. He moved to one side.

Across the street in the tiny *tasoa* the marble table-tops were covered in glasses of Valdepenas, the stone floor with prawn shells and dirty boots. The men in the boots were shouting, smoking, drinking wine and then shouting again. I applied my eyes to the soft rubber eye-pieces of the binoculars. They were trained on the window next door to the café. Iron bars divided the window into rectangles. The scene beyond was bright and clear. The Chevrolet was parked carefully with good reason. The car had more lenses, spotlights, fog lights, overtaking lights – more lenswork than a fly's eye. Now I realized that one of the headlights had infra-red beams and was still switched on. Through the infra-red binoculars I saw two men taking scientific instruments out of their packing. Shavings and screwed-up paper littered the floor. Into my ear a voice said, 'They must be nearly finished. They've been at it for nearly an hour.' It was Stewart, one of the Navy's Intelligence, who had probably been put on that frogman course just to watch me.

'They aren't setting it up,' I said. It wasn't the sort of room that would make a good laboratory. I moved aside for the other man to resume observation.

'What do you want us to do, sir?' Stewart asked.

'Who does this house belong to?' I asked.

'We've put one of the embassy chauffeurs into it since …' he nodded his head towards the house which held da Cunha's equipment.

'Perhaps he has a wife who will make some coffee,' I asked.

'Aye,' said Stewart.

'You'd better organize it,' I said. 'I have a feeling we're in for a long wait.'

After a lifetime of travelling one is prepared for transient discomfort. A good-quality dressing-gown will double as a blanket, a bed will fold to the size of an umbrella and a pair of soft slippers go into an overcoat pocket. I had all of these things – in my baggage at the hotel.

Stewart and I took an hour each at the binoculars and the chauffeur took an embassy car around the block to cover the back. I don't know what he was expected to do if they went out that way, but there he was.

At 3.30 in the morning, or what *I* call the night, Stewart woke me.

'Now there's a little van parked outside,' he said. By the time I had got across to the binoculars they were moving the fluorimeter out.

'Do you have a gun?' I asked Stewart.

'No sir,' he said. I hadn't considered the possibility that da Cunha would move the laboratory equipment elsewhere. I was waiting for him to turn up. When the van was sagging under the weight the three men locked the back doors and drove away. We followed. It wasn't a long drive to the airport.

As dawn drew a pink frown across the tired forehead of night a small Cessna aeroplane turned its nose to south-south-west and buzzed happily towards the horizon.

'Cessna'; I thought of Smith's file-card; it had to be a Cessna. We watched from the tarmac because none of the three charter planes had a pilot available. Stewart beat on the doors of the padlocked offices and damned them, but it got us no nearer to the equipment that was now at three thousand feet and still climbing. It was 7.22 a.m., 15 December.

52 I see better with this

'Do you know what time it is?'

A stout balding man in a threadbare dressing-gown barred my way.

'Step aside, fatty,' I said. 'I haven't got time for niceties.' Stewart followed me into the empty, echoing hallway.

'Get the Ambassador out of bed,' I said, 'I have special authority from the Cabinet and I want to see him at once, and that doesn't mean in half an hour's time.'

'Who shall I say is calling, sir?' said the man in a dressing-gown, aggressive but doubting. I wrote 'W.O.O.C.(P)' and the words 'Minutes are vital' on a piece of envelope and waited while he took it upstairs. I shouted after him, 'And pull the blankets off your radio officer. I want him on the radio set in three minutes too.'

My treatment of the Madrid embassy staff was causing Stewart physical pain. The sight of H.E. in pyjamas was almost too much for him.

Gibraltar answered our radio signal with commendable promptness. I spoke quickly into the microphone.

Gibraltar was very impressed with my cloak-and-dagger stuff. 'I'll put an officer on the radar set,' the senior officer there offered.

'No,' I said, 'I can't afford a botch-up. Put the usual

operator on.' They were a bit hurt but linked me to the corporal on the set. It was 8.15 a.m. 'The plane left here almost exactly an hour ago, corporal,' I said. 'If we assume it has an airspeed of 150 m.p.h. and stays on that south-southwest course, we'd expect it to be half-way between us. Can you see anything?'

There was a long silence while the corporal, sitting somewhere in the scooped-out heart of the rock of Gibraltar, watched a blue cathode tube.

'Can you see anything?' I said again to the radio. I had an awful feeling that the Cessna might have changed course or already landed.

'It's the Seville Traffic Control Zone, you see, sir. There's a great mass of stuff around there and it's almost directly on the expectation course. If it gets mixed into that traffic stack I'm not sure that I'll be able to sort it out before it lands.' His voice was brittle through the loudspeaker.

'Perhaps if you increase your range,' I coaxed. 'Look for a blip north of Cordoba, over the Sierra Morena, perhaps even as far as Almaden.' The Ambassador had combed his hair. He gave me a cup of coffee and I put down the map and microphone and we all waited while the corporal did his stuff. Every now and again his doleful voice said, 'Still searching.'

'What will you do if you get no result?' the Ambassador asked Stewart.

'This officer is in charge, sir,' said Stewart, 'I'm seconded to him.'

I let that thought settle, and then I told him, 'I'll put up airborne radar and I'll send a jet fighter plane to every airfield in the Iberian peninsula until I find it.'

The Ambassador wiped coffee off his moustache and said, 'That would take a bit of explaining, y'know.'

'I'm sure the explaining will be in very capable hands,' I said politely.

'Gottit, gottit!' The voice rumbled the loudspeaker as the radar operator sorted one pinpoint of blue light from a constellation of others.

'How do you know it's the right one?' I asked.

'I'd bet on it, sir. It's one of the larger single-engine jobs. A bit under forty-foot wingspan (I'm guessing now of course) and it's not on any of the commercial routes or charter runs either.'

'You mean it's not on a direct line between two airports?'

'Affirmative, sir. He's what we call "coasting". He's locked on to a course ...'

'You mean he has an auto-pilot. Doesn't that make that blip more likely to be a big aircraft?'

'No, sir. Even the little single-seaters have auto-pilots nowadays.'

'What do you think he is going to do?'

'Well, as I say, sir, he's probably "coasting", he'll continue on that bearing until he reaches the coast. Then he'll drift along the coast until he recognizes Malaga. Then the pilot will set himself a new course, using a wind direction and velocity according to how far he is off his original course. He probably has no navigational aids, you see.'

'Will he cross the coast at Malaga?'

'A bit east of it.'

'Would you put the Group Captain on the line, corporal.'

The corporal's voice gave a little lift of pleasure as he said, 'Yes, sir.' I suppose he enjoyed calling the Group Captain.

'Take a close look at this aircraft, would you, Group?' I said it as calmly as I could and I felt his hesitation through the ether before he said, 'We'll be over Spanish territorial waters, but if Sir Hubert thinks it will be in order ...'

I said, 'He does. I want high-speed fighters with Air Pass.*
Can do?'

'Well, I don't know. You see my standing orders forbid …'

'I want those planes over the coast by the time this Cessna gets there. Arrange a radio link so that I can speak to the planes as well as keep me connected to the radar set.'

The Ambassador gave me the merest whisper of a smile and raised his eyebrows in a tacit offer of support. I shook my head. The Ambassador and I stood looking at each other as we waited to see whether the Group Captain would give way before my brow-beating. Finally the loudspeaker gave a clip and there was a hubbub of voices before it went silent again.

'Mission 58 to identify one target. Present position Juliet Juliet five zero zero two, at flight level 120 heading 190, estimated speed point three-zero. Climb on vector 040 and make flight level 150; interception 100 miles …'

We listened as the jet fighters moved in on the Cessna.

Then suddenly a 'contact' call came through. *'Roger, keep him in sight,'* came the controller's voice.

The pilot read the registration number to me and it checked with the plane that had taken off from Madrid airport: Smith's plane. It was 9.5 a.m. As soon as the identification was made the fighter returned to North Front Air port. Radar continued to plot the Cessna. I told the Group Captain to send a fast plane up to Madrid to collect me and take me to wherever the Cessna landed.

Meanwhile the Ambassador offered me breakfast.

* Air Pass: interception radar (air-to-air and air-to-ground).

53 Long arm

Marrakech lies coiled in the shadow of the High Atlas mountains like a cobra on a rumpled blanket. By the latter half of December the season is in full swing. Livers are being ruined in the bars of the big white hotels and limbs cracked on the ski slopes of the Middle Atlas. The call to prayer ricochets down the tortuous alleys, comes quivering through the orange and lemon trees and out across the crowded palm plantations that surround the dusty walled town. Overhead, interwoven matting squeezes sunrays like orange pips and transforms the dried mud into startling dazzle patterns. Smoky fires press dust into the sunlight beams and give them tangible dimensions. Fatty kidney slices crackle in aromatic cedar smoke. Light-skinned Berbers, ruddy-faced men from Fes, blue men and the black-enamel faces from Timbuctoo and farther south crowd together in the narrow thoroughfares.

The crowds moved as a white Land Rover came to a halt. On its door I could read the word 'policia'. No sooner had the servant announced 'A gentleman to see you' than he was unceremoniously brushed aside by a short burst of Arabic. Three men entered the room. Two of them wore khaki drill, white peaked caps, Sam Browne belts and gauntlet gloves. The third man was in a white civilian suit. A soft red fez rode side-saddle on a thin brown pointed face. His moustache was sad and well cared for, and a large nose drove a wedge between his small eyes. He tapped the nose with a silver-topped cane. He looked like something dreamed up by central casting. He spoke:

'Baix of the Sûreté Nationale. Let me welcome you to our beautiful country. The oranges are plump on the trees. The date is moist and the snow is crisp and firm on our mountain slopes. We hope you will stay long enough to take advantage of the wonders of our land.'

'Yes,' I said. I watched his two policemen. One opened the fly screen and spat into the street, the other riffled through my papers, which lay on the table.

'You are conducting an investigation. You will be the guest of my department. Whatever you wish, it will be arranged. We hope you have a long and pleasurable habitation.'

'You know what capitalism is like,' I said, 'work, work, work.'

'The capitalism system is for what we work to preserve,' said Baix. One policeman was looking through the clothes closet and the other was polishing his boot with a handkerchief. Overhead I heard the whine of a MIG 17 of the Maroc Air Force.

'Yes,' I said.

'In any narcotics investigation we are most enthusiastic that the criminal is apprehensive.'

'I know what you mean,' I said.

'You intend to make the arrest of persons here in Marrakech?'

'I don't think so, but there are a few people that might be able to assist me in my inquiries.'

'Ah, that famous English words of Scotland Yard, "able to assist those in their inquiries",' said Baix. He said it again for practice. He stopped twirling his baton for a moment. He leaned close and said, 'Before you make the arrest, which I hope is not, then you tell me because it may not be permitted.'

'I'll tell you,' I said, 'but I am employed by the World Health Organization of the United Nations. They will be unhappy if you do not permit.'

Baix looked sad.

'So,' he said, 'we shall consult again.'

'O.K.,' I said.

'Meanwhile,' said Baix, 'I have transported your colleague from the railway station. Your colleague Mr Austin Butterworth.'

Baix shouted some Arabic and one of the policemen drew a pistol. Baix shouted very loudly, using one or two very rude Anglo-Saxon words. The policeman put away the gun with a shamefaced expression and went downstairs to get Ossie out of the Land Rover.

'Your friend is a specialist for the narcotics investigator?'

'Yes,' I said.

'I think I am recognizing his face, your friend.' Ossie came through the door wearing a gigantic war-surplus bush shirt, a panama hat and trousers with thirty-inch cuffs.

'Then I shall leave you to the meeting,' said Baix.

'Allah go with you,' I said.

'So long big boy,' said Baix; he tucked a smile under his sad moustache.

The Land Rover hooted its way up the narrow street.

54 Ossie moves like double this

As Baix had said, it was a country of wonders, and the days sped by as I prepared, watched and calculated. In the market we sat wrapping skewered kidney into the rich coarse bread and swallowing the smoke. We went to the cafés for sweet tea and hid in back rooms to drink Stork Beer for fear of offending the faithful. Ossie sketched plans of the local style of house and I lectured him from my scanty knowledge of elementary radio.

On the third day I visited Herr Knobel.

He wasn't a cheerful hooligan like H.K. or a sad fanatic like Fernie Tomas. Here was a special kind of brain, and you never know where you are with a brain of this sort.

Knobel was da Cunha's name. He lived in the old town. The street was five feet wide. The door was a hatch in the battered white wall. Inside the courtyard, wrought-iron gates made shadow pictures on the hot tiles. A small yellow bird high on the wall sang a short cadenza about how it would like to escape from its golden cage. A golden cage, I thought. A trap for the prisoner who has everything.

Da Cunha sat on a fine antique carpet reading *Hoja de Lunes* – the Madrid paper. Other carpets lined the walls and behind them bright coloured tilework shone with complex Arabic calligraphy. Here and there were leather cushions and through the dark doorway, just visible down the corridor, was a cool green patio; the slim leaves turning to silver swords as the breeze moved them under the hot sun.

Da Cunha sat in the middle of the room. He looked different, fatter. He wasn't fatter, he wasn't different. When I had seen him before he was trying to look like a slim, ascetic, Portuguese aristocrat. Now he was bothering no longer.

'"Investigating", your letter said' – his voice was booming and plummy – 'investigating *what*?'

'Narcotics activities at Albufeira,' I told him. He laughed a coarse spiteful laugh that was rich with gold.

'So that's it,' he said. His eyes moved behind the thick lenses like bubbles in a glass of champagne.

'I'm going to pull you in for it,' I said.

'You wouldn't dare.' It was my turn to laugh.

'They sound like famous last words,' I said.

He shrugged. 'I know that it's impossible to connect me.'

Over da Cunha's shoulder I could see through the window across the patio. The yellow bird was singing. Over the edge of the flat roof came a foot, slowly, waving from side to side looking for a foothold.

'I was the person who assisted you,' said da Cunha. 'I told the V.N.V. to contact you. I gave you the sovereign die. I gave it to you.'

'At Smith's suggestion?' I asked.

Da Cunha shrugged. 'The fool had it all wrong. He would never leave everything to me. He for ever interfered.'

'I know,' I said. 'Would you think me rude if I solicited some coffee? I just love coffee.' Da Cunha arranged it immediately.

'My friends here are very powerful,' said da Cunha.

'You mean Baix,' I said. The servant boy brought a big brass bowl and an ornamental kettle. He set the bowl at my feet and poured water over my hands. It is the Muslim custom before food is eaten. I hoped the servant wouldn't turn to da Cunha too quickly. I washed my hands slowly and efficiently. The figure that I had seen on the roof was now suspended from the parapet by both hands.

'Baix came to see me a few days ago,' I said, trying not to look out of the window. The feet came a few inches lower. I said, 'But, as I told him, I am working with the authority of the World Health Organization. There are few governments that will hinder such authority.' The feet sought and found the grille of the top-storey window.

'Really,' said da Cunha. The voluminous war-surplus bush jacket was billowing in the breeze.

'Yes,' I said. How could they fail to see Ossie? 'It's an important thing, health.' Da Cunha smiled. I finished my hand-washing as Ossie disappeared through the window. The boy took the brass hand-washing gear to da Cunha.

'You are a very clever man,' I said to da Cunha. 'You must have known what was going on at Albufeira.' Da Cunha nodded.

I said, 'What briefly were your impressions of this man Harry Kondit – and of Fernandes Tomas?'

Da Cunha unwound the gold-wire spectacles from his ear and extricated them from his white hair. 'Harry Kondit; it was a pun of your English word "conduit", of course.'

I nodded.

'Witty, physically a little over-aware of himself. Natural charm in a brash unsophisticated way.'

'His business?'

'Managed with great care.' Da Cunha answered immediately, then paused. 'He obeyed what I imagine are the basic rules of the narcotics trade.'

'Really,' I said, 'what are they?'

'Nations are two-faced about narcotics,' he said. 'Few police forces arrest people who buy narcotics and take it away

252

from that country. The rules are: never sell them in the same country that you buy, never process in the country where you sell, never sell in the country of which you are a citizen.'

'Personality?'

'He was an idealist gone sour,' said da Cunha. 'To be an idealist it is as well not to be born in America. Men like Kondit go through life acting like criminals, but persuade themselves that they are being persecuted for their ideals.'

'What about Tomas?' I asked.

Da Cunha smiled. 'I am tempted to say that men like Tomas go through life acting like idealists but find themselves persecuted as criminals; but it would not be exactly true. Tomas was a unit of a nation's strength. Anything that he finally became was due to the environment through which he passed. He was neither good nor bad; his misfortunes have always been due to the fact that he was prepared to listen to the other side of the argument. Not a very grievous fault, I would say.'

I agreed.

Da Cunha said, 'And now you want to know why I did nothing to halt these two men and their disgusting trade. That is why you have followed me, or rather followed my laboratory equipment,' said da Cunha. I nodded. He said, 'It arrived so quickly and seemed to excite so little attention en route … There is an old Spanish proverb which runs "For a fleeing enemy make a golden bridge".' I bowed.

He said, 'I knew that there was a risk of it, but …' he shrugged his shoulders. 'Without it I couldn't work anyway. What is it that you really want: the "Weiss List"?'

'I really don't know for sure.' I paused. 'You as a scientist know that you start an experiment to find a coefficient of expansion and end up with control of the world.'

'Some of us,' said da Cunha, 'prefer the coefficient of expansion.'

'London has always been very interested in your ice-melting work,' I said. Da Cunha's eyes went very bright but he said nothing.

'The ice-melting,' I said again. I unfolded a message from London. 'I sent them photos of your laboratory. This message says ... blah blah here we are, says ... "when the molecular construction of water forms regular patterns the result is ice, similarly if the regular patterns of the molecules of ice can be rearranged the ice would become water, *instantaneously*, instead of going through the laborious process of melting. Since at the present time the U.S.S.R. and U.S.A. have large fleets of missile-carrying submarines and none of them so far is capable of discharging missiles under even thin ice, the advantages of a method of making a hole in the ice (technically known as a 'polynya') are obvious and manifold. The work of Professor Knobel is vital to the Free World's stake in the Arctic."'

I folded the paper and placed it inside my wallet, taking great care not to let him see the message.

'You come to the point very quickly,' said da Cunha. He smiled a great self-satisfied smile and said, 'The military aspects of this project do not interest me at all. All I want is to be left in peace. A painter is allowed to disappear to a remote part of the world and paint, why should I not disappear to a remote part of the world and continue my studies?'

'I can imagine the owner of a flick-knife factory saying the same thing,' I said.

The servant had brought pancakes with almonds and sugar inside. He offered them and we munched heartily into the plateful. I was wondering how to handle the next part while keeping an eye open for Ossie's exit. Da Cunha leaned towards me. 'It has no military importance and never has had,' he said.

I said, 'The way I heard it, there was a plan to freeze a narrow section of the English Channel in 1940 to march a German army over it.'

'It was of no importance,' said da Cunha.

I said, 'I was on the other side of that Channel; I was keen it should stay liquid.'

'I mean it was impossible to do. The theory was correct but the practical difficulties were insurmountable. But by 1945 I had done enough research to be near a breakthrough in basic science.' Da Cunha chewed into a honey cake. 'But by 1945 it was too late. The army had disintegrated; it was too late to do anything but wait.'

'Wait for what?' I asked.

'For the renaissance of the middle class,' he said. He was oversalivating, and now he prodded my chest.

'You have come a long way to see me. I appreciate that. I am given to understand that you are highly placed in the Civil Service of your country. Whether you come offering good or threatening ill does not change the compliment you pay me. I shall give you advice to take back to your government: "Don't destroy the middle classes!"'

I thought of taking that message back to the government of my country. I imagined trotting into Dawlish and saying, 'We are not to destroy the middle classes.' I looked at da Cunha and said 'Yes.' He went on hurriedly:

'The Allies destroyed the middle classes in Germany after the war.' I realized that he was speaking of the First World War. 'The inflation destroyed savings overnight and pushed the middle classes into the arms of the Nazis. Where else could they go? The Dawes Plan gave Germany a loan of $200,000,000. It didn't go to helping the middle classes – the people you had sitting in Spitfires in 1940. Ten million dollars went to Krupp and another twelve million to Thyssen, which meant to Hitler. The industrialists and the finance houses had a wonderful time, but the middle classes had disappeared into a political whirlpool.

'And now we are reappearing. The new Europe will be a middle-class Europe. Run by people with taste, run not by jumped-up trade unionists and terrorist rabble-rousers but by men of culture, breeding and taste.' Da Cunha was looking beyond me in a fixed way. I dared not look round. His sharp, bony fingers dug into my arm, his words were laden with spittle, 'You call me a Fascist …'

'No,' I said nervously, 'I called you nothing of the kind.'

He hadn't waited for my reply. 'Perhaps I am,' he shouted, 'perhaps I am a Fascist. If Young Europe is Fascist then I am proud to be a Fascist too.'

The servant boy was hovering at the door. How he had grown! I noticed for the first time that he was well over six foot of oiled muscle.

'Take him,' da Cunha shouted. He heaved at my arm and his adroit wiriness threw me off balance. 'Take him to the cellar,' he shouted, 'give him six lashes. I'll teach these thieving reactionary friends of the Jew Kondit what I mean by discipline.' His mouth was a mousse of anger.

I said gently, 'A man like you would never imprison an envoy.' Da Cunha stretched himself to a regal height. 'I have your message for my government,' I coaxed. He looked through me for a moment or so and then gradually brought me into close focus.

He said, 'It is only because you are an envoy that you shall live.' He was speaking a little more quietly now. I caught the servant boy's eye and he gave a slight twitch of the shoulders that might have been a shrug.

'I shall carry your words to England,' I said like something out of *A Midsummer Night's Dream*. Then da Cunha and I shook hands gravely as though one of us was about to step into a space capsule.

He said, 'Could you let me have that message your London office sent?'

'About molecular rearrangements of water particles?' I said. 'I'm afraid not, I shouldn't have brought it with me really.'

'I suppose not,' he said. 'How did the last sentence read?'

'I can remember it,' I said, 'It reads: "The work of Professor Knobel is vital to the anti-Bolshevist world's stake in the Arctic".'

'When you get to my age,' he said, 'such food for the ego suddenly means a lot to one.'

'I understand,' I said. It was an understatement.

55 In me for a change

'Marvellous,' said Ossie, 'absolutely delicious.'

It was true. The jam doughnuts in the buffet at Marrakech station are among the best I have ever tasted.

'You've got it?' I asked.

'Yes,' said Ossie. He tapped the canvas bag on the table. 'Went like a dream. Just like you said. A puny little thing. The people who make shoddy safes like that should be locked up.'

'You sent the message?'

'I sent "Phase one complete. Commence Phase two. Stop. Eliminate Baker", then they sent an acknowledgement.' He smiled. 'You think that Baix will think Baker means Baix when he intercepts the message?'

'Unless he's a bigger dope than I think he is. I've used a simple one-part code. I don't know what else I can do to make it easy for him.' Ossie chuckled again. He'd taken an unreasonable dislike to Baix and loved the idea of him avoiding a non-existent assassin.

'How did it go with you?' asked Ossie. 'You keep looking at your watch; you weren't followed, were you?'

'No. Train's due in five minutes,' I said; it was 2.55 p.m.

'You won't drag it in any quicker by quizzing the watch. Tell me about the talk you had with the old nut. And have a doughnut. You are sure you weren't followed?'

'I wasn't followed.' I took another doughnut and told Ossie about the conversation with da Cunha.

'But that's not true,' Ossie told me at various places in the narrative.

'If you are going to say "that's not true" every time I say something that's not true you'd better go and gargle now or wind up with a sore throat.'

'Best liar I know, you are,' said Ossie in great admiration. 'And so that old blighter is really connected with the English Fascists.'

'With English Fascists, French Fascists, Belgian Fascists and even German Fascists.'

'So the Germans have them too,' said Ossie, like he hadn't been running his pork-sausage fingers through secrets for the last quarter of a century. 'That stuff you invented about the message from London. I liked that. What did the message from London *really* say?'

I passed him the cable that Dawlish had sent me:

```
KNOBEL   STOP   NAZI   STOP   HOAXER   STOP   WATER
FREEZING   DISCOVERIES   ENTIRELY   IRREVOCABLY
REPEAT   ENTIRELY   IRREVOCABLY   DISCREDITED
REPEAT   ENTIRELY:   DAWLISH
```

The long green modern train slid into the station. I helped Ossie with our luggage.

A man with a face like a half-eaten bar of Aero chocolate wanted money for showing us a seat on the almost deserted train. In exchange for my declining to play my part in this transaction he taught me some new Arabic verbs. The train pulled out of the neat little station of Marrakech. Ossie said, 'That Baix, I'd love to see his face.'

'That's just what I'm trying to avoid,' I said as I opened Ossie's canvas bag. We both looked at the little radio transmitter that could talk to machines under the sea.

56 Deep signal

The long flexible blades cut the air above our heads. I tapped the pilot on the arm.

'One more sweep,' I said, 'then we'll return to the ship and try again tomorrow.' He nodded.

We dropped towards the heavy sea and I watched the wave-tops, blunted by the downward thrust of air from the blades.

'O.K., Chief,' I shouted over my shoulder. Chief Petty Officer Edwards of H.M.S. *Vernon* leaned through the door and watched the ocean top.

'Back a bit,' Edwards shouted. It had always been a bomb-aimer's joke, but now the pilot obediently brought the helicopter along a reciprocal course.

'Just a floating piece of wood,' Edwards's voice said over the intercom. We moved on to the next square of the area search. Twelve miles away on the starboard side I could see the Portuguese coast at Cape Santa Maria. Through the grey sea ran black veins as the light fell across the contours of the water. 'Too dark now,' I said, and Ossie switched off his radio and the cabin glowed with the green light of the instrument panel.

It was two and a half days before our effort was rewarded. Hours of 'backing a bit' over foam-lashed pieces of flotsam and sliding over for a close look at a shoal of fish.

When we made contact the extreme long-wave radio set on Ossie's knees – the one he had stolen from da Cunha's safe – gave a 'beep beep' of response. The pilot held us steady. The wave-crests were inches under us.

'Beep beep': it was emitting a signal to us. Ossie was shouting over the intercom and I grabbed the diver's rubber-clad arm and tried to go through his instructions all over again in thirty seconds flat. Edwards patted my hand and said, 'It will be O.K., sir', then like a demon king in a pantomime he was gone. Hands crossed, face lowered, he hit the water with a splash. Only now did I see the target he had dived at. The silver metal floating amid the waves shone here and there through the green vegetation. C.P.O. Edwards had the cable lashed around the big metal cylinder within ten minutes. The winch operator began to haul it up and brought it splashing and dripping into the cabin of the helicopter.

Dawlish had done his stuff. When the helicopter got back to the ship everything was ready and waiting – even a ration of rum for the still wet C.P.O. Edwards. I was in the captain's day-cabin with the cylinder; a Marine sentry was stationed outside and even the captain knocked before coming in to ask if there was anything more I required.

Two bolts had to be chiselled off, but that was only to be expected after more than a decade under the water. The light alloy panel came free to reveal a large compartment and give access for adjustments to the barometer, thermometer, hygrometer and the motors.

Every twelve hours this metal cylinder had surfaced and its voice had told da Cunha that it was still 'alive and well'. Fernie Tomas had tried to 'home' on the signal, but failed to spot it before it descended to the sea bed again. Harry Kondit knew that his boat travelled twelve miles on each of da Cunha's trips. 'Down the coast' he had said, because

Harry Kondit thought he was the only man who kept rendezvous at sea.

I reached inside to where the instruments had once been, and found a slim metal tin with the Nazi eagle and the bright-red sealing wax. Before I opened it I sent for a jug of coffee and sandwiches. It was going to be a long task.

57 Lost letter in the mail

Christmas 1940

Dear Baron,
What a wonderful surprise to have your letter, it had taken nearly nine weeks to reach us. You may well wonder what the 'state of mind' is here in England. You would never recognize Number 20 now and it is like no other Christmas I care to remember. They have used the gardens for some sort of dump and five of the houses are full of Polish officers who are for ever shouting and singing. Gerald is in the Cameroons negotiating with the French, and Billy is with the Fleet, goodness knows where. We have only cook and Janet now to look after us and are 'camping' in the study and the gold room that you liked so much. We don't go into London at all, as there is little petrol available and the trains are blacked out and quite filthy, and now they are talking about restricting restaurant meals. That Karl is having a wonderful time in Paris we have little doubt, how we all envy him! You must send him my love when you next write.

How we agree with you about this dreadful war. The government here is completely dominated by these dreadful Labour Party people, and Sir B. is quite sure they are

*plotting with the Bolsheviks against the poor, gallant little
Finns. At least, Daddy says, they are going to have the
Daily Worker newspaper 'put down' next month. You say
that if only we had an hour's conversation together you
are sure that we could help our countries in these days of
internecine bitterness. You are right, and I must tell you
that it is not as impossible as you seem to think. Lord C.
is going to the United States in February and Miriam will
be going with him. Surely it is not impossible that you
should have to go to Lisbon on some pretence or other?
You always were able to find excuses to satisfy Nanna at
Goodwinds. Is Grandmama well? You know that Cyril is
still at the same address in Zürich; I know I would love to
see you again, it seems so long. Of course Helmut can use
the house in Nice, the agent in the village has the keys, I
only hope it hasn't been damaged, but one never knows,
the way the French have been behaving lately is past
comprehension. Please write again soon, the news that you
are well and still thinking of us has brought a breath of
fresh air to our dusty old lives.*

Your true friend,
BESS

Sunday, 26th January, 1941 London
Dear Walter,
*I shall ask you to burn this the moment that you have read
it. Tell K.E.F. that he will* have *to supply* anything *from
the factory in Lyon that you ask. Remind him that it
wasn't the French Resistance that have paid his wages for
the last ten months. I want the chimneys smoking again at
the earliest possible moment* or I will sell the whole plant.

Would your Wehrmacht people be interested in buying the place? Should you be interested I will appoint you as the agent at the usual rate. Surely a factory in the Vichy Free Zone could be useful in the light of this 'Trading with the Enemy Statutory List'?

I think these people here are beginning to realize which way the wind has blown and already a little of the bravado has disappeared. You can mark my words that should your fellows actually come into conflict with the Soviets we British will not be long in understanding what must be done.

Our plant in Latvia has gone down the drain now that they have been subverted by the Bolshies and I can only say how glad I am that the plans for the Bukovina place didn't materialize.

I am forming a 'Brains Trust' (as they say these days) of people who see eye to eye with me on these points so that when the country finally comes to its senses we will be in a position to do something about it.

You are right about Roosevelt's crowd; now that he's safely in for the third time they will foment the spiteful retaliatory attitude of the socialist mob here. However, Roosevelt isn't America you know, and as long as your people don't do anything foolish (like dropping a bomb on New York) only a small number will be willing to pick up a gun if it means putting down a cash register.

> *Burn this now,*
> *Yours,*
> *HENRY*

58 To put it together hastily

Perhaps they are not typical of the letters that I took from the cylinder. I spread them all out across the table. Some were written under engraved headings, some on paper torn from exercise books. What did they all have in common?

I shook the tiny tin of silica gel crystals that had helped keep the documents dry and I flipped through the yellow-paged, rough-printed book of names and addresses. I wondered if I would have reasoned that these things were among the great treasures of the modern world. I decided that I wouldn't have, but then da Cunha was more than a little dotty. Da Cunha who could sit and lecture me about the sanctity of the middle classes.

When Nazi Germany was falling about its creator's ears the bigwigs were busy making a grab for a souvenir of something they had known and loved – like money.

Some liked big pictures and they took old master paintings; some liked little pictures and they took stamp collections; some liked luxury, they took gold; some liked *la belle époque*, they took heroin; but one had developed a taste for power. He took these letters.

When the Wehrmacht was straining its eyes to peer through the Channel mist, the order went out to form a British Puppet Government. German diplomatic circles were asked to contact likely sympathizers, using the individual approach as far as possible. So it was that earnest, charming, personal letters reached earnest, charming people who might be prepared to be a Member of Parliament in the Nazi-backed National Socialist Government that was to have its seat in the Channel Islands until London was made ready.

These letters were filed when winter set in. They were filed again at the end of the next summer, when letters about puppet governments were addressed to earnest, charming Bessarabians, Ukrainians and Lithuanians. They had collected dust until, one day in 1945, a man realized that these letters from influential people might make life easier in an unfriendly world.

Fregattenkapitän Knobel, a scientific officer of the German Navy, took his packet of letters and his tin of heroin and went aboard the Type XXI U-boat at Cuxhaven. Da Cunha knew all about the meteorological buoys and he spent an hour sealing his package of blackmail ammunition into the canister and re-fixing the waterproof seal. Off Albufeira he ordered the commander of the U-boat to drop the canister, and then da Cunha went ashore in a rubber dinghy. The U-boat captain lost a dinghy and very soon after he lost his life, for the U-boat foundered with all hands.

What happened will probably never be known. Few Type XXIs ever came into contact with water. Most of them were packed tightly together, half-completed, on the slipways of Northern Germany, when the Allied armies reached them. As far as I know there isn't a whole XXI anywhere in the world, unless we count the bottom of the Atlantic Ocean just off Albufeira.

Tomas realized that a U-boat full of high-ranking Nazis would contain valuable loot – if you don't mind probing around rotting bodies. How much Tomas minded is another thing we shall never know. When he removed the canisters of heroin he needed help in disposing of it. He couldn't have found a more suitable helpmate than H.K., but they both stayed clear of da Cunha's preserves.

Tomas never lost his respect for da Cunha. He stiffened when da Cunha came near and answered him in the short monosyllabic tones of the German Navy. Like all Germans, da Cunha was able to master accentless Portuguese. How much Tomas knew about the cylinder is difficult to decide, but he guessed enough to blackmail at least one person named therein – Smith. Although Tomas went with da Cunha to check the meteorology cylinder every six months, until our voyage together he had made no attempt to retrieve the cylinder from the ocean bed. Tomas had only a radio receiver; from da Cunha we had stolen a transmitter which would *summon* the cylinder from the sea bed rather than just receive a signal every twelve hours. Tomas rushed to get the cylinder when he discovered that da Cunha had fled (as H.K. guessed he would).

Why did da Cunha keep the papers on the sea bed? He was a blackmailer. Smith was 'persuaded' to equip a research lab. for him. Smith was 'persuaded' to have me recalled from Albufeira. How many other people were persuaded to do things?

I took the file marked OSTRA. (An 'oyster': lying at the bottom of the sea with a pearl inside, that was da Cunha's cylinder.) I added the letters I had taken from the buoy. They made a small mountain on Dawlish's bright mahogany desk.

'So this is the lot,' Dawlish said. He sniffed contemplatively.

'Yes,' I said. 'I'd guess that most of these people have donated money to the "Young Europe Movement" at one time or another.'

'Jolly good,' said Dawlish, 'I knew you would manage.'

'Oh sure,' I said, 'especially when you wanted to cancel the whole operation.'

Dawlish looked at me over his spectacles, which can get to be very irritating.

'Furthermore,' I said, 'you knew that that girl was employed by the American Narcotics Bureau, and you didn't tell me.'

'Yes,' said Dawlish blandly, 'but she was a very low-echelon employee and I had no wish to inhibit intercourse among the group.' We looked blankly at each other for two or three minutes.

'Social,' Dawlish amended.

'Of course,' I agreed. Dawlish disembowelled his pipe with a penknife.

'When will Smith be arrested?' I asked.

'Arrested?' said Dawlish. 'What an extraordinary question; why would he be arrested?'

'Because he is a corner-stone of an international Fascist movement dedicated to the overthrow of democratic government.' I said it patiently, even though I knew that Dawlish was deliberately leading me on.

Dawlish said, 'You surely don't imagine that they can put everyone who answers that description in jail. Where would we find room for them, and besides, where would the Bonn government get another Civil Service?' He gave a sardonic smile and tapped the pile of documents. 'Our friends here are much more useful where they are – as long as they know that H.M. Government have this little pile in Kevin Cassel's cellar.'

He opened the drawer of his desk and produced an even more enormous file of documents. Across the front it said 'Young Europe Movement' in Alice's fuse-wire handwriting, and was bulging with months of work that Dawlish had never even told me about.

'You didn't understand your role, my boy,' he said in his smug voice; 'we didn't want you to *discover* anything. Somehow we knew that you would make them do something indiscreet.'

271

Last Word

I took all the material down to Kevin Cassel in his Central Register last Tuesday. He signed and embossed the official receipt and wished me merry Christmas.

'Well over the fast,' I said. Why was he always smiling?

As I drove back through Ripley an old lady was sticking tufts of cotton wool into her shop-window to spell 'Merry Xmas'. Outside a man was using a shovel to clear a path to the door.

'Now you see what it's like where the work is done,' said Dawlish, and went on to make provocative remarks about lying around in the sun. Dawlish had convened the training structure sub-committee on my behalf. It was a masterstroke in his battle with O'Brien for control of the Strutton Committee. Dawlish had put every member of the Strutton Committee on the training structure subcommittee with the exception of O'Brien. In other words it was like holding meetings with O'Brien locked out. Dawlish was all knees and elbows. He sat in his battered leather armchair and puffed clouds of smoke at the Duke of Wellington, and said that being successful was just a state of mind.

Bernhard had spread himself all over my office but had taken care not to do any of my paper work. The thirteen-centimetre lens for the Nikon had apricot jam on it, and my secretary was doing half the typing in the building. I kicked Bernhard and his twenty cardboard folders out, and although he protested volubly he set up shop elsewhere. 'And I owe you a two-pound bag of sugar,' he said as he left.

'Stealing sugar is a felony,' I grumbled. 'Didn't you learn any manners at Cambridge?'

'The only thing I learned at Cambridge,' said Bernhard, 'was how to put on a pair of fifteen-inch trousers without first removing my chukka boots.'

Alice brought me some sugar.

On Friday I took Charly Christmas shopping in the West End. She bought her father a subscription to *Playboy* and I sent Baix an Eton tie. I suppose we were each in our own way fighting the establishment. She tried to make some joke at my expense about the ice-melting theories that I had believed; but I didn't respond.

'Your old man *is* an admiral, isn't he?' I asked.

'Yes, dream man.'

'Well,' I said, 'I want to speak to him about that diving equipment. Lisbon have lost part of it. It's on my charge, you see. They want me to pay £250 towards it.'

'Come back to my place,' she said, 'I'll see what can be done.'

'You'll help?' I said.

'Console,' she said, 'console.'

APPENDIXES

1. *Telephone-tapping*

'When you talk into a telephone, you shout from the roof,' Ivor Butcher said one day. A tremendous number of phone calls are tapped in the U.K. In the U.S. wiretapping is an industry.

1. *To tap* (*in comfort*) get someone in the G.P.O. to alter wires on the frame so that your 'victim's' phone rings yours as well as the number he is calling. All you do is listen in or record. N.B. If you want to know what number he has dialled you will need a Dial Recorder to count the digits.

2. *To tap.* Take your 'tappers' (box, hand-set and crocodile clips) to the B.T. (box terminal), 'taste' the terminals with a wet finger to get the one you want. Note: a friend inside the G.P.O. who can tell you about the 'pairs' and how far from the 'victim's' phone they can be picked up will make life a little easier.

3. *To tap one call only.* You can brazenly do it from an outdoor green cabinet, but study the dress characteristics of G.P.O. engineers first.

4. *Are you tapped?* Do you get cut off in mid-conversation more often when using one particular phone? (N.B. Don't be misled by old-fashioned inefficiency, all G.P.O. phones are subject to that.) Do you sometimes find that the clarity and amplification increase after a minute or so? This is all due to

the eavesdropper carelessly replacing the handset. Moral: Don't say anything confidential over a phone, but if you really must, discuss trivia for two or three minutes in the hope that the eavesdropper will hang up.

2. *Austin Butterworth (Ossie)*

In November 1938, D.S.T., which is the French M.I.5, wanted to open an English make of safe in a certain embassy in Paris. Special Branch brought Ossie out of Parkhurst and asked him to go there.

'With the Nicks to help you,' said Ossie incredulously, and volunteered like a shot. He got on all right with D.S.T. and they kept him for nearly four months. Ossie's value to them came from his knowledge of British safes, which several of the embassies in Paris then had. Now of course any embassy in its right mind uses only safes made in its own country. However, back before the war Ossie earned himself a quite nice French civil medal, but some bureaucrat in the Home Office prevented its award.

Ossie has always been a very thorough worker, and often he would take a London office and register a firm at Bush House in order to write and inquire about the sort of safe he intended to crack. Once or twice he even bought and installed the same model to practise on. Perhaps this isn't so extraordinary these days, but in the thirties it was really scientific crime.

It was in April 1939 that D.S.T. borrowed Ossie again. This time, without telling London what they intended (and very wise, too, for the Home Office would have gone out of their small minds), they sent Ossie to live in Berlin. Big expense account and an apartment in a beautiful block of flats in the Bayerischer Platz. All Ossie had to do was to study the literature of the safe manufacturers. Sometimes they would go to one of the showrooms to look at the real thing. When war began, Paris and London were fighting over Ossie and he spent the war years travelling around the world cracking safes for various Allied Intelligence organizations. All this experience meant that Ossie had made many important friends 'across the grain', as they say in Intelligence work; that is to say, he was a link between many separate organizations.

In the normal way of operations, such people disappear when their usefulness is past. Ossie's influence was now great, and because of his friends he survived those fatal years for agents, 1945–8. Ossie had been back in prison several times since the war, even though the F.O. generally sent some tame V.C. along to the court to speak about his war record in what was ironically described as 'the Resistance'. In the post-war world of Intelligence Ossie had become a specialist on documents. Common crime was no longer for him; he got secret documents out of safes. The document business was booming. He would 'do' an aeroplane factory for the Yugoslav Embassy or the Yugoslav Embassy for an aeroplane factory. Ossie didn't play favourites among clients. 'It wouldn't be right,' he once told me. By now Ossie could read enough of a dozen languages to ensure that he wouldn't bring the wrong documents back. He had also studied photography at L.C.C. evening classes.

3. *Operation Bernhard*

The idea of producing counterfeit banknotes (£5, £10, £20, £50) in order to shake confidence in British currency is said to have been inspired by the dropping of forged clothing- and food-coupons by the R.A.F. over Nazi Germany. The original plan (to drop the notes from Luftwaffe aircraft) was named Operation Andreas but later was replaced by Operation Bernhard. This latter plan was to use the money to finance secret operations.

The notes produced at Oranienburg Concentration Camp (Special Wing 19) were used to:

1. Buy arms from Balkan partisans (so making them less dangerous).
2. Finance Hungarian radio-listening service.
3. Buy information concerning Mussolini's whereabouts (in order to arrange rescue).
4. Pay Cicero (£300,000).
5. Supply presents for Arab sheiks.

In the latter stages of the war the production centre was moved to Ebensee and to an underground factory near the village of Redl-Zipf (between Salzburg and Linz). A young S.S. lieutenant moving a consignment of the currency (and some people say the plates too) is in a difficult position when one of the lorries breaks down. Acting on orders, he tips the packing cases into the River Traun and hands the broken lorry over to the Wehrmacht. After a little distance a second lorry breaks down; it is abandoned.

When British currency comes floating down the Traun to the Traunsee Lake the U.S. Army, who are by now in occupation, investigate the second lorry. In it they find £21 million in virtually perfect forgeries. It is accepted that the remaining lorries went to the German Naval Research Station (homing torpedoes were tested in the lake).

The sides of the lake are steep, and investigation of it rendered dangerous by a raft of waterlogged timber that hangs suspended about 100 feet below the surface of the water. Divers do not dare to go under it.

In March 1946 two bodies are found near by. Both men had been stationed at the Naval Research Station. In August 1950, another death: again an ex-member of the Naval Research Station.

Many people thought that the sites of these deaths indicated that the plates were hidden in the heights above the station rather than in the water. Rumours said that the Russians organized these attempts, but there is nothing to connect them with either.

In 1953 the *Reader's Digest* financed an investigation, and in 1959 a German magazine financed another and claims to have found plates, notes and secret records in a near-by lake. The material was placed in such a way that it could be recovered. There have since been several more.

Operation Bernhard was run by the S.D. (Sicherheitsdienst), the S.S. Security and Intelligence Unit which evoked much jealousy among the other Nazi intelligence units for its extravagant access to so much finance.

4. *Olterra*

The *Olterra* was a 4,900-ton Italian tanker which sank (although leaving its superstructure above the water-line) in Algeciras Bay at the beginning of World War 2. The Italian Government offered to raise it and sell it to the Spanish Government. The price was very reasonable. The Italian salvage men cut a door in the hull below water level. It then became a secret harbour for the tiny human torpedoes (called by the Italians *Maiale* – pigs) which had arrived dismantled among the new tubes and boilers for the *Olterra*. Gibraltar harbour was just across the bay.

5. *Kurier*

Invented by German Navy during World War 2. The original device enabled a semi-skilled operator to send high-speed signals (these could be read and decoded only by means of recording gear, it was far too fast for a human ear to interpret). The dials are set to *arrange* the signal, then the cylinder is attached to the transmitter and the crank turned to *send* a signal. During the war the messages were photo-recorded at Neumünster (Holstein). The R.N. were most anxious to acquire one. After the war this improved version was designed.

6. *Lt Peterson, B.T., Court martial*

The front page said 'Court Martial' and then a list of contents. First the report of the Court of Inquiry that had repatriated this officer from Germany. Under that was the Circumstantial Letter (a report about the need for a court martial). Then there was a list of witnesses, warrant for holding the court, statements by the accused, and a batch of pencilled shorthand originals.

'Traitorously holding correspondence with the enemy (Germany) … having traitorously given intelligence to the enemy … traitorously given information to the enemy.' The difference between those was too subtle for me. I read on, 'having been made a prisoner of war he voluntarily aided the enemy by joining and working for an organization controlled by the enemy and known as the British Free Corps … failing to report his arrest to the C.O. of the establishment where he was born for pay as directed by Naval Pay Regulations Article 1085.'

The white spaces in the dossier had diagonal blue ink-lines across them to prevent insertions. As I read on, the scene came alive. The first winter after the war, the assembly hall with its kitchen tables covered with naval blankets, the senior officers in their shiny buttons, the accused in a newly issued uniform; Bernard Thomas Peterson, a volunteer reserve officer captured by the Germans during 'human torpedo' attacks on the Norwegian coast in 1943. The prosecution called as first witness Lt James who, as a member of the S.I.B. (Special Investigation Branch) attached to 30 Corps, arrested Peterson in Hanover on 8 May (V.E. Day). Lt James said that an order issued by the Montgomery H.Q. on 6 May made the use of German transport illegal. Acting on information received by phone, Lt James and two S.I.B. sergeants went to an address in suburban Hanover and there found Peterson. On his person Peterson had a *Reisepass* and a *Wehrpass* in the name of Herbert Pütz, and 200 R.M. These were produced in the court. In suitcases in the room where Peterson was found were another 19,568 R.M., a sable coat, and a 9-mm. MP18 Bergmann automatic machine-gun with ammunition. Lt James said that these could be made available to the court. The Judge-advocate, after consulting with the President of the Court, said that they would not be required but should be held available.

After the arresting officer discovered a blood-group number tattooed under his arm, Peterson was put under close arrest as a suspected member of an illegal organization: the S.S.

The S.I.B. went on, 'In the garage adjoining was found a Mercedes staff car with WM (Wehrmacht-Marine) registration. There were 108 litres of petrol in the garage and car. The car (which was the object of the visit) was handed over to the German Command Organization under Field-Marshal Busch in Schleswig-Holstein.' It also could be made available to the court. Lt James, in answer to a question, said that

Peterson's only comment on being placed under close arrest as a member of the S.S. was that 'the battle started in Seville in 1936 and it's not yet over', or words to that effect. Lt James said that in spite of Peterson's excellent English he did not suspect him of being anything other than a member of the German Armed Forces. He had encountered many German soldiers who had lived and worked in England and as a consequence spoke good English.

I turned the discoloured pages of the dossier. Peterson after capture by the Germans had been approached by two members of the 'Legion of St George' (later renamed the 'Britische Freikorps'). Its members were mostly English or Irishmen who had been in the British Union of Fascists before the war. Many of them had what are now described as personality disorders, and all were of the opinion that England would soon see sense and join a German-occupied Europe on a 'crusade' against Russia. The verbatim record said:

PROSECUTOR: You never uttered a treasonable word?

PETERSON: On the contrary, England was much loved. The name of Nelson was invoked on every side, as were the names of all Britain's heroes.

PROS.: You felt that Britain was being deliberately misled by its leaders.

PETERSON: I did sir.

PROS.: Even though these leaders were elected by public free ballot?

PETERSON: Yes.

PROS.: A ballot which your German masters never thought it expedient to institute in Germany or any of the small nations it conquered.

PETERSON: France wasn't a small nation.

PROS.: No further questions.

The defence requested permission to offer as evidence the details of Peterson's task in the Norwegian operation but this was denied. He admitted joining the Britische Freikorps and going to their training unit at Hildesheim. The transcription said:

PROS.: And what were you wearing at this time?

PETERSON: The uniform of the B.F.K.

PROS.: I put it to you that you were wearing the uniform of the Nazi S.S., a uniform that the members of this court have cause to remember with disgust and loathing.

PETERSON: It was …

PROS.: A uniform which had the notorious Death's Head symbol as its cap-badge, did it not?

PETERSON: Yes, but we wore a Union Jack armband.

PROS.: In other words, you wanted to serve two masters at once, you wanted the best of both worlds. You wanted to be on the winning side – a Hauptsturmführer SS *and* a Lieutenant R.N.V.R.

PETERSON: No, certainly not.

PROS.: The court will no doubt form their own opinion. I shall be returning to that point later.

Much of the trial dealt with the technical knowledge that Peterson put at the disposal of the German Navy, who came to the frogman and human torpedo scene very late in the war.

The German Navy had first seen a 'frogman style' demonstration at the Olympic swimming pool, Berlin, in the spring of 1943. Peterson was screened after his capture and went to a block of flats that the German Navy had in Berlin. There he met Loveless, John Amery, and Joyce (Haw-Haw), 'but they considered themselves Germans', while 'we were loyal Englishmen anxious to convert our fellow-countrymen into allies of Germany'. Peterson was persuaded by Loveless to give his services to the Germans as a frogman-instructor. He said O.K. soon enough to be at Heiligenhafen, at the eastern end of Kiel Bay in the Baltic, when the first of K force (*Kleinkampfmittel-Verband:* Small Battle-Weapon Force) was formed in January 1944. Peterson translated the British Commando Regulations and other textbooks for them and taught them how to pronounce English swear-words with impeccable accuracy to throw sentries off their guard. By this time Peterson had a German naval officer's uniform and, since K force had discarded rank badges to foster good relations, he was accepted by newcomers as a German naval officer.

PROS.: I put it to you, that you at this time had *become* a German naval officer.

PETERSON: No.

PROS.: You were wearing a German naval officer's uniform. Yesterday you said that the German Navy 'relied on you'. I am quoting: 'relied on you in their training of K force'. Did you say that, or didn't you?

PETERSON: Yes, but …

PROS.: You said it. Very well. As an officer of the Royal Navy you were drawing pay. That is to say that you knew that pay was being credited to you.

PETERSON: Yes.

PROS.: Furthermore, this pay was not just the pay of a Lieutenant R.N.V.R. of the Executive Branch, but included an extra allowance payable to you in respect of the hazard of undersea warfare and the technical nature of those duties.

PETERSON: (*No answer.*)

PROS.: Is that not so?

PETERSON: I suppose so.

PROS.: The same technical knowledge that your new German masters were so anxious to learn. Knowledge that they '*relied on you*' to impart.

PETERSON: Yes.

PROS.: What is the name given to citizens who grant reliable aid with the declared aim of overthrowing their own lawful government?

PETERSON: (*Inaudible.*)

PROS.: Speak up, Herr Hauptsturmführer Pütz, or should I say Lieutenant Peterson?

PETERSON: Traitor, I suppose you mean.

PROS.: That's right, Sub-Lieutenant Bernard Thomas Peterson, R.N.V.R., it's called Constructive Treason.

The result was penal servitude and cashiering. I flipped through the accompanying documents; a certified true copy of the sentence signed by the President of the Court; and the confirming officer's letter after agreeing the sentence.

I closed the file.